# TWISTED FATE

*A Novel*

Dana Miller

Northampton House Press

For my mom.

Thank you for always believing in me.

# TWISTED FATE

*"Fate, show thy force. Ourselves we do not owe. What is decreed must be; and be this so."*

– Act 1, Scene 5, Shakespeare's *Twelfth Night*

# Chapter 1

# Sleepless Mornings

I don't remember when I stopped believing in fate. It's hard to pinpoint the exact moment that made me feel certain it doesn't exist. As far back as I can recall, I always craved the notion of true love, the idea of destiny, and the prospect that one day I'd find the person who would be mine, forever. As a child, it wasn't difficult for me to imagine who that would be, because he wasn't a stranger, someone I'd never met before. He was Jared, my childhood sweetheart.

That was before, and we were just teenagers. These days, I've come to realize the chance of someone coming along and making me feel the way he did is pretty slim. Yes, I was young when we met, but I still could understand what it meant to have someone extraordinary in my life – a person who understood me without needing to ask, who made me not only believe fairytales existed, but that I could be part of one, as well.

Now I know they exist only in movies . . . and sometimes in my dreams. Waking life feels more like it was written by Shakespeare. Sometimes a comedy, sometimes a tragedy. And you don't get to choose which one you'll be featured in, any given day.

Maybe that's why, late on this cool spring morning, I'm still lying in bed, awake but unwilling to rise. I'm settled into the most perfect, comfortable position beneath a toasty comforter. Plagued, though, by a bright burnt-orange glow from the sunlight seeping through my eyelids. Why do I always find the most ideal sleeping spot, which feels as if the bed is hugging me, only as the time to rise creeps nearer? And all the while the sun's surly rays poke at me like an impatient child.

I sigh and turn over. Only in dreams can I drift back to a time when my world wasn't turned on its head. Why can't I just stay here a little longer? I'm twenty-nine years old, for crying out loud! I should be able to sleep all day, if I choose.

But the loud clattering from the kitchen says otherwise. My roommate Preston is stirring. So drifting back now is out of the question.

I brace myself. Time to sit up and –

At the precise moment my phone alarm clock plays, Preston bursts in with his usual early morning gusto, to begin the daily routine of torment until I surrender and crawl out to face the world.

"Morning, honey!" He prances around to Walk the Moon's "Shut Up and Dance", blaring on my cell phone. He's all dressed up in a suit, for some reason, which makes his hip-twitching dance look all the more disturbing.

I fall back and yank the covers over my head. "Go away."

"Laina, time to get up!" he announces.

I lie as still as a baby animal hidden in tall grass, hoping he'll be unable to see me and leave as quickly as he came.

A vain hope, it turns out.

"Laina, let's *go*," he repeats, with more urgency. He fumbles around the room, cursing as he trips over something. His footsteps pad back to the bed. He grabs my shoulder and wildly shakes it until my entire body is flopping like a dead fish.

I remain as limp as possible. "Five more minutes," I croak, swatting at his hand, trying to shoo him away. "Too cozy in here."

"No! No more minutes. You've slept long enough," he scolds, though he does let go of my shoulder.

This has been our morning ritual ever since we moved in together, about two years ago. It always ends the same way, so at last I give in and prepare to fling back the covers.

Preston is grunting in disapproval while haphazardly tossing various items of my clothing about the room. He's definitely spiffed up and looking dashing in a light gray suit with an electric blue tie, his thick, dark brown hair meticulously parted and swept to one side.

"What're you doing?" I growl. "You're making a bigger mess." I grab a pillow and launch it at his head. It strikes his arm instead.

He ignores the attack. "Excuse *me*," he snips, straightening the knot on his already-perfect tie, "but this room was already trashed. I don't know how you can tell which clothes are clean and which are dirty." He lifts a blue tank top by one finger and gingerly sniffs at it, then grimaces and tosses it into the overflowing wicker hamper against the wall.

I snicker through my nose at his repulsed expression. "Oh, please. There's no way it smells that bad. Leave my stuff alone, why don't you? I'll never find anything again with you throwing stuff around like a lunatic."

"Seriously? How anyone can function in this chaos! Your messiness gets progressively worse every day, I swear! When we met in college, you weren't nearly this disorganized."

Suddenly his nose twitches like an outraged rabbit's. His gaze shifts away from the mess and onto something else a sixth sense appears to detect. His eyes narrow and he stiffens, standing at attention like a meerkat sensing a predator. "What in the world is *that smell?*" He sniffs the air in quick little snorts. "Is that old chicken? Did you eat *chicken* in here?"

Preston has the nose of a Bloodhound. He should work for the police.

"Just a few wings. A midnight snack." I shrug.

Throwing his arms up, he allows all the clothes he gathered to fall back to the floor. "Okay, it's official now: you're disgusting! There are *literally* rotten chicken bones hidden somewhere in this vortex you pretend is a bedroom." Pacing back and forth, stepping on anything in the way, he fumes, "I don't get it, Laina! This is not you! I can't keep doin' the same thing *every friggin' morning!*"

As he works himself into a tizzy, the thick, Italian, New York accent he worked hard to shed creeps back, until he sounds like an old Robert De Niro movie soundtrack. "Theah ain't even piles a' clothes on tha floor. It's just a massive fabric dump! Can't even see my own shoes standin' in this shit! Who knew yah *had* so many clothes! What, do yah buy new ones so you don't have ta do a load a' laundry? And yah used to freak if *I* dropped a single French fry in da cah. God forbid a crumb fell on da seat! Now yah eatin' greasy wings in bed? What are yah, a gavone? Did yah use da pillowcase as a napkin? Sure, it's been tough the last two years, but yah can't stop livin' because Tyler died."

Red in the face, he finally puffs to a halt.

The mention of my brother's name sends a bolt of agony straight to my gut. I will always blame myself for what happened. For the accident that killed him while he was on his way to come save me from myself, again. My mother blames me too, even though she'll never come right out and tell me so. We haven't spoken a single word to each other since his funeral.

The urge to cry swells again at the back of my throat. "No, Preston. You can't have a relevant opinion about this. You never lost a sibling."

His shoulders slump, his eyes briefly close, and he slowly exhales, as if taking the time to choose his next words with extreme caution. Stepping closer to the bed again, he sighs. "True. But I lost a friend. And I know he wouldn't be happy with how you've completely let yourself go. Come on, Laina! I've never known you to be okay with livin' like a slob."

I curl onto my right side to face the nightstand, which holds a framed photograph of Tyler and me. It was taken on the happy day we opened our Staten Island bookshop, Viola's Hideaway. That perfect day is now tainted, too. It's the last photograph of us together. His hopeful eyes and bright smile send a wave of emptiness through me. I focus on his handsome, smiling face and imagine I can hear his voice telling me everything will be all right.

"It's not like I *want* to be a mess, Preston. I just don't know how to fix myself. I still feel . . . broken." All I want is to close my eyes and drift back to sleep. Listlessly I curl my fingers around the seafoam green pillowcase beneath my cheek.

"The problem is, you've been like this too long. You've forgotten how to get back to the way you were. Well, today's gonna be exactly what you need." He dramatically flings an arm out, toward the curtained window. "And now, for the really good news!" He pushes the drapes apart to reveal an eye-watering blast of blaring sunshine. "The sun is out!" His sounds like Mary Poppins about to burst into song. "Great for the big day, huh? We got no rain in April or May. Then June, it seems like wet is all we get. But not today!"

Am I not fully awake yet, or has my brain decided to put a concealing fog over what is supposed to happen today? I stare baffled at Preston, mouth agape. "What're you talking about? What's today?"

With a sideways glare, he stomps over to the framed corkboard on the wall over my desk, which is heaped with junk mail, discarded bras, and at least one take-out Chinese carton. Empty, I hope. He untacks an engraved wedding invitation pinned up between an outdated New York *Times* Bestseller List torn from the newspaper and a poster of Shakespeare wearing sunglasses.

A single groan escapes my throat as he hands over the glittery invitation.

*You are cordially invited to celebrate the wedding of*
*Francesca Lazzaro*
*and*
*Rick Collins*
*At Belvedere Castle in Central Park*
*Saturday, June 3*
*at*
*Four o'clock in the afternoon*
*Reception to follow at the Loeb Boathouse*

Boy, do I not want to go. But Fran is Preston's cousin, and I did promise, so . . .

"Don't people say rain means good luck on a wedding day?" I yawn, letting out a short squeal at the tail end of what started as a good stretch, but ended with a cramp in my right calf. That's just how life works for me, most of the time.

"Francesca is not one of those people." He holds up his pointer finger and waves it around freely. "Plus you know damn well that's only said so brides won't take it as a bad omen and cancel the entire wedding." He skips back over to the bed and slaps my charley-horse leg. "Come on, up and at 'em."

I cringe. "Ow!"

"Get up! It's party time, Sleepin' Beauty!" Preston must've added too many sugars to his coffee this morning. His manic look shouts Hidden Agenda, and I don't like it one bit.

I feel utterly exhausted by the prospect of plastering on a fake smile for an entire day. No doubt at some point during the reception I'll be forced to perform the *Cha Cha Slide* against my will and be obliged to engage in small-talk conversations over and over with people I don't know.

I fake another groan. "Oh, Preston, I can't go. Got my period and the cramps are just…" I roll my eyes dramatically, to illustrate that I'm in agony.

He doesn't even stop what he's doing to look over. He simply continues to tidy up. "You had your period a week and a half ago. Remember, you made me go on an emergency tampon and brownie mix run? You were poppin' Midol like they were M&M's."

"Oh. Then maybe it's the flu. Feel my forehead. Do I have a fever?" I scoot to the edge of the bed and pathetically lift my head, asking him to be my human thermometer.

Face impassive, he deadpans, "You don't. Have. A fever." He sniffs at another shirt and chucks it into the hamper. "God, Laina, don't you own *any* clean clothes?"

"Must be a hangover, then."

A brief silence. Maybe he's relenting?

He bends to retrieve a crumpled skirt from the floor, then turns to stare at me impassively. "You should've led with that one. At least it's believable."

"Oh, come on. It's not like Francesca will care if I'm there or not. She's so self-involved, she wouldn't notice if the Pope showed up to her wedding."

He snorts. "Now you really *are* being ridiculous. You actually think Fran knows who the Pope is?"

"Preston, you already have Jack as your date. And I'm not in the mood to play third wheel today."

"Okay, I can understand that . . . but all the more reason for you to come. We gotta find you a man. One you can stand to be around for more than fifteen minutes." He flashes a big crooked smile, opens his eyes wide, then bats his lashes.

I can never keep a straight face when he does this. "Come on," I say, laughing. "I just haven't met anyone I can see a future with."

"You never date anyone long enough to find that out. When was the last time a guy spent the night?"

I wrinkle my nose. "You make it sound like that's a bad thing."

"Of course not." He rolls his eyes. "You're just afraid to let anyone get close because of that one in a million chance they might actually make you happy. I want you to be the woman you used to be, before vintage chicken bones became a real concern in my life."

"Getting me back to the way I was before Tyler died would require more damage control than you might want to take on."

"That's fine!" He perks up. "The first step to recovery is admittin' your life needs a major overhaul. And for the second step, start by helpin' me locate your purple dress in this disaster zone. I put it on the chair last night." He holds up random pieces of clothing. "But it appears to have wandered off. Unless." He flits over to the bed, and in one swift motion whisks the tan comforter off, revealing me, already wearing the plum-colored cocktail dress.

I try to snatch the comforter back.

"Are you kiddin' me?" He gapes. "You actually wore it to *bed*? I should've realized. Your hair and makeup are already done. You're insane. You do realize that?"

"But I saved a lot of time, right?" As I get up I glimpse my reflection in the triple-dresser mirror, my chocolate-brown hair only slightly disheveled. Nothing a little primping can't fix. My dark eyes are still outlined in smoky, catlike liner and eye shadow. I chuckle. "*Now* I remember. I stayed up late last night getting ready so I could sleep in. It's not *my* wedding today, after all." I reach for the comforter again.

Preston yanks it entirely off the bed. With a *woosh* it slithers to the floor.

I hang my head. "Come on, I seriously don't want to go."

"You know, I should thank you now. You're already dressed." He eyes me critically. "That makes my job much easier." He frowns at the dress, though. "How on earth are you planning to get the wrinkles out of that thing? And you know it's not good to sleep in makeup. You're twenty-nine. Cherish that beautiful skin while you can, or one morning you're gonna wake up looking like my old Aunt Giuseppa. The bags under her eyes go down to her chin. You want that?"

I shiver at the thought. Aunt Giuseppa is pretty scary looking.

He squints. "And what's wrong with your right eye? It looks... lopsided."

I reach up and touch both eyelids. The right one feels naked compared to the left.

We both peer at my pillow. "Is that a *spider?*" Preston shrieks.

"No." One of my faux eyelashes is stuck to the pillowcase. I gently peel it free. "I'll just stick this back on."

He looks as though he wants to say something else, but is holding back. Finally he sighs, then mutters, "I just don't get it", and leaves.

As I start to lie back down, he shouts from the living room, "And don't you dare go back to sleep! We have to stop at work before we head into the city."

"Okay, I'm getting up," I growl, and force myself out of bed. I never liked weddings, even before. Going to this one will be sheer torture.

Because my brother isn't the only person who's lost to me. Today of all days I don't want to think about my first love. I don't want to think about Jared.

# Chapter 2

# Viola's Hideaway

An hour later we arrive at the Staten Island bookstore and café Preston and I co-own at the Hylan Plaza, a five-minute walk from our apartment.

Shakespeare's *Twelfth Night* was the inspiration behind Viola's Hideaway. That comedy of errors was Tyler's favorite play. He liked the way the characters all got confused, and everyone kept posing as someone else, yet it all turned out fine in the end. That was my brother, in a nutshell: the optimist of the family. He always believed, and never gave up on anyone. Not even me, though with all the mistakes and dramas I put him though, it must've been hard.

The walls here are a single mural, one massive, continuous painting of scenes from the play. It flows throughout the bookstore. As you walk from room to room, they tell the story. The first painting, by the front entrance, is of a shipwreck caused by a terrible storm. There's Viola, lying on the sand after being washed ashore on the island of Illyria. It's the moment before she awakens, and assumes her twin brother Sebastian has died at sea. Though, in the painting, he can actually be seen lying far away, also washed ashore. I always hurry past this part of the painting now, eyes averted. These days I prefer to look at the walls where Viola is posing as someone else, dressed in medieval tunic and britches, under the assumed name of Cesario.

If only it were that easy to change your identity in real life!

In the second part of the mural Viola is dressed in boy's clothing, both to hide and blend in to this new place. She's standing before Duke Orsino as he hands her a love letter written for his secret crush, Olivia. The next painting shows Viola as Cesario, attempting to convince Olivia to allow Duke Orsino to court her. Orsino's letter lies forgotten at Olivia's feet, though. She appears more intrigued by Viola's boyish charm.

The fourth is a confrontation between Sir Toby Belch and Sir Andrew Aguecheek against Sebastian, who is of course still alive. In this comedy of errors they believe him to be Viola, or rather her as the boy Cesario. Distraught at the fight—and mistaking Sebastian for her beloved—Olivia is on her knees, weeping, reaching out as if to save him. The next painting shows brother and sister reunited and unharmed, while Duke Orsino and Olivia look on in understandable confusion. In the last part of the mural Viola is in Duke Orsino's arms, while Olivia clings lovingly to Sebastian. All's well that ends well . . .

Besides the mural, we have comfortable oversized armchairs, tufted brocade couches, and leather ottomans scattered around four rooms to enhance the cozy atmosphere. Built-in bookcases stand row after row from floor to ceiling. Our employees maneuver antique wooden ladders, which slide around the perimeter of the rooms on wheels, in tracks, as they retrieve out-of reach books on the highest shelves for waiting customers. It's truly an old-fashioned bookshop, a moment preserved from the past, which is what Tyler always wanted.

When we were still kids, one year he received an illustrated copy of the play for Christmas. After he read it, he used to tell me the story. Sometimes we even acted it out. I liked the drama of the shipwreck, of course, but I've always felt most drawn to the destinies of Viola and Duke Orsino. Their love story is the one I turn to when I want to remember a better period in my own life – a time when fairytales, fate, and the notion of true love were still very much alive in me.

Preston and I head over to the checkout counter where one of our two part-time employees, Tammy, is handing a bag to a departing customer. An undergraduate at the College of Staten Island, she's thoroughly mastered the rolled-right-out-of-bed look. Her creamy blond hair is pulled atop her head in a messy bun. She's wearing plaid pajama pants and a white t-shirt. Preston has asked her repeatedly—actually, pleaded over and over is more like it—for her to at least yank on a pair of jeans before she comes to work.

Somehow this always goes in one ear and out the other.

"Good mornin', Tammy," Preston says in a chipper tone. Then he does a double-take at her outfit. "You're looking so...so *comfortable* today." He winces and shakes his head.

"Morning, Mr. De Luca," she replies mid-yawn, and turns to me. "Miss Jorden, that book order came in, so I signed for it. I put the box in your office." She slumps over the checkout counter, an old wood and glass pharmacy display case, propped on one elbow, the palm of her hand supporting one cheekbone as if that alone is holding her up. She chews gum like a cow slowly munching grass, not bothering to conceal that she's totally bored out of her mind. On the bright side, she's honest and always on time, and the customers seem to love her. Go figure.

"That's fantastic. Thank you." I neatly restack some untidy literary journals on display atop the checkout counter since the mess doesn't seem to have caught Tammy's attention.

"Are you and Cristin okay with holding down the fort today?" Preston asks, rifling through a stack of invoices. He tucks them inside a large yellow envelope and looks up.

"Yeah, sure, of course," she says in a lethargic monotone, like a human version of Eeyore from *Winnie the Pooh.* "We got it covered. Don't worry about a thing."

Flashing a strained grin, Preston squints at her in a way which I know indicates he's irked. "Ah," he retorts. "*Ex*cellent."

"You guys actually got me out of a camping trip with the fam," she adds, "so it worked out. I hate camping."

"Really?" I chime in. "I love it."

Preston turns to stare, looking as if there's a fish hook tugging on his upper lip. "When on *earth* have you ever gone camping?"

"Every summer when I was a kid."

"And where exactly did this *camping* take place, Central Park?"

"No, smart-ass. We used to pitch tents out in the woods, in Pennsylvania."

He shudders and glances back at Tammy. "Well, there you go. Learn somethin' new every day." Leaning against the counter, he turns back to me. "I'm guessing your dad took you and Tyler?"

"What? Um, yeah...that's right." I stop myself in time, to avoid revealing who else was always in attendance on those weekends.

Preston narrows his eyes as though he knows I'm withholding the full roster of the camping crew. You see, our next door neighbor and his son Jared went on camping trips every year. My father, Tyler, and I were always invited to tag along. But of course, I won't mention that to Preston. He'd roll his eyes. Over the years I've mentioned Jared's name to Preston an insane number of times. He believes it's unnatural for an adult woman to still harbor feelings for a childhood sweetheart. So, after he'd heard the never-ending list of nostalgic stories from my childhood many times over, he decided enough was enough. From that moment on, I have not been allowed to so much as whisper Jared's name in front of him.

"Okay!" he says now, clapping once. Conversation over. "So I'm going to check on a couple things. Then we can head out." He dashes away to his office, a closet-sized room adjacent to my own, at the back of the store.

As Tammy oh-so-slowly organizes a small shelf of books beside the register she turns to look at me. "Oh, Miss Jorden, I almost forgot. This woman in here a little while ago asked to leave these flyers by the register. I wanted to check first to see if it's okay, before I put them out." She slowly reaches for a stack of lavender paper on the shelf beneath the register, and sets it in front of me. "Her name is Desi Chase. She's, like, a fortuneteller."

An old engraving of a crystal ball is centered on the paper. Below it is the following advertisement:

*Come See the Mystical Desi Chase, and Learn Your Fate!*
*Located next to the St. George Theatre*
*Dial 718-5-5-5-F-A-T-E to schedule your appointment today!*
*Walk-Ins Welcome.*
*Available for events and parties!*

"Huh. Guess she's looking to drum up business in the neighborhood." I chuckle. "Suppose it won't hurt to leave them out. Some people actually believe in this sort of thing."

Tammy tugs the rubber band from her head in slow motion, roughly tousles her hair, and re-sets the still-messy bun. "I don't know, she seemed pretty legit. Like, her clothes and all?"

Tilting my head, I purse my lips and stare at Tammy in disbelief. It's just the sort of thing I would've been gullible enough to fall for myself, a few years ago. "Please don't tell me you buy into all that mystical see-the-future voodoo."

She flutters her eyelashes and shrugs. "You don't think some people have a natural gift to predict the future or even see your fate?"

"I believe some people have a natural gift for convincing others they have that ability. But it's all a scam. Until someone proves me wrong, *that's* what I believe."

"Really? But you couldn't have always thought that." Tammy snorts, pulls two long locks of hair from her freshly-made bun, and tucks them behind her ears.

Caught off-guard by the question, I stare for a moment before saying, "I suppose not. When I was a kid, I believed in pretty much everything. But then…" I look away and fiddle with a mug of colorful pens, as if it's crucial to straighten them until they are just so. "Reality struck. I grew up."

Tammy hunches over the counter and slides one of the flyers in front of her. She reads it intently, picking clumps of mascara from her lashes and flicking the flakes onto the floor. At last she sighs. "So, should I chuck these, then?"

Now I feel like the stereotypical grumpy, rigid boss. "No, no, it's fine. You can leave them out for now."

Preston emerges from his office, smoothing his tie, all set to drag me off to Francesca's wedding, and we depart. I fail to notice, until after we climb into his car, that one of Desi Chase's advertisements is still crumpled in one hand. Not wanting to clutter up his car after the morning's neatness lecture, I tuck it into my clutch, intending to throw it away at the first opportunity.

* * *

A half-hour later, as we board the Staten Island Ferry with Preston's boyfriend Jack, Preston says in a judgmental tone, "You were mumbling Jared's name in your sleep last night."

Did he seriously just bring up The Forbidden Jared as a topic of conversation? And how can I possibly control what comes out of my mouth when I'm unconscious?

While Preston is a true friend who looks out for and even takes care of me, I think he doesn't really understand me. Yet he's pretty much become the only family I have now. My father's been out of the picture since I was sixteen. He and my mother decided to divorce not long after Jared and his mom, Evelyn, moved away without a hint or a word as to where. This was shortly after Jared's dad, William, suddenly passed away. That was one of the most difficult times in my life, too. My childhood sweetheart moved, his father died, and mine vanished from my life, as my parents split, all in one summer. That's a lot for any teenager to process. Sometimes I think I never really did . . . but still.

Now I fold my arms across my chest and sigh. "You said that like I should somehow have control over what I dream about, or what I say in my sleep."

He snorts. "No, I didn't."

Preston and I met in our freshman year of college at Fordham University. We were both studying business, and clicked from the very first day. But we only became roommates five years later, when he answered an ad I put on Craigslist, and we reconnected. We now live in what is actually a two-family home in Oakwood on Staten Island; one our landlord, Mr. Cangiano, creatively transformed into two separate apartments. We have the entire ground floor, which we enter through the side door of the home. Timothy and Erica, a newly married couple, occupy the second floor. The basement is where the communal washer and dryer are located, along with Mr. Cangiano's workbench. He tinkers in the basement from time to time on woodworking projects, or whenever he's doing renovations.

Preston drops the subject of Jared and sleep talking as the three of us climb the staircase of the ferryboat. We head through one of the side doors to find seats outside, overlooking the water. On a humid June day, a nice saltwater breeze is always more welcome than being crammed in a stuffy cabin with strangers, all of whom are sucking up whatever oxygen is trapped inside. This way we can enjoy the Statue of Liberty, Ellis Island, and the New York City skyline as we drift into Lower Manhattan.

The horn blows, indicating the ferry is about to depart from the terminal.

"I'm not an idiot," Preston says suddenly, looking at me again. "I know you can't control it. I'm just saying, it's not healthy to still obsess over Jared. You've had feelings for him since kindergarten, and he's still not out of your system. What would your brother think?"

Most of the time, whatever Preston has to say has some sort of clear logic behind it. But this really takes the prize.

"Tyler would probably be trying to help me track him down. Just like all the other times he tried to help me in the past. He was always on my side." My voice quivers and I blink rapidly, afraid I will cry, and that I won't be able to blame it on the stiff breeze coming off the water. "He knew how much Jared and I cared about each other. Tyler only wanted me to be happy. He was Jared's best friend. He would understand."

"Okay, okay, I'm sorry." Preston holds both hands up. "I know it's a touchy subject. But you'd think if it was meant to be, you'd have been able to track him down by now. Or that he would have tracked you down."

"I've searched the name Jared Grant online a thousand times. Nothing comes up. At least, nothing but a seventy year old in a retirement home in Mendocino. I've tried to find a Facebook page, a Twitter profile – even searched the internet White Pages. I don't know what else to do. Hire a detective? Who has the cash for that?" I try to say this casually, as if the thought hasn't seriously crossed my mind several times.

"Now that's just desperate, and sad." Turning away, Preston swipes an abandoned NY *Post* someone left two seats over. A picture of the president is on the front page. "Can they possibly ever write about anything else again besides the Hookergate scandal? Everywhere I turn, that's all anyone is talking about," he fumes.

"Maybe Jared changed his name," says Jack suddenly.

"What? Oh, be realistic." Preston rolls his eyes as he skims the crinkled, windblown pages of the *Post*. "What, you think he's in the Witness Protection Program or something? Nobody else ever *does* that."

* * *

Once we're off the ferry and at the West 81<sup>st</sup> Street entrance to the Park, on Central Park West, I hesitate. I haven't been here since the day Tyler died. Of course the cobblestone sidewalk, the trees, the horses and carriages – nothing has changed.

"Why are we going in this way? I thought the wedding was at the Boathouse." My voice quivers. I wipe my sweaty palms down the sides of my dress, dreading the thought of having to walk through the Shakespeare Garden again, the place the three of us – Tyler, Jared, and I – used to hang out.

"Well, yeah, it is. But the ceremony is at Belvedere Castle," Preston replies. "Laina, you know this. It was all on the invitation."

The short hairs on the back of my neck stand on end as if I've received an electric shock. A tennis-ball-sized lump weights the pit of my stomach. How could I not have taken in that the ceremony was going to be at Belvedere Castle?

"Are you sure that part was on the invitation? Maybe they forgot to print it."

Surely they would have *had* to include that information, though. Otherwise how would Preston or any of the other guests know where to go? It's not like he chats with Fran on a daily basis. In fact, he usually makes sure to avoid her at all costs. They aren't exactly close.

My head swims as I try to recall the exact words printed on the invitation, but I can't freaking remember. Did I block that part out? Did my eyes jump over the dread words *Belvedere Castle*? Or did my brain simply refuse to process this volatile information?

What the hell is wrong with me?

A wave of nausea washes over me. I can't do it. Can't go in there. "Oh, um, right. It's just that, well . . . see, I didn't realize we were going to Belvedere Castle *first*." I back away, fingertips tingling, hands trembling at my sides. My heart is racing so fast I can feel the rapid beats thumping inside my head. Even though it's been two years since Tyler . . . since I've been to the Shakespeare Garden and Belvedere Castle . . . I know everything will come flooding back. Too many memories live behind the walls of the park.

I hyperventilate, making myself even dizzier.

"Hey." Looking bewildered, Preston touches my arm. "Okay but, well, why the big deal? What is it? What? Do you have a fear of castles, or somethin'?"

With a curled lip, Jack mumbles, "Who on earth wouldn't like castles?"

Waving a hand flippantly in front of my face as if everything is fine, I continue retreating, stepping slowly backward. Unfortunately, I take one step too many, and fall off the curb and into the street, legs flying over my head.

I'm struck with not just pain but sudden mortification, realizing I've just given the fifteen or so onlookers parading past a juicy view of my lacy purple panties. My cheeks burn as though they're on fire. I try not to make direct eye contact with anyone who might've witnessed my fall. Most continue past as if I don't exist, anyhow. It's New York, after all. I greatly prefer this callous reaction to that of the others, who pause to gape in sheer horror and pity, glancing back over their shoulders as they whiz by.

It's okay, I tell myself. What are the odds you'll ever see a single one of these people ever again in your whole life?

Ugh. With my luck at least one will move in right next door, and the second they come over to introduce themselves, it'll be like, *Oh, hey! I remember you! You're that girl who took a flop in front of a horse and carriage outside Central Park!*

Preston and Jack hasten to my side and endeavor to lift me, both looking baffled by my behavior. I can't blame them. It must appear that I've lost my damned mind. My knees knock, my legs are unsteady as they set me back on my feet. I feel like Bambi when he learned how to walk. I try to shake off the inelegant topple, to look serene, almost as if I meant to do it. I also thank my lucky stars I managed to not land in any horse shit, since this is usually where the horse-drawn carriages stand around waiting for customers.

"Laina, what the hell is up with you?" Preston gapes. He grips my arm too tightly, as if he's worried I'll drop right back to the ground should he let go. I'm sure glad he is, too, because I wouldn't want to find out this is a real possibility.

And then it hits me, worst of all. Through heavy breathing, I gasp, "Honestly? I think I'm going to be sick."

\* \* \*

I'm sure to those around us it must appear as if Preston and Jack are holding me hostage because I am staggering along, doing my best not to look at my surroundings as they drag me arm in arm through the Shakespeare Garden to Belvedere Castle. It doesn't do much good, however, because every step I take evokes another memory.

I can't help but notice that Preston and Jack are exchanging *what the hell is wrong with her* glances.

We finally reach the first level of the castle, where a gigantic white tent is set up. Preston turns to me. "Could you please stop actin' like an extra from a serial killer flick? It's going to freak everyone out. I don't know what your problem is today." He sounds annoyed but there's worry beneath the sharpness. He makes an effort to sound giddy, chirping, "Weddings are happy! This is a *happy occasion!*" Folding his arms, he eyes me up and down. "Jeez, we're in Central Park at a nice event. With free food and champagne! You're actin' as if we're draggin' you through Seaview Hospital."

"Which hospital?" Jack frowns.

"It's this old, abandoned one in Staten Island. Super creepy and supposedly haunted." Preston turns back to me as Jack's face falls. He slips one arm through mine, and leads the way to the next level of the Belvedere Castle. "Let's just say a quick hello to Francesca, then grab seats. The sooner we do that, the sooner the ceremony will be over. Then we can head to the reception to get you good and sauced."

Inside the tent, complete and utter chaos is unfolding. The interior is overflowing with bright pink bridesmaids whose dresses appear to have been transported from an Italian wedding in the 1980's. All that's missing is the tall, frizzy, big hair. They scatter like cockroaches at the end of the world when Francesca's shrill voice, which rises above all other sounds, barks orders from her throne—a folding stool—as the finishing touches are applied to her up-do.

One bridesmaid in particular appears utterly traumatized, huddled in a corner, crying.

"Where the *hell* is my mother?" Francesca blares. Her freshly-dyed poppy-red hair is pulled back so tightly her eyebrows have been elevated about two inches farther up her forehead, giving her the slightly pointed, sinister appearance of a Disney cartoon villainess. In the two years I've known Francesca, she's always had a sour look plastered on that long, thin face, as if she's permanently disgusted with the world and every single person in it. I have no idea how she managed to convince Rick to willingly marry her. My conclusion is, the poor guy must be certifiably insane, someone who in former times *would* be on his way to Seaview Hospital.

"Um, I think she went to the bathroom," a young, skinny bridesmaid hesitantly replies, as she touches up another bridesmaid's lurid pink eye shadow.

Francesca's eyes bulge out of her head, further enhancing the cartoon look. "Well, what the hell are you *doing*? Stop fooling around and *go get her*!"

The bridesmaid gasps, frantically throws the eye shadow and makeup brush on the ground, and skedaddles out of the tent.

Francesca screams, "*Tiffany!*"

I swear I feel the ground quake beneath my feet.

A profusely-sweating bridesmaid darts into the tent, crying, "I'm here! I'm here!" Grabbing a glass pitcher of water on the table beside Francesca, she savagely chugs it down until there isn't a single drop left.

Francesca glowers and chides through gritted teeth, "Tiffany, where's my something blue? I *need* my something blue."

The dehydrated bridesmaid slams the pitcher onto the table with an audible *thump*, and wheezes while simultaneously gasping for breath, "I'll . . .I'll be . . . back. As soon . . . as I can." She takes a bracing lungful of air before dashing off again on the Wedding 10K Marathon.

"Hang on! Hang the hell on!" Francesca roars after her. "Get the photographer! Tell him pictures in *five minutes*, and not a second later. I don't care if he needs a cigarette break, or a coffee break. I don't even care if he needs to use the toilet so bad he can't stand up straight. I'm sick of everyone's heads being up their asses today."

The bridesmaid pauses in midstride, in case maybe there is something else coming.

When Francesca sees her still standing around, her face swells until it's in danger of bursting, and disturbingly close to the exact shade as her fiery hair. "Why the hell are you still standing there? *Go! Go!* Something blue! Photographer! *Head! Out! Of! Ass!*"

Tiffany bolts from the tent, as Francesca heatedly adds, "Son of a *bitch!*"

Preston, Jack, and I stand frozen, clinging to one another in sheer terror. Finally brave Preston bucks up the courage to approach his cousin.

When he isn't beheaded, he waves for Jack and me to follow.

We both shake our heads and stay put, a safe distance away. The look on Jack's face eloquently illustrates what I'm thinking: *The hell is wrong with him? I don't want to get close to those jaws. What is he, insane?*

He waves us over again, with more urgency. Now we have no choice but to unwillingly comply. Jack and I take baby steps over to Preston's side, still clinging to one another for safety.

"Hey, Fran," Preston's voice cracks. "Congratulations. You look absolutely stunning." He braces himself for a typhoon-level blast.

She curls her thin lips and flashes a phony, sour snarl. "Yeah. Thanks. Right out of a freaking fairytale," she sneers.

Preston flinches but doesn't flee. "Okay, well, I can see you're busy gettin' ready for your big moment, so we're gonna go find some seats. Just wanted to pop in to…"

Francesca's gaze slowly shifts, snakelike, in my direction. Her eyes widen as they land on me. Gaze still riveted, she shoves an outthrust palm about an inch from Preston's face, nearly smashing his nose.

He instantly stops talking.

Her eyes light up. She beams at me, actually perking up in her seat, as if I'm suddenly her most favorite person in the world. Or maybe her next meal.

This is even more frightening than the raging outburst and the swollen fuchsia face. My stomach churns, because her happiness could only mean trouble for me.

"*Laina*, thank goodness you're here!" She actually laughs, and breathes a giant sigh of relief.

The woman working on her hair is having difficulty following Francesca's erratic movements, lunging around with the comb and can of hairspray like a frantic little dog who needs to pee.

Francesca glances around. Her basilisk gaze settles on the huddled, sobbing bridesmaid. "Courtney!"

The girl's tear-streaked face snaps around to look in our direction. Her bloodshot eyes bulge with fear.

"Courtney, sweetie, come make yourself useful. Bring over Sara's dress."

Courtney levers herself up and shuffles convict-like to a table where an extra bridesmaid's dress is lying unattended. Clumsily wrestling the voluminous folds of the monstrous dress, she staggers slowly toward us with it.

"Today, Courtney! I'm getting married *to-day*," Francesca wails.

Courtney instantly picks up the pace.

"Thank you. There you go." Snatching the dress away from the trembling bridesmaid, Francesca thrusts it at me. "Put this on. My bridesmaid, Sara, went into early labor this morning. Isn't that just *perfect* timing?" She looks down at her phone, then back at me. "I need you to take her place. Otherwise we'll have an extra groomsman with no one to take down the aisle."

Fighting not to drop the horrible, hefty dress, I inspect it. The thing is so heavy, the hem must be packed with lead. The material seems to be the offspring of an unfortunate mating between some pink cellophane wrap and a Brill-O pad. It comes equipped with an oversized, droopy bow plastered right to the bodice. Oh, goody.

Jack feels the material gingerly and mumbles, "What color do you think this is, Bubblegum?"

Francesca must have overheard him. She sniffs and bluntly replies, "*The shade* is Pole Dancer Pink."

Jack nods. "Yeah, sure. That would've been my second guess." Whirling away from her, he covers his mouth, then bites the side of his hand, obviously fighting a terrible urge to giggle.

I struggle to hold the cumbersome dress out in front of me, for a better look. I estimate it's about twelve sizes too big. There's no way I can wear this thing.

"It's…um…it's really lovely," I force through my teeth. "But I'm pretty sure it isn't going to fit." Then I brace myself for the response.

She rolls her eyes and slumps her shoulders, as if thinking I'm a complete moron. "Ye-es, I understand that. Were you *not listening* when I *specifically told you* the dress was meant for a woman who is *now in labor?*" She takes a slow, deep breath. "I'll just have my mother pin it around you. You'll look fabulous. Now, let's go! Chop-chop. Pictures in…" She glances back at her phone for the time. "*Son of a bitch!* Where is the photographer? Where the hell *is* everybody?"

The tent does seem to have cleared out within the last few minutes. As Preston ushers Jack and me outside, I plead with him not to make me do this, to which he responds, in a snippy tone, "Well, I'm sorry, but you've got to. I'm not goin' back in there. I think she's possessed! She'll rip me to shreds. Is that what you want?"

"It's definitely not what *I* want," Jack quips, smirking.

"I begged you, literally *begged* you, not to make me come today," I cry, "and now look at what I'm going to be subjected to." I heave the atrocious dress up inches away from his face, so he can get a closer look at the giant pink scrub-pad I'm being forced to put on my body.

He nods apologetically, scratching the back of his head, shading his eyes like he has a migraine. "Yeah, good point. This one's on me. Don't worry, I promise we'll get you good and drunk at the reception. I owe you big time, honey."

"You're going to owe me for the rest of the century after today," I snarl.

Preston leans in to hug me, whispering, "I swear, somehow I *will* make it up to you. It'll be somethin' huge. Down the road you'll look back at this day and it will all have been worth it."

"I sure hope you're right," I reply through gritted teeth, "because I want to hurt you so very badly right now."

# Chapter 3

# Drunken Disasters

I'm never going to meet a guy looking like foam on a mad dog's lips," I grumble as we sit at our table and the reception begins. Preston rushes off and returns with a whole tray of assorted alcoholic drinks. When he slides it in front of me, I scoop a cocktail in each hand and slurp from each drink's straws simultaneously. I hate to be so crass, but the fancy beverages do make this situation seem a bit more bearable. I feel that I've earned them. Especially since I'm seated across the table from Preston's disgusting Uncle Murray, who doesn't know how to properly chew food or even use a fork. He's notorious for slopping stuff in the general vicinity of his face. Half of it ends up in his lap.

The Reception Hall of the Loeb Boathouse is lined with floor to ceiling windows. Rustic and charming, the vintage Boathouse overlooks a lake, giving the illusion you've suddenly, magically escaped from the City to an elegant country retreat. On the down side, the tall, chaotic floral centerpieces Fran picked out happen to match the feisty Bridesmaid dresses perfectly.

I guzzle the first two drinks within seconds.

Preston holds up a hand to halt me. "Uh, actually the drinks were meant for all of us."

I shoot him a warning glare as I push the two empty glasses away.

He pauses briefly, taking in my heated gaze. "But of course you clearly need them more than we do. Have at it."

As soon as I finish my second round I select another two. I don't bother to ask what they are, nor do I care if they'll taste complimentary. I simply drink.

"You might want to slow down. You know what happens when you imbibe too much," Preston reminds me, as I finish off my next round of liquid courage.

"Right now," I huff, "I don't care! You should've let me stay home. Then this all could've been avoided."

God, the dress is scratchy. I'm itchy all over, as if I recently fell, naked, into a patch of poison ivy. I can't even reach the places it is irritating the worst. "Shit," I mutter, "I have to readjust this." Geographical layers of tulle are bunched around my knees, and the under-slip lining is twisted like a tourniquet from the waist down.

"What the hell are you doing?" Preston mumbles, looking around nervously as I squirm in my seat.

I flash him another heated scowl. "I look awful! And I can't even begin to express how uncomfortable I am. Your cousin Francesca is an evil woman who enjoys inflicting pain on others."

"Oh, what a news flash. Just sit down and relax," he commands, tapping my arm. "Because you're just gonna make it worse with all the fidgeting. And you may feel uncomfortable, but you look totally fine."

I know he's full of crap, because he wrinkles his nose as he tells me this.

"You're the worst liar in the world! I look like I clawed my way out of a Zombie Barbie Halloween catalogue." I reach for a back-up drink.

"No, really, it could be worse. You just..." He pauses and frowns at my chest, then leans back in his chair. "Did your boobs grow?"

Now *my* eyes bulge from my head. "No, they didn't grow! What, you think I magically sprouted bigger boobs in the last few hours? This is tissue paper! I had to stuff the cleavage like a turkey so I wouldn't walk around flashing everyone the whole night." When I press in both arms to squeeze my chest, the paper crinkles audibly.

Preston's mouth drops open in horror. "Oh, you poor thing! I had no idea!" He claps a hand over his mouth, peering inquisitively, then reaches out and pokes at my chest. "Sorry," he adds, no longer able to contain his laughter. "Just couldn't resist."

"You jerk. I felt like a voodoo doll, Preston! Poked, prodded, pinned, and stuffed for over an hour. Do you have any idea how humiliating this feels?"

"No, but I can guess. You do look kind of like a toy-train wreck."

"That's putting it mildly. But at least you're being honest now."

As the first course arrives he spreads his pink dinner napkin over his lap, then reaches over and swipes mine, tucking it into his shirt collar.

I stare at him, confounded.

"What? This is an Armani suit. Like you're really gonna care if you get food on that hideous thing," he points a fork at my dress.

I flap a hand indifferently. "Go ahead. Take it."

Six drinks and three tequila shots later, I drag Preston and Jack to the middle of the dance floor. Strobe lights flicker like spastic lightning, making me feel like a robot stuck on slow mode. I know I'll hate myself tomorrow for the amount of alcohol I've already consumed, but right now, I simply don't care.

"Were you always this horrible at dancing?" Preston comments, looking somewhat embarrassed at my unpolished dance moves.

Ignoring his cheeky comment, I proceed to strut my stuff. Yet I can barely enjoy myself, since the pins holding the massive dress to my body refuse to stop jabbing into me. The longer I'm out on the dance floor, the more I begin to notice something else – the itchy cellophane material has found a way to superglue itself to my skin. It now feels as if I'm trapped in a vinyl sweat suit. The scratchy layers of tulle underneath the hot, sticky fabric scrape against my calves and thighs. I feel like a prisoner in a straightjacket full of needles and hot wool.

Since there doesn't seem to be enough time to devise an alternative solution, I rip. In a haphazard manner, I tear off portions of the dress and fling them to the dance floor, piece by piece.

Preston stops dancing once he realizes what I'm doing. Appalled, he shouts, "Whoa! Whoa! Whoa! What's happening?" He grabs my arm in an attempt to stop the frenzied ripping.

"I'm puttin' this dress out of its mishery," I slur, still tearing off sections of tulle.

"Yeah, well it looks like you're attempting to perform the world's most disorganized striptease. Come on, let's go outside and get you some fresh air."

After my first couple of steps after him, I feel a tug, then a wrenching tear down one side of the dress, followed by a cool breeze on my legs. It feels incredible. I sigh with pleasure, as if I've had a tiny orgasm, then glance down and notice there's a fresh slit snaking to my upper thigh.

As I turn to look for the nearest restroom, I nearly collide with a man who's staring at me in what seems to be wide-eyed horror. He's also exceedingly handsome and muscular, with short caramel-brown hair and bright blue eyes.

"Oh my God! I'm so sorry!" he cries. "I stepped on your hem."

Preston slowly backs away, flashing his Mr. Bean grin. This handsome stranger clearly has The Preston stamp of approval.

I quickly check to make sure my nether regions aren't exposed, so that's a plus.

"I actually think you improved it," I shout above the blaring music to the attractive stranger, pleased with his handiwork.

He notices the torn-off chunk of dress on the floor and bends to retrieve it, along with the giant bow that once pathetically festooned my tissue-enhanced chest.

I grab it and fling it over one shoulder. It lands on a nearby table, smacking into Preston's Aunt Mona's plate of food. She jumps and glances around like a startled squirrel.

The handsome stranger's mouth hangs open. He stands before me in a frozen daze. The other pieces of fabric fall from his hands. He glances quickly around, as if making sure no one will suspect the tossed bow came from him. "And what were you planning on doing with the rest of the pieces?" he asks.

Indifferently, I shrug. "Bury them. Burn them. Scrub out some pans. I haven't decided yet."

He grins, revealing perfectly straight white teeth. "What's your name?"

"Laina Jorden." I extend a hand.

He takes it, holding on longer than a normal handshake would typically last. I don't pull away, partly because having someone else to hold on to helps steady me in my current inebriated state. Now that I've stopped dancing, though, the room spins, and I feel even more off balance. It's a difficult task to keep my feet firmly planted and not keel over.

"I'm Mason Hartley. I went to law school with the groom." He peers over at his buddy. Rick is spinning Francesca around the dance floor. Turning back to me, Mason adds, "I only hope the poor bastard knew what he was doing. I know he loves Frannie, but damn, she seems like a handful!"

I hoot with laughter. "You have no idea! I wasn't even supposed to be a bridesmaid. I was enslaved against my will." I stagger and trip over my own feet.

Luckily Mason is there to grab my arm and stop me from falling.

I straighten, then clumsily lose my footing once more. It's actually not possible to stand still any more. "Oh, jeez!" I exclaim, and bend to inspect my right high heel, finding exactly what I anticipated – a broken heel. Kicking off the shoe, I twist to look up at Mason. "Are you good with your hands?"

He looks taken aback by my bold question, blinking at me, then staring blankly for a moment.

I hold up the crippled shoe.

He nods and follows me as I hobble to a nearby table and snatch up a random steak knife. I hold out one hand. "Can I borrow you for a moment, counselor?"

He sniggers, and takes hold. "Uh, sure. As long as you're not forcing me to be an accomplice to murder."

"Don't be silly. I just need you to help me make some flats."

\* \* \*

Mason and I remain glued to each other for the rest of the reception. It's strange, but I somehow feel drawn to him, as if the universe had plans for us to meet. It's a feeling I hadn't really expected to come around for me again.

We drag two chairs over to a far corner of the hall and huddle together so we can hear each other speak over the earsplitting music. Our conversation is easy, light, and enjoyable. He seems much more fascinating than any other man I've met in some time. His playful nature is a welcome escape.

As the wedding reception begins to die down and the guests depart, Preston spots us lost in our own little world. He carries news of the plan for the after-wedding party. "The arrangement is, everyone will meet at Francesca's parents' house in Massapequa."

I'd figured on going home early. But it's pointless to object. There is no way Preston will allow me to cut my time short with Mason. To be honest, a tiny part of me doesn't want this night to end.

We gather our belongings and Mason gives me a piggyback ride so I won't have to hobble through Central Park on wobbly, dissected heels. Preston, Jack, Mason, and I discuss our plan of action as we arrive outside the entranceway to Central Park. Mason is nice enough to run across the street to a vendor's cart and buy me a pair of souvenir flip-flops. We call a Lyft to take us to the Long Island Railroad Station, where we'll hop on the train to the Massapequa Park exit in Long Island. Luckily, Francesca's parents' house is within walking distance from that stop.

On the train, Mason and I sit across from Preston and Jack. They can't seem to stop making goo-goo eyes at each other. And maybe the alcohol is wearing off, because after a while I find myself constantly fidgeting in my seat, barely able to concentrate on what Mason is saying. The stupid dress is driving me nuts.

Unintentionally, I cut Mason off mid-sentence and tap Preston's knee. "Where's my purple cocktail dress? I've got to get out of this itchy thing," I pull the fabric away from my chest, trying to calm myself down with Lamaze breaths. Not that I've actually had instruction in that, so who knows if I'm doing it right.

Looking guilty, he says, "Now, don't be mad."

"Don't even say it." Pinching my eyes closed, I shake my head vehemently.

"I don't have it. I was given specific instructions not to let you change out of the bridesmaid dress under any circumstances, so I had to hand yours over. Francesca insisted."

"Preston, this isn't funny anymore! I've got pins poking me in places that are too embarrassing to mention, the itchy tulle has worn away the first three layers of my skin, and the other crap feels like a sandpaper tourniquet around my body. I can't handle this torture much longer. If I can't change soon I'll have no choice but to show up at Francesca's parents' house in nothing but my birthday suit and pink flip-flops. And don't think I won't do it, because I will."

Rolling his eyes, Preston groans, "Now, let's not get dramatic."

Jack, however, seems extremely uncomfortable with the conversation. He shifts in  his seat, as if considering fleeing the scene. He knows me well enough to realize what I'm saying is anything but an empty threat.

I turn my back to Mason. "Could you please unzip me?"

His eyes widen as if he's unsure if he's being serious or not. I assure him that I'm perfectly serious.

"Cut that out!" Preston leans forward, swatting my arm. "You're gonna get us all arrested." He doesn't let up on the smoldering glare until after he sits back in his seat, to be sure his message has sunk in.

Mason leans in closer. "Don't worry. We'll be there soon. I'll give them ransom money for the release of your kidnapped dress." He follows with a wink that's sly and sexy, yet so fleeting, if I'd blinked, I might have missed it entirely.

I crack a smile and nudge him with my shoulder. "Thank you."

Preston sits arm in arm with Jack, smirking, a rapt audience to our flirting. At least *he* is clearly pleased with the way the night is turning out.

* * *

We arrive at the Lazzaros' newly-renovated Colonial-style home in Massapequa a little after eleven. Various uncles crowd the large porch, lost in a haze of cigar smoke. Preston says hello to each one, though I'm not entirely sure how he could distinguish who's who lurking in that thick, hazy cloud. I hold my breath to avoid inhaling the pungent stench of cheap tobacco. Finally Preston ushers us through the front door. I flash a general wave at the uncles before we enter in a puff of smoke. A hot shower will surely be required by the end of this night.

The moment we're inside, Mrs. Lazzaro greets us. Francesca's mother is an elegant woman, tall and slender. She clearly isn't afraid to wear what appears to be her finest jewelry—all of it at once—and she offers to give us the grand tour. The home seems to go on forever, each new room pretty much identical to the last, all filled with chunky, gaudy furniture, in a style I can only describe as Gilded Mediterranean. She doesn't fail to boast about how each piece of furniture was custom made and shipped straight from her family's hometown in Italy.

As we stroll through, all I can think about is raiding one of her many closets in the hope of finding a pair of stretch pants and a t-shirt. I desperately need to get more comfortable. But I never get a chance to slip away and explore, unobserved. As big as the house is, it still seems entirely too crammed with guests. Music drifts in from the backyard, where many more partygoers surround the in-ground pool.

Once the long, drawn-out tour is over, we decide to head for the kitchen and get drinks. But before we can make our way there, a few friends from law school pull Mason away to talk shop. Then Preston's mother steals him and Jack from my side. I have no choice but to go solo and make myself a cocktail.

But as I reach for a bottle of Belvedere from the counter it's snatched from my grasp.

"Excuse me!" I snap at the young man who took it. He looks so clean cut and baby faced, he can't possibly be twenty-one.

Acting jittery, he blurts out, "Sorry, but we've been given strict orders from Mrs. Lazzaro that only the waiters can pour or serve drinks." He sets the vodka bottle back on the counter. "I can't let you touch this. My dad will kill me if I get fired from another job."

"Okay, buddy, just relax. It's not *that* drastic." I sigh. "Mrs. Lazzaro seriously hired waiters for her daughter's After Reception party?"

"Um, well, yeah." He nods like a dashboard toy. "And normally I wouldn't say anything, but she scares the shit out of me. To be honest, I could use a swig myself." His hands shake as he takes fresh champagne flutes from the counter and sets them on a tray. Trembling like a frantic rabbit, he hastily fills them with champagne. More liquor lands on the tray than inside them.

"So, if I need drinks, I have to hunt you down?"

"Well, no. There's two other waiters." He hands me an empty flute and fills it with champagne.

"Thank you." I chug it all down. Unsatisfied, I hold out the tiny, skinny glass for a refill. "See, here's the thing. I'm going to be requiring a lot more alcohol than this." I shake the empty flute and eye the other glasses on the tray balanced on his hand. "What's your name?"

"Ian," he gulps.

"Well, Ian, if you don't mind, you have just become my new best friend for the night."

* * *

An hour later, I'm still following Ian around, since I have no idea where Mason, Preston, or Jack have gone. I eventually break away from Ian's hip and duck outside for some fresh air. Shuffling across the back patio, I abandon my champagne flute on one of the tables. Loud rock music is still booming despite the late hour. I figure the only reason the police haven't been called about noise complaints is because the entire neighborhood must be in attendance. It's certainly crowded enough. Or maybe that's double vision from all the drinks I've had.

The night is hot and sticky, the air almost too thick to breathe. I stare at the sky to see if I can make out any stars shining behind the dark blanketing clouds, but the longer I look up the dizzier I feel. There are too many people on the patio so I decide to take a stroll around the pool. The light around its outer rim illuminates the water and changes colors every few minutes. I'm mesmerized by it. Fixated on the glow, I mosey over to the water. The first step I take in that direction, however, the killer dress tangles around my feet and I trip. Again.

I feel frustrated, desperate, but a hazy idea is forming. I swipe an unattended lighter from a table and drunkenly stagger off, clumsily edging around the pool. Once at the far end, away from everyone, I madly flick the lighter. A flame appears. I lean over and hold it to the now-ragged bottom of the dress. Clearly I'm not thinking straight, but I also know I am too drunk to care whether or not I burn myself.

The dress ignites in seconds. I stand frozen, not knowing what to do next, rapidly going up in flames.

In the distance, I hear what sounds like Preston's voice, though it is roaring incoherently. Next thing I know, without a moment to brace myself, something slams into me and I'm tackled into the pool. I open my eyes underwater, panicked, but see only blurry, pale-green pool water. A rush of cool chlorinated liquid thrusts itself up my nose, harshly burning as it bustles its way down my throat.

As I sink deeper, what flashes before my eyes is the near-death experience I had when I was sixteen.

It was the last summer Tyler, Jared, and I would all share together, though we didn't know that yet. Our mothers had taken us to Point Pleasant beach in New Jersey. The water was bitterly cold and murky, and I remember feeling panic at the thought of not knowing what could be in there, swimming around me. I spotted something out of the corner of one eye. Maybe nothing much. Then again, it could have been exactly what I thought I'd seen – a shark fin. The idea wasn't far-fetched. The shark attacks that inspired Peter Benchley's novel *Jaws* happened at the Jersey Shore.

At the same moment I decided it was really a shark fin, Tyler had yelled at me, "Hold on tight! Giant wave coming!"

And just like that I was submerged beneath the salty water, tumbling, flailing my arms and legs. Fighting to find the surface, but too tossed about by the swirling current to even know which way was up, deeper and deeper I seemed to go, as if an anvil was tied to my ankles. I was at the mercy of the sea. Filled with fear of the shark sniffing me out, I felt powerless, unable even to remember the basic motions of how to swim.

And now, as I drunkenly flail beneath the water at the deep end of the pool, my body is being dragged deeper into this new, tiled abyss by the sheer weight of my stupid dress. I kick as hard as I can but the heavy, sodden fabric pulls me even deeper. There has *got* to be lead in this thing.

I feel a sharp tug on my arm but jerk away out of fear. The grip snags me tighter and I am relentlessly dragged up, up, up. Engulfed with panic, I can't claw my way out fast enough.

I bob to the surface. Preston gives me a boost up the ladder as Mason and Jack rush over to help.

Mason shouts, "Are you okay? What happened?" He pulls me onto his lap and cups my cheek with one hand, as I slump there, limp as a beached jellyfish.

"Oh, honey," Jack begins, as he takes in Preston, who stands dripping beside me. "Oh, you poor baby!" He runs a hand over Preston's sodden suit jacket.

"Wait, are you talking about me or the Armani?" Preston pants, still slightly out of breath.

Ruining one of my roommate's beloved designer suits is sure to land me in some serious hot water. I don't have the courage to look him in the eye. For all I know he's on the verge of tears. I'm not sure I could move anyway, since my dress feels so heavy now, it must have soaked up half the water in the pool. I know I won't be able to stand on my own. I close my eyes and cover my face with both hands.

This is the last thing I remember before I black out.

\* \* \*

My head is thumping. It won't stop.

Now awake, I realize the problem: I'm hung over and it's bad. A groan escapes my throat as the drumming in my head intensifies. I can feel my heartbeat pulsating throughout my entire body. I open my eyes a slit, just enough to be blinded by the sunlight pouring into my bedroom. Shuffling, clattering, and clinking comes from the kitchen, and with each passing moment, the noises grow louder, more painful to my ears. The hand I extend to reach for the nightstand is shaky and unsteady. Once I manage to pry the drawer open, I rummage around until I find an old, scratched pair of bug-eye sunglasses. Settling them carefully over my eyes, I stumble out of bed, catching a shocking glimpse of my tangled, wildly disheveled bed head in the triple dresser mirror.

*Ugh, super classy. Good job, Laina.*

Peering down, I notice I am also wearing a pair of black boy short underwear, a pink tank top put on backward, and one blue sock. Lumpishly I emerge from my bedroom and slink to the kitchen, wondering how this all happened.

Preston is at the stove, his back turned to me as he whips up bacon and eggs. The charred meat and greasy sulfur aroma churns my stomach.

Spinning to look, he takes in my haggard appearance. "Oh my, Sleepin' Beauty's finally awake. Party too hard, princess?"

Staggering and zombie-like, I step into the kitchen and choke out, "She's severely hung-over and needs more beauty sleep."

Jack barges through the front door of the apartment with a plastic bag and a tray of coffees from Dunkin' Donuts. A bit too loud for my liking, he chirps, "Good morning! Who wants bagels and coffee?"

"I do!" Preston sings out, flipping bacon with a pair of tongs, careful not to splatter any grease from the pan. "Did you remember my Cinnamon Raisin bagel?"

"Of course I did," Jack replies, before planting a kiss on his cheek.

The thought of putting food into my body is sickening. Still trembling, I grab vodka from the liquor cabinet and cranberry juice from the fridge, setting them on the mahogany kitchen table. My hands shake as I take a two-fisted swig of vodka, then one of cranberry juice.

"Use a glass!" Preston shouts. "Ugh, you are such a pig!"

"That would require an extra step," I grumble, closing my eyes.

"Shouldn't you be drinking water?" Jack's staring at me as if I have grown ten heads.

"I'm trying to get rid of my hangover." I take another gulp of vodka and then one of juice.

"Right, but how do you expect to get rid of a hangover if you keep on drinking?"

"It'll level me out." I gently rub my tummy, hoping that will help it feel better. No such luck.

"I'm pretty sure a hangover is the body's way of saying it's dehydrated and needs water, not that it's thirsty for more vodka," Jack observes. He glances at Preston, who closes his eyes and holds out both hands as if to say, *Don't bother.*

Jack sets the bagels and coffees on the kitchen counter and takes a sip from one of the steaming Styrofoam cups. "Want your coffee?" he asks Preston. "I got it just the way you like. A splash of cream and two sugars."

Preston wrinkles his nose. "That's how I take normal coffee. You know how much I appreciate the bagels, but I can't drink that slop."

Jack props a hand on one hip and exclaims, "*Excuse me?* Dunkin' Donuts makes delicious coffee!"

"It's not delicious," Preston says matter-of-factly. "Their coffee tastes like burnt pretzels. Burnt pretzels are not appetizing."

The coffee pot beeps, signaling it has finished brewing. Preston hops to retrieve a mug from the cupboard and pours himself a fresh cup. "Thank you for the thought, honey, but I'll stick with my Chock full o' Nuts."

I groan, leaning my elbows on the kitchen counter, cradling my thumping head in my hands.

"Laina, do you think you could muster the energy to grab us a couple o' plates?"

Trying to make as little noise as possible, I inch two plates from the cabinet above my head and oh so gently set them on the counter next to Preston. As I slowly glide back over to the kitchen table to take a seat, Jack snaps, "Laina, you do realize cabinets don't close on their own, right?"

Preston shuts the cabinet door sharply behind me, as I flippantly wave a hand.

Just then a phone rings, painfully shrill. I cringe and clamp both hands over my ears. "Oh, please, make it stop!"

"I believe that's the land line ringing, not my phone," Preston says.

The answering machine clicks on from the living room and I hear my own muffled voice on the greeting message say, *"Hey, it's Laina. Sorry I'm out, or too busy with some crazy shenanigans to take your call. Leave a message after the beep!"*

"Laina? It's Mason, from last night." The deep, sexy voice radiates from the machine like peppered honey.

I frown, thinking. "Mason . . .Who's Mason?"

Jack and Preston's heads excitedly snap in my direction. They do a giddy little dance around the kitchen, Preston still holding greasy tongs in one hand and a spatula in the other. Both are cheering as if their team just won a football game.

I walk back into the kitchen. *"What?* Who is he?" I ask again, this time poised to cover my ears in case of any more unwelcome bellowing.

"You met him at the wedding." Jack wiggles his eyebrows with wholehearted approval. "I refuse to believe you don't remember that Greek god you danced with."

I think back through blurry memories, like a series of jump-cuts, from the day before. Finally he pops into my head. *Mason.* Blond. Sexy. Suave.

"Oh, yeah." I tilt my head as I try harder to piece together the fuzzy images of Mason's handsome face and chiseled body from the previous night. Did he really at some point buy me a pair of flip flops? "How did he even get our number?"

Preston raises an eyebrow. "We exchanged phone numbers last night. I gave him ours after you couldn't remember the last four digits of your cell number. And you're calling him back right now," he demands, pointing the drippy tongs at me.

Turning aside to Preston, Jack mumbles behind one hand, "I can't believe he called after what happened."

They exchange an odd look which makes me shudder.

Nervously I ask, "Oh God, what? What happened?" I stumble to the kitchen table and drop into a chair. "How much did I have to drink?"

Gritting his teeth, Preston begins, "Well, after lighting yourself on fire, you took a dip in the pool at Fran's parents' house. Of course we had to get you out of there before you caused any serious damage. So, Mason helped. He carried you all the way to the train stop, because after a couple blocks you passed out. You woke up when we got on the train. Mason called a Lyft once we got into the City, and then you passed out again."

"Yeah, you did that a lot," Jack chimes in, nodding, looking thoughtful.

"He rode all the way to Staten Island with us and even helped me get you out of the taxi and to the front door. But then…" Preston trails off. He scrunches his nose, seeming hesitant to continue. "Well, once we got to our door you kind of got sick."

Jack purses his lips and shakes his head. "All over him."

My jaw drops. I have never felt more humiliated in my life, and that's saying something. What an awful thing to do to a nice person, and I barely know the guy.

"So, he's either calling for a date, or to ask where he can send his dry-cleaning bill." Jack flashes a wide grin and chuckles.

"Call him back," Preston demands, as he scoots over to turn off the burner on the stove.

"No way in hell! Not after what I did. I'm despicable and disgusting and mortified. And *please*, stop with the shouting. My head! The throbbing. Ugh." I press a hand to my forehead to hold my brain securely in place as I hobble over to the freezer.

"It hurts so, so much," I whimper, grabbing an ice pack from the freezer, and a dishtowel from the countertop to wrap around it. I lay this across the top of my head, and the cool pack provides almost instant relief.

But what kind of wackadoodle calls a girl after she pukes all over him? He must be insane. Still, I absolutely to need to apologize, though I can't even fathom that conversation ending well. He couldn't possibly be calling to make a date! Any normal man would run for the hills, screaming, stripping off his ruined clothes, only stopping to set them on fire and bury the ashes.

So he must simply be calling for a formal apology. He probably thinks I'm a lunatic, though, after my behavior last night. So, definitely no date. What man would bother to call such a hot mess?

"He's a criminal defense lawyer, did you know?" Preston says, clearly impressed.

"Yeah, that I surprisingly *do* remember," I add, biting my lip, wondering now if he might even want to sue me.

"You never know, maybe you somehow managed to turn him on even though you upchucked all over him," Jack suggests, though he makes a repulsed face. After a moment he adds, "Nope, can't see that being the case. I was a witness. There was nothing elegant or sexy about what you did to that beautiful man."

"Oh my God, this is awful. Possibly the most repulsive thing I've ever done."

The nausea increases so I crawl out into the living room and onto the couch, to curl into a fetal position, making sure the ice pack remains securely against my head. When I open my eyes again I see a pair of mutilated high heels strewn in opposite corners of the living room floor. "Oh my God, what the hell happened to these?" I reach down and snatch one shoe from the floor to inspect it more closely. "My best satin heels! They're completely destroyed. I *loved* these." I clutch the shoe to my chest. "How did this happen?"

Frowning, Preston shakes his head. "You really don't remember? You butchered them with a steak knife. I think you made Mason help."

I gape at him and move the ice pack to the back of my neck. "No way in hell can I call this guy back. Ever."

He folds his arms, drumming his fingers on one forearm. "Would that have anything to do with Jared? Be honest."

After a long moment of silence, I decide it's best to lie. "No, of course not."

"I don't believe you. Come on! You liked Mason yesterday, and for some reason he clearly likes you. Even after the events that unfolded like a horror movie last night, he still called. That's tellin' you something." He takes a seat beside me on the couch. "Laina, please. Don't screw up another possible adult relationship because of a childhood thing with Jared a million years ago. And don't say it's not because of him! I know you. Every relationship you start always ends because you compare each man to a fairytale prince in your head."

"What? I don't —"

"No one ever forgets a first love, and I sure as hell don't expect you to, totally. But the sooner you realize no one will ever *be* Jared, maybe you can allow yourself to move on to someone else. A man who can potentially be just as wonderful."

Jack emerges from my bedroom with the cordless phone in hand and places it at Preston's side. Preston grabs his wallet from the coffee table, pulls out a business card tucked inside, and dials some numbers written on it.

Wait, what's he doing? No! No, no, no! He better not be calling Mason back!

Preston thrusts the phone into my hands. The earpiece is faintly ringing. I spring from the couch and fling the cordless onto one of the cushions, as though it just bit me. In that moment of panic, I also launch the ice pack and dish towel clear across the room like a caped Frisbee.

"Hang it up! Hang up *now*!" I shout, my heart thumping so hard I can practically feel it thudding against my ribcage.

"No! Don't be such a weirdo," Preston barks, scooping the phone up from the couch and pressing it against my ear again. "Grow a pair! Just talk to him."

The phone rings once more. Then a deep voice says, "Good morning, beautiful."

# Chapter 4

# Desi Chase

The following Monday, after Preston heads off to the Hylan Plaza to open Viola's Hideaway, I sit by the mirror in a pair of jean shorts and a lime green tank top, putting on makeup. It's not even eleven o'clock yet and I don't need to be at the bookstore until four.

I wonder what I should do with those free hours. It's such a beautiful day out there, I'd hate to waste it by sitting inside. I dig through the makeup bag in search of my favorite lipstick, then recall I tucked it into the clutch I carried to the wedding. Of course, it takes over an hour to find the damn purse in my messy bedroom, and while flinging clothes and digging through piles I demolish the place even further. One of these days I swear I'll get around to cleaning it up.

"Ah-ha!" I shout as I spot the lipstick inside my clutch, happy not to have lost it at some point during that drunken escapade. When I dig the tube out, though, a folded paper it was nestled inside of flutters to the floor.

Desi Chase's fortuneteller flyer.

I smooth the creases out on top of the bed and examine the flyer once again, curiosity piqued. Not that I believe in this stuff, but . . . what sort of prediction would she about my own future? Or even just my upcoming date with Mason? Of course, I know it's silly nonsense, but it could be fun to at least see what this woman is all about. And while it is a bit of a hike to get down to St. George, I do have time to kill. She's advertising this stuff in my store, after all. I should be able to vouch for her abilities, right?

I drive with the windows all the way down to embrace the warm summer breeze and smell the scent of fresh cut grass, on the way to St. George. The parking situation there is horrendous, of course, and I end up with no option but to walk three long blocks. Just as the flyer states, Desi Chase's store is located beside the St. George Theatre, and it is impossible to miss. A wide neon *Fortune Teller* sign illuminates the front window of the small brick storefront. The same crystal ball pictured on the flyer is repeated in a big decal on the plate glass window.

I hesitate on the threshold, but at last enter the dimly lit store, telling myself, *You're here. No turning back now.*

A blue velvet Victorian loveseat stands against the wall in the foyer, next to a small round mahogany table with New Age magazines stacked on top. Toward the back, a red curtain hangs from a ceiling-mounted rod, providing privacy to whomever is in the back. At the other end of the entrance are shelves with patchouli and sandalwood candles, tarot cards, astrology books, Hindu statues, and handcrafted Celtic jewelry. The store emanates a sharp, woodsy, spicy aroma. The scent itself is pleasant, even if slightly overpowering.

"Um, hello?" I call.

A slim hand pulls the curtain aside, revealing a tall, sleek, brown-haired woman of maybe thirty-five, with flawless golden skin, wearing a brightly-colored dress that looks vaguely like a loose-fitting sari.

"Ah, yes. Come in, my dear. Come, come," she insists in a soft tone, waving me in, as if she was already expecting me. "Please sit. I'm Desi Chase. I would like to welcome you to my humble little shop."

She leads me to a round table draped with a blue velvet cloth. A stack of tarot cards sits on top. The table is flanked by two carved, oversized mahogany chairs with blue velvet cushions. I sit, then introduce myself, and wait for her to begin.

She takes the seat across from me. Numerous rings encircle every other finger on both hands. She has a mysterious air, yet also a friendly and open manner, which should seem contradictory, but why this is so . . . I can't seem to put a finger on it.

"How…how does this w-work?" I splutter, to break what feels to me like an awkward silence.

She, however, is obviously unruffled. Her eyes meet mine directly, and she smiles. "This is your first time."

I nod, shifting in my seat, feeling like a child.

She picks up the tarot deck from the table and thoroughly shuffles the cards, which flitter against her fingers as quickly and lightly as a hummingbird's wings. "I will explain. Through the tarot reading, I can reveal your past, present, and future. There are often times during a reading that I get a feeling about certain things, or underlying messages from the cards. The message is not always direct. Call it a sixth sense . . . call it whatever you like."

I nod and then frown, staring blankly. I can tell she's picking up on my skepticism. Glancing around the dark, quiet store, I ask, "And do you get . . . a lot of customers?"

A smirk tugs at the corners of her mouth. "I believe I am immensely good at what I do. My gift brings in many satisfied clients who praise my reputation. So many, in fact, that I have had the privilege of traveling all over the world."

"And you, um, perform at parties and stuff?" My tone sounds unintentionally patronizing, and I quickly apologize.

She doesn't look offended, though. "People sometimes seek my gift for their important lifetime events, yes. I have been most recently asked to attend a few weddings, here and elsewhere. I enjoy helping people, by giving hope and guidance where I am able." Then she takes the freshly-shuffled deck in one hand and wildly mixes and scatters the cards in a big messy heap across the tablecloth. She tells me to collect them again, stack them face down, then shuffle and reset the deck in the center of the table.

I do as she asks.

Then, one hand hovering over the neat stack of cards, Desi fluidly swipes it across the table, this one graceful motion fanning the cards out in a perfect arc. "I would like you to casually run one hand over the surface of cards, like so." She demonstrates, gingerly sweeping one hand in the air a few inches above them. "Select three cards, and put them face-up, in the center of the table. Align them next to each other in the order you selected each. The first card will tell me about your past. The second will inform me of your present. The third will determine your future."

Feeling completely awkward and self-conscious, I do as she says. My hand stops and hovers over a card. Without giving it much thought, I flip it over and position it in the middle of the table, then do the same for the next two I choose.

Desi sweeps the remaining, unchosen cards into a pile, stacks them neatly, and sets them to one side. She combs her fingers lightly over each of the three I selected, examining them intently, brow furrowed.

"Miss Laina," she says at last, tapping the first card I chose, "this, here, is the Nine of Swords, and it reflects your past."

I peer at the card, which depicts a person sitting up in bed, hunched over, face buried in their hands, as if they have just jolted awake, crying, from a nightmare. A chill harrows my spine.

"The Nine of Swords tells me you live each day carrying tremendous remorse and sorrow everywhere you go. You place heavy blame on your own shoulders. You can't seem to untangle yourself from this sorrow because of your past, and because of that past you can't move on. I sense quite a bit of loss here."

*I'm going to throw up. Is she serious? How could she know this?*

"And now, this one," she continues with barely a pause, tapping on the center card. She lays the other hand over her heart. "It is the Queen of Cups. She appears to us reversed, you see?"

I nod. The card depicts a woman wearing a crown and sitting on a throne, an ornate goblet cradled in her hands.

"Your present is showing me you have reservations about allowing yourself to experience love. You prefer your own dreams to reality. I get the sense that you rely heavily on the decisions of another, rather than making any on your own. I believe a high underlying level of fear is the culprit in this behavior. Not necessarily fear of that other person, who is your advisor, but rather fear buried deep within yourself. *You* are afraid to make choices."

Flustered, I shake my head and blink in sheer disbelief. This stranger is describing not only my life, but also my innermost feelings. "But . . . how could you know all of this?" My heart thuds harder in my chest in anticipation of what the next card will tell her.

She simply smiles, and continues. "Your final card is the Judgment card. This one is reversed, as well. And, see here? It goes hand in hand with the Queen of Cups."

Just like the Nine of Swords card, this one doesn't give off a warm, fuzzy vibe either. The illustration is of an angel playing a long, straight trumpet as it hovers above a crowd of naked people who are . . . yes, standing in their own coffins.

*Nope, not liking this card at all!*

"It means you will find yourself at a fork in the road, soon." She nods. "But you mustn't be afraid, at last, to go forward." Looking up to catch my eye, she pauses, apparently just noticing that I'm getting spooked. Though possibly that's the normal state for customers in here.

"My dear," she whispers in a calming, silvery tone, "I do hope I'm not making you too uneasy."

"Just a bit freaked out is all," I confess a bit sheepishly.

She lays a hand on top of mine, giving it a gentle squeeze. Her eyes close. A moment later she shivers, as though a deep chill is coursing through her body. Her shoulders, in fact her whole demeanor, is suddenly extremely tense. At last she inhales deeply, and her eyelids flash open. For a moment her gaze locks onto mine. Then her eyes close once again and she tightens her grip on my hand. She gasps, and her eyes snap open once more, gazing at me as if she suddenly knows all my secrets.

My heart thumps as I wait for her to break the silence.

"I want you to relax now." Smiling, clearly pleased with herself, she adds, "You will receive the help you need in order to guide you on your true path. Signs from the universe, which are all around us, will help steer you the way you're meant to go. But you *must pay attention* to the signs. You will need to determine how best to interpret them and then decide which path to choose from there. If you don't pay attention or listen closely, you may come to regret it. But truly, I don't want you to worry. You won't be alone. *He* will be there to guide you."

With intense curiosity and excitement, I lean toward Desi. My heartbeat accelerates. "Who will?"

"Who?" She leans in closer. Her voice quavers a bit as she whispers, "Why Tyler, of course."

\* \* \*

Friday night, as I dress for my first date with Mason, it commences to rain. Not a drizzle, nor even the kind of storm where massive puddles will accumulate every few feet. No, it's a full-on torrential downpour which, even from inside, is clear will make it physically impossible to see two inches in front of my face. I drag myself into the living room, all dolled up in a sundress and high-heeled sandals, to discover Preston and Jack cozied up together on the couch, watching a cooking show as they snack on an oversized bowl of popcorn.

"I'm cancelling the date," I announce. "And before you object, have you seen the weather out there?" I pull open the living room curtains so they can witness just how bad the weather has gotten.

Preston waves a hand dismissively in front of his face. "It's just a little rain, honey. No big deal. There's a nifty little invention they have out nowadays that will help. We actually keep one the coat closet. It's called an umbrella. So go on, and have a wonderful date!" He turns his attention back to Netflix.

"*Just a little rain?* It looks like a hurricane outside! I'm going to have to take a row boat just to get to the train and then another to get to the ferry."

"Okay, now you're being absurd." Preston rises from the couch and joins me at the window. "Let's see . . . hmm, it's not even *that* bad. Just a little standing water."

Thunder cracks, lightning flashes, and we both flinch, though Preston recovers first. The lights relentlessly flicker inside the apartment as if we're on The Haunted Mansion ride at Disney World.

I turn to stare at Preston, hands propped on my hips, as the bulbs continue to buzz and flicker. He stands there still snacking on his bowl of popcorn, pretending he doesn't notice the light show in our apartment.

"Do you want to know what I really think?" I ask.

"Sure, honey. Lay it on me." He crunches a fistful of popcorn like a ravenous animal that hasn't eaten in a month, not meeting my narrowed gaze.

"I think this is a sign. That it is exactly what that woman Desi was talking about. Tyler is clearly sending the rain to show I shouldn't be going on this date."

Wide eyed, Preston grits his teeth and stops crunching the popcorn in his mouth. "Yeah, well, she also told you not to be afraid to travel down your intended path. So if you cancel the date, you're ignoring her advice. And since when did you start believing in fortune tellers?"

"Since now!" I shout, waving a hand at the window and the sodden City that lies beyond it. "Clearly she was spot on!"

"Her reading does sound oddly contradictory at the moment," Jack admits, from the couch.

Preston shoots him a fiery, quelling glance. "You can't be serious, Laina! It's rained almost every day this month. But now, just because it also rains on the night of your date, you choose to believe it's a supernatural sign telling you to cancel? Seriously, that woman must have been looped! Forget about what she said. Stop allowin' it to mess with your head. For once, please just let yourself experience something possibly wonderful."

"And sexy!" Jack chimes in, he gets up and comes to Preston's side to swipe some popcorn from the bowl.

"Yes, and sexy," Preston concurs, hugging the huge bowl closer to his chest. "Oh, Laina, look! It's your favorite." A half-popped kernel is pinched between his thumb and index finger. "These are the kind you like, right?"

I smile and nod, pretending that they are my favorite pieces. When actually, it was Jared who always preferred the half-popped kernels.

"Sexy or not, I'm not going," I declare, raking my fingers nervously through my hair.

They holler in unison, "Oh yes, you are!"

Just then, the power goes out. We're left standing in complete darkness. The only thing audible in the room is the sound of Jack crunching a mouthful of popcorn.

After a moment Preston mutters, "Okay, then. Maybe reschedule."

\* \* \*

Night after night, attempt after attempt, Mason and I cannot seem to successfully go out on our first date. It isn't as if I'm not making an effort, either. After the extreme downpour and the blackout comes the flat tire on the Staten Island Expressway, after I decide to drive into the City rather than hop on the train and ferry. Another attempt a few nights later, I accidentally lock my keys in the car. Then the following week Mason comes down with a horrific stomach bug.

Even through all of this, Preston continues to urge me not to give up. And, just to be sure, I decide to give it one last try.

A lot of good it does me, too. On the way to Mason's apartment, where he has planned to make dinner, I get attacked by a mugger, a skinny kid in a ski mask. As I erratically pepper-spray my attacker with the little canister on my key ring, I get a whole bunch of blowback in my eyes from a sudden breeze that springs up out of nowhere. The attacker runs off then, at least, and without my bag. I have no idea how I actually groped my way to Mason's apartment after that, but soon there I was, pounding away on his door, raving about how it's another sign from the universe that we shouldn't be dating.

Instead, he guides me inside and offers a cool washcloth for my eyes.

As I stare at my tearing, swollen, bloodshot, blurred reflection in Mason's bathroom mirror, I can't help but feel foolish. He must think I'm a complete lunatic. He's probably out there right now concocting a way to get this crazy woman out of his apartment as fast as humanly possible.

"Laina?" he calls from the other side of the bathroom door, "Please come out. I got a fresh damp towel for your eyes. I know you're upset about tonight, and no wonder. And I realize our last few planned dates were a bust, but . . . I really like you. And if you agree, well, I think this could turn into something great."

Okay, so maybe I misread the situation.

Clutching the edge of bathroom sink for support, I reflect on Desi's reading of my present card. She couldn't have been more accurate. I *am* afraid to open my heart to someone and allow myself to experience love. Here is this wonderful, dreamy man offering me his heart, yet I'm still hesitating. Something truly *is* wrong with me. I actually might regret it later if I don't give Mason a real chance now.

"Come on," he urges. "We can stay in, I'll order some food delivered, whatever your favorite is, and we'll keep cool compresses over those poor swollen eyes. I'll pour you a *really* big glass of wine to take the sting away." He pauses for a moment, then adds, "You know what, forget the glass. If you want, I'll let you drink straight from the bottle. What do you say?"

I can't help but smile. He, at least, is trying exceedingly hard to make this work. I should at least give the guy a fair shot. "Okay," I choke out, still wiping flaming tears from my eyes. "Just give me a minute. I'll be right out."

In a heated fog of pain, I stagger over to the toilet and lower my shorts. I sit, falling immediately into the bowl, splashing myself with cold toilet water, shrieking as I shoot back up to my feet again. Not knowing where to even stand, dripping, I begin pacing around the bathroom with my shorts still hobbling my ankles, cold toilet water trickling over my knees, and then my ankles, leaving a trail across Mason's beautiful tiled floor.

"Oh, God. Oh, God. Oh, God. Why didn't I check? *Why didn't I check?*" I mutter, over and over.

Because as any idiot knows, it's a rule when visiting a guy-only house – always check to see if the toilet seat is down before sitting. Ugh, come on, Laina. Such a rookie mistake!

Gritting my teeth in disgust, suddenly wishing only for a shower and my own comfy bed, I wonder: Who could have predicted Mason would just happen to leave the toilet seat up?

"Laina?" He knocks again. "Sure you're okay? Is there anything you need?"

"Actually, yeah," my voice croaks. "Do you mind if I take a shower?"

"Uh, well . . . sure. Go right ahead. Towels are under the sink. I'll leave you a change of comfy clothes, if you like."

"Sounds perfect!" I blurrily grope around in the bathroom sink cabinet for a fresh towel.

"Hey, Laina? What's your go-to comfort food?"

"Sushi. Always sushi." Turning on the shower nozzle, I stick a hand beneath the warming stream, waiting for the ideal water temperature before bothering to undress.

"Sushi it is!" He exclaims. His footsteps recede into the other room.

After washing the hideousness of this night, so far, from my body, and changing into a comfortable t-shirt and plaid boxer pants Mason thoughtfully left outside the bathroom door, I finally emerge with no makeup and damp, tousled hair. Settling onto his living room couch, I watch in open-jawed delight as he unpacks at least ten large sushi containers with enough sashimi, dragon rolls, and grilled eel to feed fifteen people.

"Hopefully this makes up for everything that's happened tonight, and all the previous failed attempts to get together. I promise to do whatever I can to turn this date around." He pries the clear lid off the final container and hands me a set of chopsticks.

Suddenly ravenous, I lift a California roll and pop it in my mouth.

He gazes down at me, still leaning on the coffee table. "As a matter of fact," he adds, and slips one hand under my chin. He leans in, lightly brushing his lips against mine.

Surprisingly, my stomach floods with butterflies. I hastily swallow the sushi roll.

He smiles a bit sheepishly. "Sorry, but I wouldn't have been able to wait until the end of the night to kiss you."

"I'm glad you didn't," I reply. And it's true.

We smile at each other, and then dig into the sushi, intent on salvaging the remainder of our first date.

# Chapter 5

## Sleepless Sleepovers

As the weeks pass, the dating disasters seem to die down. Mason and I spend a great deal of time together, and whenever I begin to second-guess the newly forming relationship, Preston and Jack are there, nudging me forward, urging me to keep trucking along because they 'have a feeling about him' and believe I 'met him for a reason'. Suddenly *they* are fortune tellers, too.

I, on the other hand, remain cautious, waiting for any indicators I should hightail it out of the relationship quickly, before things get too serious.

To be honest, the only reason there's still this much hesitation in me is because I'm slowly noticing how he does a number of things that have always been pet peeves of mine, such as not putting the toilet seat down, ever, and chewing food with his mouth open. Plus, biting his nails to the point where it crosses over from nibbling to actual, audible crunching. He also frequently mispronounces words, saying 'supposably' instead of 'supposedly' or using them in the wrong context, such as substituting 'broke' for 'broken' or 'froze' for 'frozen'. So much so that there is a growing urge to repeatedly slap the palm of my hand on my forehead.

And don't even get me started on his incessant need to always be right, in any situation. I often find myself giving in and agreeing to do whatever he wants, just to save time. Whether it determines where to grab dinner, which road to take, or what to do on a particular night, he always gets his way. I suppose it's in his nature to be this way. He is a lawyer, after all.

According to Preston, these are all fixable traits and I need to just let such trivial things slide. He has a point. It's not like I'm perfect, either, and I understand that.

For instance, it turns out Mason isn't a fan of my snoring habits, and it just so happens that snoring is one of *his* pet peeves. As he and I begin to spend nights at each other's apartments we've fallen into a routine: he heads to bed before I do so he can attempt to fall asleep first. Then, once Mason is safely deep in Slumberland, I crawl into bed—ever so gently—so as not to disturb him. However, I have also come to discover he's a bit of a bed hog, with an unfortunate tendency to sprawl across the entire mattress like a giant starfish. So when it's finally my turn to come to bed, I'm lucky if there's a sliver of the edge of the mattress left to cling to.

But I understand. Being at court bright and early requires him to get a good night's sleep to be as alert as possible for his clients' sakes, so, I've decided to do my best to accommodate him. What I've been noticing, however, is that I'm so self-conscious about not waking him, I hardly ever sleep. On the nights where he stays at my apartment, I've gotten into the habit of falling asleep on the couch instead of joining him in my bedroom. I hardly spend any time in my own bed anymore.

The more I say I want to throw in the towel, though, the more Preston reminds me of Mason's admirable qualities. Such as how he takes care of himself and his appearance, the way he dotes on me constantly—even when we're in public—and always tries to make me smile. He even occasionally surprises me with lunch or flowers while I'm at work. So there are days when our relationship does seem surprisingly wonderful. But by the end of the night—or should I say, the middle of the night—when exhaustion sets in, it honestly feels like I'm going through the motions and shoveling shit against the tide. The sleep deprivation is starting to have a frightening effect on me. I've been jumpier and more on edge, especially with Preston.

Finally, three whole weeks of inadequate rest, I'm utterly frustrated and have reached a whole new level of sleeplessness, one I've never encountered before. It features clumsiness, hallucinating, short term memory loss, and talking to myself more than I'd care to admit. Each night, as soon as Mason is sound asleep in my bed, I decide to give sleeping together another try, since I'm beyond exhausted. But after twenty-minutes of playing tug-of-war over the sheets, and attempting to roll him over to keep from being inched out of the bed and onto the floor, I decide I've had enough shenanigans for one night. The sun hasn't risen yet, and since there's no chance of falling asleep, I decide to make a cup of tea and watch some television in the living room.

Tiptoeing on the dark hardwood floor, I'm careful not to step on any of the loud, creaky sections.

I turn on the burner, fill the teapot, and flip on the television to an old black-and-white episode of *The Honeymooners*. It's the one where Ed Norton sleepwalks – how fitting. I cozy up under the soft, teal blue, plush blanket we keep draped on the arm of the couch as shadows from the television show flicker and dance around the living room walls. Ralph accompanies Norton while they sit in Norton and Trixie's bedroom, waiting for the doctor to arrive. They discuss how Norton got the bump on his head, and slowly, slowly, I drift off into a daydream.

It's funny, but I wish I were a sleepwalker. At least then I'd be asleep, even if in motion. Staring dazed at the television, I wonder if there's any NyQuil in the apartment. I'm edging past that point of exhaustion where, even if I want to sleep, no matter how tired, it is impossible to turn off the brain.

While digging through the medicine cabinet in the bathroom, groaning with frustration as I toss things around, I open and close drawers, oblivious to the amount of noise I'm making, until Preston clears his throat from the open doorway.

I flinch, still clutching a tube of toothpaste and a disposable razor. "Did I wake you?" I squeak, suddenly wondering if he might be a hallucination.

"It's 3:45 in the mornin'. Of course you woke me. I think you woke every bird in the neighborhood, too." He scrunches up his face. "What are you tryin' to do with *these?*" Snatching the toothpaste and razor, he tosses them back in the drawer. "Colgate should never be used as a substitute for shaving cream."

The teakettle abruptly screams then. I sigh out of sheer exhaustion as I hobble to the kitchen to remove the teakettle from the stove.

Preston follows. "Another sleepless night, huh?"

Lethargically I glance back at him with an 'I will kill' expression.

"Well, since I'm awake, would you mind pourin' me a cup?"

"Sure," I reply, my voice practically buzzing.

He flops onto the couch, hoarding my blanket for himself, chuckling as Ed Norton shouts for "Lu Lu" in his sleepwalking state. I take a sip of tea even though it's still practically bubbling, scorching my mouth and throat as I fight to quickly swallow. The tea slowly claws its way through my insides, blazing a path to my stomach. To avoid taking another imprudent sip, I set the teacup on the pinewood coffee table.

Slumping one arm over the back of the couch, fist resting against the side of his head, Preston stares at me. "So, what's been goin' on with you lately?"

Without peeling my eyes away from the screen, I mumble, "Nothing. Same old."

He snorts. Clearly he doesn't buy it.

So I decide to open up. "Okay, fine. I can't remember the last time I felt like myself. I know you think dating Mason is good for me. I mean, maybe on some level it's good that I'm actually dating, and he is a great guy. But I don't think he's the one I'll end up with."

Preston looks like he's about to chime in.

I cut him off. "I know you're going to tell me it's too soon to know that, but it's not." I reach again for the tea. "It's just...I've also been waiting for signs from Tyler. I know you believe Desi Chase was looped, but she was spot on with everything. How could she have known about my past, or about Tyler? I mean, look at what's on T.V. right now: Ed Norton, and he's sleepwalking. Not only is *that* my nickname, but he's walking when he should be in bed sleeping. It's a sign. I know it is."

Shaking his head, Preston remarks, "I thought your nickname was 'Scutch'. Isn't that what Tyler used to call you?"

"I wasn't talking about Tyler." My voice trails off to a whisper.

"Oh, Laina." He closes his eyes and slowly exhales. "So, let me get this straight, Tyler called you 'Scutch' and Jared called you 'Ed Norton'?"

"No, just 'Norton'."

"Do I wanna know why?" He asks in a way that shows he's actually curious.

"Jared used to tease me that it took me forever to complete a task, just like with Ed Norton's character."

"Oh, I get it. Like cleaning your room?" He smirks. "These two sure had a knack for nicknames. I gotta admit, they were both creative. You know, I've always believed you learn something from every relationship, good or bad."

"Maybe so," I grudgingly admit.

"How else are you gonna know what works for you and what doesn't. Or what you really want in a companion if you don't test the waters? Mason may not be *the* one, but something tells me he's the one for you right *now*. Did you ever think maybe he might lead you to *the one?*"

Feeling drowsy, maybe thanks to the chamomile tea, I shake my head. It seems too difficult to figure out how it could be possible for Mason to lead me to the man I'm supposed to be with.

Preston continues, "Look, I'm not sayin' you *have* to date someone to be happy, because I know that's not true. But you've been alone for so long, maybe you don't know of any other way to be, or what it feels like to be vulnerable and let someone else in. If there's a problem with the sleepin' arrangements, talk to him. Make adjustments. Maybe try to explain that, for the time being, it would be best if there weren't so many sleepovers. I think he'll understand."

"I hope so. Do you realize he's the first guy I ever dated who spent the night?" I ask.

He stares at me incredulously. "What?"

"Well, you should know; you live here."

His eyes go blank as he stares into the distance. "How did I not notice this before?"

"I prefer to sleep alone. I can snore all I want, as loud as I want."

"Wow." He gapes, shocked. "Well, how are things aside from the lack of sleep?" He playfully nudges my arm.

"What do you mean?" I ask.

"You know, *things*. The hanky panky between the sheets." He wiggles his eyebrows suggestively.

My mouth flies open. "I'm not going to tell you that!"

"Ah, why not," he pleads. "Come on, I need some girl talk." He bounces in his seat like an impatient child.

I pause, but am unable to fight the smirk forming at the left corner of my mouth. I don't want to talk about this. However, he won't leave me alone until he gets his fill of gossip. "Okay, fine," I begin. "That part is surprisingly good. No complaints there."

"See, not every aspect of the relationship is so bad!"

"Right. It's just that . . . I can't help but think…" I trail off self-consciously.

He sighs, but it's not an impatient huff, this time. "I know you're still thinking about Jared."

"Believe me," I cut him off, "I understand how much easier my life would be if I didn't think about him anymore. So no need for the usual lecture." I settle deeper into the couch, arms folded.

Preston lays a hand gently on my arm. "Laina, I hate to say this again, but . . . in order to live, you have to let him go."

"I know I do," I glumly answer, staring at the television screen, where Ed Norton is sleepwalking again.

Preston takes a long sip of his tea, then leans over and kisses my forehead. "Try to get some shut-eye. This sleeping arrangement with you, the couch, and Ed Norton clearly isn't healthy." He stands, stretches, yawns, and retreats to his bedroom.

And me? I mull over having a talk with Mason, and end up watching an *I Love Lucy* marathon until the sun rises, ready to shine itself on a new day full of unknown possibilities.

# Chapter 6

# The Catalyst

The next day is one of those off-kilter ones where no outfit feels comfortable on my body. Sifting through the untidy closet, digging through mounds of clothing on my bedroom floor, I find nothing seems to work, once I put it on. I spot a plastic bin on the top shelf in the back of my closet with *SUMMER SHIRTS* scribbled on it in black Sharpie. I stand on tiptoes and scoot the box to the edge with a hanger. Just as I'm about to grab it, it falls, along with a bunch of other belongings I didn't realize were stashed on the shelf. I sit on the floor to peruse the mess. As I lean to inspect what has fallen, I'm struck in the head by another falling object.

"Ouch!" I press a hand to my head, then notice a journal now sitting on top of the pile. I'm sure it wasn't there before. The cover is a classic white and black swirl design, the kind you see on composition notebooks. A pale blue page-marker ribbon is attached at the top of the spine.

*No freaking way!*

I haven't set eyes on this journal in years. In fact, I don't even recall stashing it on that shelf.

Jared gave it to me when we were kids. He filled a large portion with stories about his, Tyler's, and my shenanigans over the years. Then he gave it to me so I would never forget all the adventures we shared. The same day he gave me this, he also gave me a necklace with a tiny blue Forget-Me-Not flowered charm on it. I still wear that necklace every single day.

As I flip through the pages and gaze longingly at Jared's familiar scrawled handwriting, it suddenly it hits me. Now I know exactly how I want to spend the remaining free hours of my day.

\* \* \*

Something enchanting happens as soon as I enter Central Park and leave the chaotically charged New York City streets behind. Some sort of invisible bubble encircles the park, one that repels all feelings of anxiety and obligation. The rest of the world seems to go unreservedly silent. At around one o'clock, I go in through the West 81st Street entrance. Unlike the day of Francesca's wedding, I am entering willingly and with no hesitation, only fresh, hopeful feelings. It seems right to be here. I can feel my destiny relying on me to take this leap.

I pass a jazz quartet near the Swedish Cottage and carry on toward my favorite bench at the top of the tall stone steps. The sun beats down directly overhead, making the eighty-five-degree day feel much hotter than it actually is. But I'm not complaining, since the warmth hugs my body. As I wander to the old spot, I admire the winsome surroundings, the flower beds and tall shady trees. It feels like home, but one I've felt compelled to abandon the last two years. Yet, it still welcomes me back as if no time has passed at all.

I breathe in the sweet perfume of fuchsia and ginger flowers and admire a lavender butterfly bush situated just behind the bench. A handful of tiny white butterflies elegantly flit back and forth around it. Only the clouds seem in a hurry here. They briskly waft past above me, as if in a rush to get somewhere.

I sit for a long while reminiscing about all the wonderful times Tyler, Jared, and I shared right at this very spot. Everything about the garden takes me back to my childhood — the smell of the flowers, the songs of birds, the muffled scuffing of feet along the stone walkways, the bronze plaques with Shakespeare quotes hidden amid the flowers. I spot one from the corner of one eye while sitting on the bench. I get up and go over to stand above the plaque, for a better look. It's one of my absolute favorite quotes, which Viola says in *Twelfth Night*.

*"Oh time, thou must untangle this, not I.*
*It is too hard a knot for me t'untie."*

I feel the true meaning of her words now. Viola finds herself tangled in a love triangle. While disguised as a man and renaming herself "Cesario", she falls in love with Duke Orsino. He, however, believes himself to be in love with Olivia. In an odd turn of events, Olivia then falls in love with the charming young Cesario, who is really Viola attempting to play matchmaker, to help Duke win Olivia's heart. Soon Viola has no idea how to free herself from the mess she's in. Time is the only thing she believes will help her situation.

Stuck in my own internal love triangle, I find myself torn between the lingering longing for Jared and new feelings for Mason, with no idea as to how I should proceed.

I pull the journal from my bag, along with a pen. The pale blue ribbon page marker peeks out at the bottom. I open to a blank page. If, as Desi Chase claimed, she was truly able to tell my fortune, and is correct that Tyler will be sending me signs, why not do my part and reach out to him, as well? If nothing comes of it, at least I can say I put myself out there. That I tried. In any case, I no longer want to ask the question, *What if?*

So, I write:

*Dear Tyler,*

*Writing you a letter now may seem a bit odd, and in a way, even silly. It's not like you're going to write back. I am hopeful you will find a way of communicating, though. I'm writing for two reasons. The first is, I just don't know of any other way to gain some closure over losing you. I'm desperate. I never got to actually say goodbye.*

*So many nights all I want to do is pick up the phone, dial your number, and hear your voice on the other end. Even just once more. If I could have our last conversation back, I would never allow myself to take it for granted. I would tell you how much I love you, will always love you, and how lucky I was to have been blessed with you as my older brother.*

*People expect me to move on from the past, but that's easier said than done. For them to pass judgment as if they understand what I went through, what I continue to go through, isn't fair. It's a hell all its own. I'm simply left wishing for one more opportunity to say I love you, one more embrace, one laugh — one more chance to say I'm sorry. I'm left wishing for one moment I know I will never have.*

*I'd like to believe it will get easier with each passing day. But enough time has gone by now to realize it never will. I want you back. I miss the way life was, growing up. We didn't have a care in the world back then. I miss everything about the way life used to be. I'm doing my best to stay strong, though there are moments when I feel I'm fighting a losing battle. If only there was some way to know if I was making the right decisions in life. None of the men I meet seem like the right fit for me. I know it's pathetic to hold out hopes that one day I'll miraculously be reunited with Jared, but I can never seem to stop that wishing thing there, either.*

*The second reason for writing this letter is just that. I can't wait around for Jared to magically come back, and I know you would want to see me settled. But I also know you would never want me to settle for second best in love. What should I do?*

*A woman I met recently told me you would be sending me signs. Am I waiting for something that may never come? So here I am, throwing it out into the universe. I know it's a little ridiculous of me to ask, and I don't exactly know what to look for. But I must stop fixating on the past when I should be looking to the future. I can't keep it up, and I know you wouldn't want me to.*

*How I want to hear your voice right now telling me to stop overanalyzing. To just live. Then my life will fall into place the way it's meant to. I suppose I should take my own imaginary advice from you. I'll be keeping my eyes open, just in case.*

*I miss you more than words could ever say. I love you.*

*Scutch*

* * *

I remain in the park for hours after I write my letter to Tyler. In fact, I completely lose track of the time. It's strange to look back and see how everything has changed over the years, and how I've changed because of it. Growing up, Tyler and I were so similar—two dreamers. Possibilities seemed endless. Together, nothing could stop us from conquering the world. Jared was a major part of that. When we were young, the three of us often talked about opening a bookstore together. We all loved to read, we loved to play make-believe in the garden, and we loved to tell stories. We also loved to pretend we were characters from Shakespeare's plays, even though at the time we didn't fully understand what those roles were about. We felt connected to Shakespeare simply by being in the garden as often as we were and by going to see Shakespeare in the Park every summer.

After Jared moved away, I slowly stopped believing in happily ever after. When my parents split, they sold the apartment we grew up in. My father moved to New Jersey, where he married a woman named Jane. Tyler and I moved into a tiny apartment with our mother in Murray Hill. She went back to using her maiden name, and the hope of Jared somehow finding me again grew fainter each day. We had different addresses, different phone numbers, and different lives.

After a few years Tyler and I slowly drifted apart. I didn't realize it at the time, but looking back, I hate that I allowed that to happen. He fought so hard to keep us close, but I selfishly chose not to notice. While he kept working hard to achieve the dream of opening a bookstore, I grew less interested in the future than in trivial distractions. I went through a whole "bad boy" phase. Dating all the wrong guys made it easier to forget the unwelcome changes.

What I didn't see was that I was actually destroying my relationship with Tyler. Eventually he talked me into moving to Staten Island to open Viola's Hideaway. He must have hoped it would be a new beginning for us both. No one, especially me, ever imagined he would die so young, and leave us behind.

One memory in particular haunts me—the day Tyler died, I had an argument with my mother about Sean, a man I was dating at the time. She couldn't stand the sight of him, and I knew he was no good, but I stayed anyway. Back then I figured being with someone—even the wrong someone—was better than being alone. I was so wrong. This is partly why I'm so cautious now when it comes to my dating life.

That day, too, I fled here, to the park.

"How did I know I'd find you here, Scutch?" Tyler had joked, as he climbed the stone steps, clad in his favorite beat-up jeans and a *Beetlejuice* t-shirt. He sat on the bench facing me. We shared the same dark brown eyes, though his looked droopy from lack of sleep.

"What are you doing here?" I asked bitterly.

He shook his head. "I stopped at Mom's since I don't have to be at the bookstore until later."

Of course he knew the Shakespeare Garden was the place I always went to hide, to get away. He then attempted to convince me to listen to my mother, to break things off with Sean.

I didn't want to hear it. I was going out that night with Sean whether she liked it or not.

"What's up? Feels like I don't even know you anymore." He glanced at the sky, which was quickly darkening. "You really shouldn't go all the way out to New Jersey tonight. We're supposed to get a bad storm. If you and Sean have another fight and you call me to come pick you up again..."

Enraged, I jumped to my feet. "Don't worry. Your little sister can take care of herself. I won't call you to come rescue me."

He shrugged. "I'm just saying, I hate driving when the roads are wet." But he had a pained expression.

I simply stared back, resentful he was siding with our mother.

"Come on, Laina. Great things are happening for us. Don't turn away from it all now. Not for someone like him."

I just folded my arms across my chest and glared.

Obviously sensing he wasn't going to win, he got up and went to the stone steps, to leave. "You know the drill." His voice was low. "Text me if you need a ride."

I didn't even turn to look as he walked away.

I did text him that night, though, and he was involved in a terrible accident on his way to pick me up. That's how he died . . . trying once again to save me.

I still think about how we shared a great love for Shakespeare's comedy, *Twelfth Night*. I suppose we felt attached to it from such a young age because the characters Viola and Sebastian were siblings, and the story seemed to follow us, eventually inspiring his vision of the bookstore.

In the play Sebastian was believed to have died during a shipwreck caused by terrible weather. Tyler died in a car crash caused by a severe thunderstorm. There is no pleasure then, only chills, when I think about this part of its strange connection.

In those final moments with Tyler, how I wish I'd listened. Why not just stay home for one night? How selfish I'd become! How I wish I could reverse the clock, throw my arms around my brother and never let him go. Ever since then I've been too nervous, too uncertain to make any big decisions, for fear of the outcome hurting someone I love. I suppose that's why I've relied on Preston so much the last two years. He is the one friend from college I've remained close to, the one I depend on to get me through tough situations, to roust me out of bed on the days when it feels impossible to face a world without my brother in it.

\* \* \*

Returning to Staten Island after my visit to the Shakespeare Garden, I see there's still an hour left free, so I head straight to the Moravian Cemetery to visit Tyler's grave. It's been a while, and I generally don't let too much time pass without stopping in.

I turn off Richmond Road, drive through the double iron gates, and curve around the circular entranceway, passing the white farmhouse office building to my left. Beautiful old, stone bridges arch over small lakes, where ducks and geese swim merrily below. Enormous, thick-trunked oaks, maples, weeping willows, and flowering cherry trees fill the cemetery, along with vibrant flowers and bushes in beds situated between wistful statues and cement benches. Some parts of the cemetery have no headstones, so for a brief moment it is easy to forget where I really am.

I drive along the winding, one-lane path toward Tyler's grave, enjoying the tranquility. It may sound odd, but this cemetery truly is exquisite.

I park, reach into my bag and pull out my coin purse, then pop open the glove compartment for the roll of scotch tape I keep stashed in there. Digging through a bunch of coins, I locate a nice, shiny dime.

Tyler collected dimes, because, he said, F.D.R. was the best President we ever had. So, whenever I come to visit, I tape one to his headstone to let him know I've been here. That way he can go on collecting his favorite coins.

Shutting my car door, I wander across the grass, stopping about ten feet from his resting place. I stand for a few moments in silence, because as it turns out, I'm not here alone.

My mother is kneeling at Tyler's headstone. It seems we both had the same idea today. The last time we spoke was at this very spot on the day of his funeral.

As I contemplate turning back to make a mad dash for my car, she looks around and spots me, then turns away again, wiping her eyes.

"Um, sorry, I was just …" I begin to say, but she cuts me off.

"It's fine." She rises to her feet and clears her throat. "I was just about to leave anyhow." Her brown hair blows with the breeze. We stand facing each, neither of us speaking or making eye contact.

"How have you been?" I ask at last, voice high and jittery.

She thumbs a last tear away. "Oh, you know . . . some days are better than others. Today was difficult. I thought coming here would help, but it didn't."

Another long and awkward pause follows.

"Uh, Mom…"

"You know," she cuts me off again, "when you're a mother, you try everything in your power to do the best you can for your children. But somehow, with our family, it all fell apart and I don't even know where to begin to fix it."

I feel sure she must be referring to me. And so, as if I still haven't blamed myself enough for what happened, I recall Tyler's funeral recess. As it concluded, my mother turned on me and angrily shouted, in front of all our relatives, "When are you going to grow up and realize your actions affect other people? This is all your fault!" Then she had let out a bloodcurdling cry of pain, and slumped, clinging to my uncle Toby. "I can't even look at you!" she snarled, before he whisked her away. Leaving me to stand there all alone, with at least twenty pairs of hostile eyes burning into me like heated iron daggers.

Now, as I look at her quivering chin and bloodshot eyes while she fights to hold back tears, I desperately wish I could make things right again.

"Do you think it can ever be fixed?" I ask meekly.

She lets out a single sob, more of a gasp. "It's just so . . . difficult right now. Hopefully, one day." She sighs once more and walks slowly to my side, leans in and lightly kisses my cheek. Just as quickly she scurries off like a startled rabbit, mumbling, "I have to go. Work."

"Bye," I whisper as she disappears up the slope and out of sight.

I don't stay very long after that. I say a few words to Tyler, read aloud the letter I wrote to him, tape the new dime to his headstone, and blow a kiss goodbye, promising to come and speak to him again soon. Then I get back in my car and drive to the bookstore, to go to work as well.

* * *

The following night, as Preston, Jack, and I gather in the living room to eat our weight in Chinese takeout while we binge-watch *Friends* re-runs, I find myself distracted.

I took a big step yesterday by willingly going to the Shakespeare Garden. But now that I've gone and managed to get through it without a panic attack, I want to go back. As I absently stir my beef and broccoli with chopsticks, staring at the screen, I once again think about Jared. Maybe I should try one more time to find him, perhaps secretly hire someone to help me track him down. I won't divulge this new idea to Preston. That would be insane. He definitely wouldn't approve.

I'm snapped back to reality when Preston says loudly, "Hello? Earth to Laina!"

My eyes dart over as he wildly waves from his chair to get my attention. "Are you even listening to me?"

Trying to look apologetic, I say, "No, sorry. Guess I was daydreaming. Did you need something?" I turn my gaze back to the television and toss a piece of broccoli in my mouth without waiting for his response. I don't do it on purpose, but a million things are racing through my mind.

He flings a fortune cookie, which hits the side of my face before dropping onto the couch cushion. I turn and scoop it up, babble, "Oh, gee, thanks," through a mouthful of food, then drop the cookie onto my plate.

He clicks off the TV. Before I can even protest, he says, "Laina, I've been going over the numbers. I know you're aware that managing the bookstore has been a struggle lately, but . . . well, we need to do something drastic or we'll risk losing it."

I snort. "Let's not be dramatic. It can't be *that* bad."

"Well, it is, actually. I've been wantin' to talk about this for a while. If not for me, the place would've fallen to the ground by now." He frowns. "We need to come up with new ways to bring in customers, unless you're content with losing everything your brother spent so much time building."

I stop chewing then, and look back at him, petrified and speechless. Lose the bookstore? No, that cannot happen. "Okay, first thing tomorrow we'll sit down and brainstorm. I promise."

Looking relieved, he nods and flashes a smile. I turn back to the television.

Preston and Jack start bickering beside me, which falls on deaf ears because somehow it sounds like the *wah wah wah* ranting of Charlie Brown's teacher, only tenser and with two voices.

The next thing I know, the front door vehemently slams shut.

Before I can figure out what has happened, Preston hurls a handful of fortune cookies, all of them pelting my head and arm. I twist to look at him with a 'What the hell!' glare. Only then do I notice Jack is now nowhere to be seen.

"What just happened?" I inquire.

"You're on a whole new level of distracted tonight." He shakes his head, finds one last fortune cookie on the couch beside him and flings that one as well.

I lift my arm and successfully block it this time.

"Come on, what's got you in a fog?"

I shrug. "Nothing, I'm fine."

He raises his eyebrows, but his crestfallen look says he isn't in the mood to pry details out of me tonight. "Okay, okay," he concedes at last.

Setting my chopsticks on the coffee table I proceed to describe how I spent yesterday in the Shakespeare Garden and composed a letter to Tyler in my journal. I go get the journal and show him the letter, even permitting him to read a few of Jared's stories. He doesn't say much while I explain everything to him.

But when I get to the part about waiting to see if Tyler would send me a sign, he holds a hand up to stop me.

"We discussed all this. I thought we had agreed you'd let this go for now. That you were gonna give Mason a chance." He's obviously displeased, and staring at me as if I've lost my mind.

Disheartened, I grab the journal back from him.

"Laina, it's okay not to know what you want right now. All I'm suggestin' is that you let yourself live a little. Don't get totally caught up in a fantasy that some wacko planted in your head about your deceased brother sending you signs from the Great Beyond. That's like taking ten steps backward instead of moving on with your life. Why are you freakin' out about this so much, anyhow? It's not like you and Mason are getting married. Not even all that serious."

"That's not exactly true. A few days ago, he invited me to go with him to his stepbrother's destination wedding in the Bahamas. I'd be meeting his entire family." My mouth turns dry at the thought.

Preston's face freezes. Wide-eyed, clearly taken aback, he mumbles, "Okay, I'd say that's pretty serious."

We sit in silence for several moments.

"When is the wedding?"

"September."

"Wow, that's fast." He bites his lip. "What did you tell him?"

"I told him I'd have to think about it. He's inviting me to a big family event in a month, when I don't even know where we're going to dinner tomorrow night. It kind of freaks me out."

"That's completely understandable. It's sudden, but I think you should say yes."

"*What?*" I look at him with alarm. Suddenly I'm feeling queasy, and wonder if I got a bad piece of beef.

He holds his hands up as if he's not done speaking. "Hang on, just hear me out. You can always change your mind. Cancelling a plane ticket isn't the end of the world. And besides, you might regret not taking him up on the offer later on if you say no now.

Plus, think about it. You can never say no to a free vacation, right?"

"You're so twisted," I bark. "Unlike you, I would never stay with someone just to get a free vacation out of it."

"Then don't look at it like it's a free vacation." He leans forward and props a hand on the cushion beside me. "Look at it like, well . . ." He shivers dramatically, as though a spell has been cast over him, "it's your destiny."

I really want to slap him on the side of the head. "You're an ass." I roll my eyes and turn back to the television.

"Okay, okay," he chortles, "I'm sorry. I shouldn't make fun. But in all seriousness, just consider it."

I heave a deep, put-upon sigh. "If I say I'll think about it, could we change the subject?"

He sits at attention, looking smug as a cat. "Yes! Absolutely! Now that that's settled, I can finally have my cookie."

He looks around for a cellophane-wrapped fortune cookie, to no avail. I now possess them all.

"Erm, could you toss me one? I don't think I have any."

"Oh dear. Well whose fault is that?" I dangle one temptingly for a moment, then relent and toss it his way.

He catches it one-handed, and grins.

Now it's my turn. I stare at all the possible scattered fortunes around me on the couch cushions. I skim my fingers over the crinkly wrappers until I find one that simply feels like just the right cookie, the same way I selected the tarot cards. I tear off the plastic and crack the crisp almond cookie in half.

Twisting to look at Preston, I ask, "What does yours say?"

He appears disgruntled. "It was empty. Throw me another." I comply, and he slashes through the plastic like a starving bear at a campsite.

I stare down at my fortune, hardly able to believe my eyes. I read the fortune over and over. There's just no way it can say what I think it does.

Beside me, Preston grumbles, "Another empty one! Is this some stupid practical joke? Was the fortune-stuffer at the cookie factory on an unauthorized potty break?" He drops the broken bits into the brown-paper Chinese food bag on the coffee table, then grabs it and stomps off to the kitchen.

The coast is clear. Scooping my journal up from the coffee table, I scurry off into my bedroom, tucking the fortune safely away in one of the pages as I flee the living room. Once the door is safely shut I can hardly flip through the pages of the journal to my letter to Tyler fast enough. When I reach it, I skim down to where I wrote, *I can't wait around for Jared to magically come back, and I know you would want to see me settled. But I also know you would never want me to settle for second best in love. What should I do?*

I take in a deep, bracing breath. This is it. This is my sign! Pulling the fortune from the page I tucked it away in, I hold it right beside my letter, eyes fixed on the tiny paper fortune before me. Because typed out in a bold red font are the words, *Never settle for second best in love.*

* * *

After my exciting fortune cookie surprise, I find myself consuming Chinese food for dinner a little too frequently. Not because I'm constantly craving Cashew Chicken or Lo Mein, but for the fortune cookies. Because it seems this is the new portal to communicating with Tyler. Insane? Maybe. Probably, in fact. The new fortunes I receive say the most absurd things, too. On the last night I decide to order Chinese, every single fortune cookie I open says the same thing: *Your fortune is in another cookie.*

I ultimately decide I've eaten enough Asian food for a while when the night concludes with a horrific stomachache and me guzzling half the bottle of Pepto-Bismol. Clearly my body isn't accustomed to such elevated levels of MSG.

After I stop looking for signs from Tyler in my food, and after Mason and I hash out some of our relationship kinks (like fewer sleepovers) I start to look at him a bit differently than before. Relaxing, and actually enjoying his company, I find myself laughing and smiling more, and begin to question the first fortune's meaning.

Is Mason no longer what I once would consider second best? Despite our initial differences, he and I now flow into a more manageable routine, once the nightly visits no longer last until morning, and I stop dissecting every little thing he says and does. I realize I am finally making an honest effort. Not because Preston has urged me to, but also because, for the first time in ages, I truly believe fate has my back, and will not steer me wrong.

# Chapter 7

# Paradise Island

Before I know it, it's September, and Mason and I are landing in Paradise Island for JP and Liv's destination wedding. Stepping out of the airport doors, and into the humid Bahamas air feels stifling. The heat penetrates my skin, possibly to the internal organs. Everything around seems to pulsate, even after I step out of direct sunlight. Our driver, a lanky, delightful Bahamian man named Dave, instructs us to jump in while he loads our luggage into his van.

We receive the grand tour as he drives us to our hotel. Majestic Royal Palm trees seem common as weeds on this island, as we curve along the gorgeous shoreline and view the sparkling turquoise water.

Dave says, "Many movies are filmed in de Bahamas, you know. One *Jaws* film. And de James Bond one, *T'underball*."

I gulp as the word 'Jaws' passes his lips. All I can think is, *giant sharks*. I don't care if I am in the Bahamas or how beautiful and clear the water may be; I refuse to go swimming in the ocean.

We see stucco-walled villa after villa, as well as huge exquisite mansions on private gated estates. After another five minutes we pass the Cloisters to the right and the Versailles Garden to the left. It will be the location of JP and Liv's upcoming wedding ceremony and reception.

A couple minutes later we hook a left onto Garden Drive, which takes us to the Paradise Island Beach Club. Dave follows the circular drive and pulls to the front entrance of the villas, underneath a canary-yellow archway. Two big French doors lead to the front desk and sweeping lobby seating area. A grand coral-shaped chandelier hangs from the ceiling in the center of the room.

As Mason and I walk through the grounds of the villas, I'm entranced by the beds of fuchsia and other flowering bushes, and what appears to be a tunnel of greenery encircling us. The place is overflowing with alluring shades of pink, set off by the white cement walkways and creamy stucco walls, which make it seem as though we're walking on a cloud.

"Oh, by the way," he says, "we won't be sleeping together."

*Oh, thank God! More rest for me.*

"Oh, really?" I affect a hint of disappointment. "Hmm. How come?"

"Aunt Tina and Uncle Frank are a bit old-fashioned when it comes to the unmarried sleeping in the same bed thing. Actually, that's mostly just Aunt Tina. But we're going to be staying in their villa, and it's their rules, so…"

"Sure, okay, I get it. So where will I be sleeping?"

"I think with my two younger cousins. We'll try to make the best of it."

I nod as if to insinuate that I'll do my best to bear up. But to be honest, I'm hugely relieved to have my own bed. Since Mason and I are still implementing the whole separate apartment sleeping arrangements back home, the sleeping situation down here now is working out better than I could have hoped. He won't have to hear me snore and I won't have to fight for my share of the covers.

We continue up a white zigzag staircase to room 35, which is located on the second level. He heartily knocks on the door.

The burly man who answers has a thick gray mustache, shaved head, and wears a navy-blue t-shirt, plaid shorts, and flip-flops. "Mason! Wonderful! Hey, everyone, they're here!"

His wide grin is so like Mason's, it's immediately clear they're related.

"And you must be Lina," he adds, looking over at me. "Great to meet you, sweetheart. I'm Thomas, Mason's father." He extends a hand.

I take it, and smile. "It's Laina, actually." I glance at Mason, one eyebrow raised. He appears befuddled about the name confusion, as well.

Thomas' eyes widen regretfully. "Oh! So sorry, dear."

I assure him it's perfectly fine.

Peering beyond the pale pink and peach kitchen to the living room at the back of the villa, I spot twin bleached-blond teenage girls. These must be Mason's cousins, Becky and Allie, who are about sixteen and right now fixated on some T.V. program on a huge flatscreen, apparently unable to peel their eyes away.

Thomas points to each girl in turn. "That one is Becky, and Allie is on the right. Their parents weren't able to get vacation time off work, so my brother Frank, Mason's uncle, and his Aunt Tina brought the girls along for the wedding."

A short, plump woman, her lobster-red hair wrapped around dozens of tiny curlers, traipses into the living room from a back bedroom, shuffling along in flip-flops, wearing a bright yellow sundress. "My Mason's finally here!" she squeals, looking elated, before turning her attention to me. "Hello, my love. I'm Aunt Tina." She extends both arms to Mason, wiggling her fingers as if she's enticing an infant to come get a hug.

Mason steps over and she squeezes him tightly, then turns again to look at me. "You must be Lina! So glad to meet you at last, dear."

She grabs both my hands and squeezes them so hard I feel the small bones sift and pop. She doesn't seem to know my actual name, either.

I glance at Mason again, then back at Aunt Tina. "I'm sorry, but it's Laina, actually." I am beginning to wonder if Mason's family thinks I'm someone else.

"Oh dear." Aunt Tina blushes. "Afraid we've all been calling you 'Lina' these last couple months." She chuckles shrilly, turns to look down the hallway, and shouts, "*Frank!* Come meet *Lay-na!*" She cautiously glances back at me, as if to double-check she said my name correctly this time.

I smile and nod to reassure her.

"Who?" A man resembling Thomas, though slightly older and shorter, shuffles into the living room in a plain gray t-shirt, cargo shorts, and beat-up leather sandals that could pass for something Hercules might have actually worn back in ancient times. They do look comfy, though.

"*Laina* is here," Aunt Tina informs him, rolling her eyes as though pronouncing my name correctly has already proven to be a big hassle. "We've been sayin' it wrong all this time. Can you believe that? Can you ever . . . " her voice trails off.

"You two have perfect timing," Thomas eagerly cuts in. "A bunch of us are going snorkeling. We'd love for you both to come too." He turns away to stuff a waterproof camera into a small backpack.

"That sounds like fun." Mason turns to me with wide, expectant eyes, then back to his father. "JP and Liv going too?"

"Don't count on it," Becky chimes in, peeling herself from the couch. I was wondering how I would be able to tell them apart, but now I see Becky has longer hair and a broader face. So, not identical twins.

"Oh, Liv, the poor dear," Aunt Tina mourns. "She worked so hard on the wedding plans, only to find out nothing was done the way she'd expected. JP has been trying to help her sort everything out. We feel just awful. I don't understand how this could have happened. I said it from the moment we got here – it's that budget wedding planner she found back home." She shakes a finger wildly, as if this helps prove her point. "She shoulda had someone local down here, a person familiar with the area to take care of everything. Such a shame! Hope it all smoothes out before tomorrow. The poor dear . . . " Her voice drifts off again like a boat slipping its anchor.

"Evie even volunteered to help get everything in order." Thomas chimes in, then turns to me, explaining, "Evie is my wife. Mason's stepmother."

I nod and politely smile. "I see."

"Believe we're meeting up with them for dinner tonight at Montagu Gardens. They both can't wait to meet you, Lina. I mean *Laina.*"

"You'll totally love JP," Becky gushes. "He's, like, the *best* guy there is." She glances over at Mason and teases, "No offense, Mason. You're, like, a super-close second."

"Ha-ha, very funny," he scoffs, and I can tell he's not amused. Turning to me, he mutters, "Yeah, and she's my cousin, not JP's. Nice, huh?"

I pat his arm consolingly.

"So where are we at with the snorkeling? Those fish won't wait around all day," Thomas interjects, clapping once, then checking his watch.

I can see it written all over Mason's face: he's itching to go. And I want to be a good guest, but my insides churn at the idea. "Um, well, I'm not really a great swimmer," I admit. "Maybe we could go exploring, just for today?" I hold my breath, expecting Mason to make a pitch for the snorkeling instead.

But he half-heartedly turns to his father and shakes his head. "Guess you should count us out for now, Pops." Then he walks down the hall with our suitcases and disappears into the front bathroom, leaving me with Aunt Tina. We continue chatting, but a few moments later, she and I nearly jump out of our shoes when Mason shouts and swears from the hall bathroom, his muffled voice echoing off the walls.

"What happened?" Aunt Tina shouts, scurrying to the bathroom door, flip-flops flapping at her heels. She opens the door.

Mason steps out, looking apologetic. "I think I pulled too hard on the door handle. I couldn't get out. Someone better call the front desk," he adds, shaking the loose door handle.

"My goodness, how on earth?" Aunt Tina cries. "You must have some grip, honey!"

"I forgot I locked the door and just pulled on it a little too hard. Guess I don't know my own strength." He winks at me.

\* \* \*

As Mason and I bop along in a taxi on the way to the Straw Market, he grabs my hand. I smile at him, then stare down at our entwined fingers. Nice, but . . . I can't help but feel as though there should be something more there. I know deep down I don't quite feel what I should. But I want to, and wish I did. No doubt it will happen, in time.

Turning my attention to the exquisite homes and trees around us, I gaze out the window of the cab, acting as if I'm simply enraptured by the beautiful tropical landscape. While in reality my mind prickles with guilt for allowing the relationship to go on as long as it has.

The cab driver turns down a narrow dirt road and lets us out. I spot a lime green Señor Frog's sign propped at the far end of the street. Above it, a cartoon frog lies on a hammock beneath a stand of palm trees, welcoming us to paradise.

Mason runs into one of the liquor stores to buy alcohol, enough for the next few days, so we can save some money on drinks while we're hanging around the villa. While I wait outside and have a look around, I take it all in: the friendly-looking people, the colorful buildings, that laid-back island energy, the reggae music that trickles from every storefront— it truly is paradise.

I allow my feet to lead as I wander about, until, distracted, I bump into a tall wooden pillar. It's a makeshift events bulletin board with flyers and postcard notices tacked up all over it. Before I turn away, my eye is drawn to three words at the top of one colorful flyer:

*Shakespeare in Paradise*

And just below that headline, the details:

*August 26 – September 16*
*At the Dundas Bahamas Historical Society*
*Contact the Dundas Box Office for Tickets*

My heart flutters. Who knew that all this way distant, there would still be something just like Shakespeare in the Park!

Then I frown, wondering, could this be a sign from Tyler? I haven't received any more since the fortune cookie. Maybe this is his way of telling me I should start going to these shows again.

Just then Mason exits the store with a cardboard box filled with various bottles of alcohol. "You won't believe the deal I got on all this."

"Great!" I point to the flyer on the pillar. "Did you ever go to see a Shakespeare in Paradise play out here?"

He stares blankly at me. "I have no idea what that is."

"They put on Shakespeare performances, like, *Romeo and Juliet*, *Twelfth Night*, *Macbeth*..."

He continues to stare, expression vacant.

"They have performances this week. I don't suppose . . . you wouldn't be interested in going to one, would you?"

"No, not really," he flatly replies, wrinkling his nose dismissively. "Wouldn't you rather go out drinking? Experience the laid-back Bahamas culture?"

"But this is also part of their culture," I argue. "Their appreciation for the arts."

He sighs. "But it sounds like work. And I could really use some down time. I'm drained from working on that new case. I need a break. If you want art, how about we sit on the beach and have one cocktail after another until the sunset looks like Van Gogh's *Starry Night*?" He nudges me with an elbow.

"Ha. Ha."

"Come on, you love boozing. Doesn't that sound more appealing? But we'll talk more about it later. Right now, we should hit up Señor Frog's for a drink." He walks rapidly away down the street, shouldering his gigantic box of booze.

I follow after him, walking more slowly. Because I know by now that talk actually won't ever happen.

But as we follow the blaring music coming from Señor Frog's, I come to a decision. This trip is not all about me. I refuse to be the cause of family drama before Mason's stepbrother's wedding by breaking things off and leaving before the event even takes place. It would be rude, even cruel. Still, once we return to New York, I'm going to end things with Mason.

I take a long, deep breath, content with my choice. I feel a bit more at ease now that I've decided to not let anything or anyone sway me into doing otherwise. It's only what's right. So for now, if the only Bahamian culture Mason is interested in partaking of involves getting plastered . . . then hell, I guess I'm going to drink.

\* \* \*

Sometime later, who knows how long, brief flashes of blurred images creep to the foreground of my mind, in between long spans of blackness. Bright, piercing sunlight. A bathroom stall toilet. Me crouched over it on hands and knees. An upside-down image of the back of Mason's shoes as I'm flung over his shoulder. Me again, sobbing in a cab while trying to talk seriously to Mason in what I can only recall as drunken gibberish.

I finally awaken on a cot in the front room that I'm sharing with Becky and Allie, bending my head to see their perfectly made twin beds. Banging and shuffling noises boom from the other room. I'm nauseated, and so dehydrated I can barely swallow. My hands tremble and are filled with pins and needles.

Is it possible I was roofied? What time is it? How long have I been asleep?

Slowly propping myself up on both elbows, I notice I'm now dressed only in a t-shirt and a pair of underwear. My jean shorts lie on the floor beside the cot. I grope for them, and unsteadily put them on. A bitter taste lingers in my parched mouth. Lumpish and achy, I drag my hungover body to the bedroom door, which opens the moment I reach for the knob.

Mason steps in, wearing a tan linen suit. "Oh good, you're up. How you feeling?"

"Glorious," I whisper sarcastically, voice quivering, throat as scratchy as if I've swallowed a sheet of sandpaper. I slowly, carefully take a seat on the edge of the twin bed closest to the door. "You look all fancy. Is it time for dinner? I'll try to hurry but I don't think I'm going to eat anything."

He raises his eyebrows. "No, it is not dinner time. Today is JP and Liv's wedding." He checks his watch. "Actually, in a couple of hours."

"What! But . . . are you telling me I slept half the day away yesterday and the entire night?" Breathing slowly, I force down a surge of acid reflux that blitzes my throat.

"Yeah, and half the following morning. You didn't want to listen when we were at Señor Frog's. I kept saying slow down, but you didn't want to hear it. So many tequila shots were bound to catch up with you. I had to carry you through the villa draped over one shoulder. My family has been really worried. They keep asking how *Lina* is." He shakes his head and snorts. "I have no clue why they're calling you that, by the way."

I cover my face with both hands. "What a great first impression to make. They're probably thrilled you brought me along."

"Well, Becky and Allie aren't too happy with you right now." He smirks. "They told Aunt Tina you kept them up all night, snoring."

"Perfect." I slump down farther on the bed. "Now I won't be able to sleep the entire time we're here. I'll be so self-conscious that I'm keeping them awake."

"Don't worry about it. I think JP and Liv are a little disappointed, though. They didn't get to meet you yesterday. We were all supposed to have dinner last night," he reminds me.

I massage my temples. "Oh God, I'm so sorry. What did you tell them?"

"I didn't actually see them. I hung back here to make sure you didn't choke on your own vomit. Told Dad to send along our apologies. I'm sure they understood."

"Mason, I feel horrible. I know you were looking forward to seeing JP. I promise I'll be on my best behavior today."

He shrugs. "It's okay, really. Everyone has been driving me crazy all morning. I've just about had it."

"Why, what's going on?" I rub my eyes, no doubt smearing the day-old liner and mascara crusted to my lids.

"For one thing, everyone won't quit calling you 'Lina' no matter how much I correct them. Plus, there's an actual dilemma I have to deal with. JP has been missing all morning . . . but you didn't hear that from me." He taps an index finger over his lips in a 'hush-hush' manner.

"Missing! Do you think he's okay?" I frown.

"Dad saw him earlier in the morning chugging Pepto-Bismol straight from the bottle. I think he may have cold feet. So now it's up to me to hunt him up and get him down that aisle before Liv finds out." He rolls his eyes. "That's all we need. She'd be devastated. Plus, the reception arrangements are still a mess at the Cloisters. So, I also need to head down there and give my stepmom a hand."

"I'll jump in the shower and start getting ready, then meet you there to help out."

"Sounds good. All right, I'm heading out." He kisses my cheek. "See you in a bit." He briskly walks off down the hall. A moment later I hear him shout to the family, "See you guys down there!"

"Okay, good luck," a few voices respond.

I cautiously emerge from the bedroom, hoping to tiptoe into the bathroom without Mason's family spotting me.

"Lina, you're awake!" Aunt Tina announces, shuffling into view. I slowly turn on the balls of my feet until I'm facing her, and crack a faint smile. "Oh, hi."

Her hair is in curlers once again and she's wearing a white slip. Her eyes widen. "Holy moley, you look *dreadful!*" She shouts down the hall toward the kitchen, "Thomas, why don't you whip this poor thing up some eggs?"

I cup a hand over my mouth and try to push away the sickening thought of putting food into my body. "Really, I'm okay. Maybe just some coffee."

"Nonsense! You haven't eaten a thing since you arrived yesterday."

She insists I follow her to the dining room. Here, take a seat." She pulls out a chair.

Thomas is standing behind the pass-through kitchen counter drinking a Kalik beer.

"Don't you think it's a little early to be drinking?" Aunt Tina scolds.

"My stepson is missing on the day of his wedding." He lifts the beer in a salute. "So, no, I don't."

Aunt Tina taps my arm. "I bet the poor thing just has pre-wedding jitters."

"Maybe he ate a piece of bad fish or something at dinner last night." Uncle Frank chimes in, as he strolls into the dining room, clucking, clearly amused with himself.

I cover my mouth again and try to focus on breathing slowly, in and out, to quell the rising nausea.

*Do not get sick. Do not get sick.*

"No, no. I'm sure it's nerves," she firmly disagrees, traipsing around into the kitchen.

She comes back with a cup of coffee for me. I take it away from the table, and the smell of food in the kitchen, to sit instead on the pale blue living room couch, and switch the TV station from the cooking channel to local news. The meteorologist onscreen says a hurricane is expected to hit the northeast coast in four days' time.

Thomas comes in and takes a seat beside me.

"Did you hear about this? The hurricane," I ask, concern for the bookstore tightening my voice.

"Oh yeah, wouldn't worry about it too much. They always blow these storms outta proportion," he replies in a gravelly tone. "Helps the supermarkets make money when people rush to buy batteries and jugs of water. You see it happen all the time."

I take a few more sips of coffee before excusing myself to shower. In a dash, I throw on my sapphire lace dress and do my makeup and hair in record time. But there is a severe, lingering knot in my stomach I can't seem to shake. Luckily, according to the mirror, there is no visible clue I happen to be nursing the worst hangover of my life.

Saying goodbye to Mason's relatives, I head to the main gate and stroll along the path to the main road, hooking a right once I reach Paradise Island Drive. Arriving at the Cloisters only a few minutes later, I stop before a beautiful stone statue. In the middle of the front garden, a patch of tall bushes surround the figure of a woman bowing her head. White basket weave chairs are arranged at the bottom of the large stone steps surrounding a circular gazebo overlooking Nassau Harbour.

A few wedding guests are already arriving, taking shelter from the sun under a big stand of Royal Palms. Mason is down at the bottom level, near the gazebo, rearranging chairs, clearly flustered. As I approach I can see sweat trickling down his face. He is also frowning.

"Are you okay? Find your stepbrother?" I ask, carefully stepping over the grass in my high heels.

"Uh, not yet. That's the next order of business," he sounds frazzled as he grabs another chair to line it with the others. "Everything's a mess here, nothing is getting done. I can see why Liv is so upset."

"Is there anything I can do?"

"Well, I know you haven't been introduced yet, but my stepmom could probably use some help. She's doing the flower arrangements. Maybe you can give her a hand?" He tilts his head in the direction of a woman whose back is turned to us, standing at the top of the stone steps.

Carefully climbing them again in my slender, somewhat wobbly heels, I finally reach Mason's stepmother. Her medium brown hair is pulled back in loose, dangling curls. "Excuse me, Mrs. Hartley?"

She slowly and gracefully turns, like a rotating mannequin in a shop window, one hand daintily grasping a lily. "Yes?" she asks, in a cordial, calm tone.

I take in her familiar features and suppress a gasp. Long, thick lashes flutter over caramel-colored irises. Her soft brown hair is a bit shorter than I remember, and bangs now frame her pretty, slender face. Before I can think about it, *"Mrs. Grant?"* slides through my lips, almost in a whisper.

"Excuse me?" Her eyes widen, and she looks taken aback. "Do I know you?"

"I'm...I'm..." I splutter, unable for a moment to spit any more words out. All I can think is, *It can't be. But it is. It's her!*

Pulling her attention from me, she leans out to wave at Mason, and then turns back. "You're Lina, Mason's new girlfriend? I'm his stepmother, Evelyn . . . though everyone calls me Evie." She shakes her head, confused. "I'm sorry, but did you just call me Mrs. Grant a moment ago?" She stares fixedly, as if she's trying to figure out if we've ever met before.

We most definitely have. I can't even swallow now. A lump forms in my throat, and the knot in my stomach is pulsating. There must be an ulcer brewing, or something. I fear this time I will be sick. "Laina," I manage to force out. "Not Lina."

Her face falls then, and she looks at me with obvious dismay. "Laina *Jorden?*"

I nod, then scan the surrounding area, half expecting Jared to emerge from the bushes. But what could they possibly be doing at Mason's brother's wedding? Then I recall who she is: my boyfriend's stepmother, so . . .

Jared Parker . . . JP . . . his mother is the stepmother . . . I'm suddenly living out a horrible nightmare.

Evelyn seems to agree. She stares at me with alarm. She takes a short, stunned gasp as her eyes narrow. She suddenly seems extremely nervous. "Laina, please..." her voice quivers as she uneasily twirls the stem of the white lily between her fingers.

Horrified, I choke out, "This . . . this is Jared's wedding, isn't it?" The certainty hits like a knife to the gut. Jared is JP! Jared, my Jared, is getting married! My legs tremble and threaten to collapse under me. "But I thought Mason told me the last name was Hartley. JP Hartley," I say frantically. "Wait...did you change Jared's last name?"

Tears well in my eyes. I hold my breath, hoping it will keep them from spilling down my cheeks. "Why would you do that? When did he start going by JP?"

"Laina, please," she begs, laying one soft, cool hand on my arm. "We can discuss all of this later."

"N-no," my voice quavers. "We can't. Please, I need to know right now."

"Okay, okay," she says in a lower, edgy tone, sounding a bit sullen, as if she hopes that providing any explanation will satisfy me enough so that I won't cause a scene. "JP is a nickname for Jared Parker. I'm sure you must remember that. We moved away to Pennsylvania after William died. We had family out there. After I married Thomas, he adopted Jared, so I changed our last name to his."

"But *why*?" I squeak.

She pauses, squinting to study my reaction, as though she is astonished by my obliviousness. "You...you really don't know, do you?" she replies, looking dumbfounded.

"Know . . . know what?" I must be hyperventilating at that point, because a wave of dizziness washes over me. I bend over and count slow breaths to make it stop. "Pennsylvania," I mumble, as if it is foreign and exotic, like Katmandu or Belize. She could have told me she dragged him off to live in Neverland and my reaction would probably still be the same. "Where is he? Where is Jared?"

"You're not children anymore, Laina. Please don't go messing with his head. He's getting married. I hope you can respect that." Her voice quavers now, too, and her face is twisted with worry.

Quickly surveying the banks of flowers, all the wedding preparations taking place around me, I can hardly breathe. I want to shout at her for taking Jared away from me. I want to ask why she would just pick up and leave without a single word to his friends. But I can't. I'm frozen. The thick island heat is suffocating me. My head swims as I think over and over again. *This is Jared's wedding. My* Jared. Within the next hour my first and only true love will be taken away right before me, forever, and I will be forced to watch!

Without thinking of what I am doing, or where to go next, I race back to the entrance and dart across the street, neglecting to look both ways, and hook a quick right back to the villa. As I run, I feel as if I am suffocating, unable to suck in enough air in the thick island heat. I want to drop to the pavement, curl into a ball, and cry hysterically. I want to shake my head hard, like an Etch-A-Sketch, and erase the last five minutes.

Am I really, truly a guest at Jared's wedding? How shitty can my luck be? I never thought fate could be this cruel. So sick, so twisted.

I want desperately to find Jared and tell him to leave his fiancée, to convince him not to go through with the wedding. I, the best man's girlfriend, am seriously considering breaking up with him before his stepbrother's wedding and stealing away the groom! Of actually stopping the wedding, like a dramatic scene in a movie, objecting to the proceedings as she professes her lifelong love for the groom.

In the midst of sprinting down the sidewalk, I run right out of my high heels and only notice this a few steps later when the hot cement scorches the soles of my feet. I rush back to retrieve them, panting, and start running again.

What if Jared has forgotten all about me? Clearly, he *has* moved on. What good would it do to look him in the eyes and ask him to leave his fiancée? And if he refused . . . it would crush me to hear him say he's forgotten all about me. Oh my God! Out of all the people in the world I could have possibly dated, why did it have to be Jared's stepbrother?

I wish I could believe life eventually works out, that everything happens for a reason. But what the hell could be the reason for this mess? My stomach churns. The island seems to be spinning all around me and I can't manage to pull myself together. My tear-clouded vision makes it hard to see where I'm running, and I veer off the sidewalk, stumbling into a wall of bushes to my left. Scratched by the tiny, thorny branches, I refuse to stop. As if still drunk, I clumsily collide head-first into a STOP sign, then fall backward onto the grass. For a few moments I sit, dazed, on the tiny patch of lawn trying to regain my composure and catch my breath, as my head throbs and my body trembles.

I need to get back to the villa soon, before I bump into anyone. I don't want to have to explain my condition. Luckily, I arrive after Mason's family has already left for the wedding. I close the door and my shoes slide out of my grasp, clunking onto the tile floor. I fling my shoulder bag at the nearest chair and, trancelike, I float toward the bathroom, feeling hollowed out and hopeless. I flick on the bathroom light and stare at my swollen, red, tear-streaked reflection.

"I'm at Jared's *wedding*," I inform my mirror image, wiping my leaky nose with a thumb. "Look at me, I'm a mess. Why would anyone, let alone Jared, want me?" I sob, feeling sorry for myself. My chin uncontrollably quivers. Salty teardrops trickle into the corners of my mouth. Turning the cold water on full force, I try to splash away the evidence of a shattered heart from my tearstained face, only smearing the ruined makeup deeper into my pores.

Never would I have imagined an otherwise healthy heart could ache so, as if it is a separate being with another heart inside itself, which is breaking as well. I can't breathe. Gravity feels heavier with each passing second, pulling me lower with every breath. Gasping, I cling to the sink counter to prevent myself from collapsing, as my legs quiver like Jell-O.

Finally I feel stable enough to hobble to the roll of toilet paper, grab one end and walk away, leaving an unraveling trail behind me as I wipe my leaky nose.

"This isn't fair!" I shout, grabbing hold of the bathroom door, smashing it shut as hard as I can. The walls of the villa shake. The noise reverberates throughout the bathroom.

I imagine what Tyler would say if he were around. I doubt he would try to talk sense into me. He, better than anyone else, would know any chance of that is long gone. But if he *was* here, right here, right now, what would he say?

I think I know.

"He would tell me to go to him," I whisper. "To try and stop the wedding, until he knows I'm here. This might be my only chance."

The idea perks me up and terrifies me at the same time. But how would I even go about doing that? I'd have to find Jared first. He went missing. So now I have to think. If he wanted to be alone on the island, where would he go?

Suddenly the answer is so obvious. Versailles Garden.

I thrust my shoulders back, ready to take on the pavement once more. Maybe there's still a small chance left to get my happy ending after all. "You'll never know unless you give it a shot," I pep-talk myself.

Now in a desperate rush to leave, I clutch the doorknob, yank it toward me, and nearly pass out as the handle detaches from its base, and falls into my hand. As I stare down in horror at the knob of betrayal cradled in my palm, the other half clunks to the tile floor on the other side of the door, out in the hallway.

No. No, no, no. This can't be happening!

I'm afraid to move. I'm afraid to do anything, really, because the moment I do, I will have to come to terms with the fact that this is real. I have trapped myself in the bathroom, and each moment that passes, Jared is one step closer to walking down that aisle.

# Chapter 8

# Forget-Me-Not

For what seems like hours, I scramble around like a trapped animal frantically trying to escape a cage. If I could chew or claw my way through the door, I probably would. Though I'm not normally claustrophobic, the more time I spend in this windowless little bathroom, the more it feels as though the walls are closing in.

My cell phone is in my handbag, which is of course lying on a chair in the dining room. So, there's no way to call or text Mason. After relentlessly pounding on the door and shouting on the top of my lungs for help, I take a moment to regroup, until remembering once again that I'm running out of time to find Jared. Determined to break free, I switch back over to panic mode, slamming my body repeatedly into the door. A wasted effort, since the hinges are locked on the inside with me, but I do it anyway. I can't let myself stop trying. I pray there is hidden adrenaline buried within me somewhere—or perhaps an inner Hulk—that will miraculously emerge, giving me the super-strength to free myself.

In between pretending to be a battering ram, I try to jimmy the jammed door lock with anything I can find in the bathroom. However, the tools at hand are limited to a flimsy plastic hair comb and a worn-out toothbrush. Nothing works, of course. I bang on the door until my hands are crimson, sore, and throbbing. I scream until my voice is hoarse and raspy. At last, thoroughly worn out, I slink onto the tile floor, clutching the silver doorknob like an evil talisman in my aching hand.

In the silence, my mind busily races. I'm left alone in a quiet villa with nothing but my troubled thoughts, and can't help but ponder everything that has occurred up until this moment. Is this indeed my fate, to be within arm's length of having the one and only person I've ever wanted my entire life, only to be bitch slapped by fate's cruel hand? Fate repeatedly mocks me, and I allow it to. I've squarely placed myself in this role: the person that bad things happen to, and then all I do is pity myself, rather than seriously try to change my own fate.

Has it all really been a string of coincidences – meeting Desi, finding Jared's journal, meeting Mason, Jared being Mason's stepbrother, and being at Jared's wedding? Is it truly my fate to be sitting here on this floor at the precise moment Jared about to give himself to another woman? Where is a freaking fortune cookie when I really need one? And if locking myself in the bathroom wasn't supposed to happen then why didn't Tyler send a sign to stop me from coming back here?

Tucking my knees to my chest, I hug my legs and let my head rest tiredly on my knees. A twinge of pain makes me wince when one knee grazes a bump on my forehead. A souvenir of when I ran head-first into the stupid STOP sign.

*The STOP sign…*

I bolt upright and cry, "Oh my God!" Jumping to my feet, I frantically pace in the cramped bathroom, reanalyzing my trip back to the villa. First, I ran straight out of my shoes. Who actually does that, aside from Cinderella? Then I ran head-first into a STOP sign! Duh. Those *were* my signs, and I ignored them! Also, last night I was supposed to eat dinner with Jared and Liv, but I was too focused on drinking myself into oblivion. Sabotaging yet another opportunity to see Jared before things even got this far.

I wish I could call Preston and thank him for convincing me to stick out the relationship with Mason. I want to commend his gut instinct for intuiting that this is what I was meant to do. He was right; he definitely paid me back big time for stepping in as Fran's bridesmaid. If not for Preston, I wouldn't even be here right now. I never would have crossed paths with Jared. I would never have been granted the opportunity to change my fate.

Oh, how I could kick myself!

After what feels like an eternity, the villa door clicks and creaks open. For a moment I think I may be hearing things.

"*Laina*," Mason shouts, "are you in here?"

My heart leaps with joy. I'm not hallucinating! Unsteadily I climb to my feet. "Mason! Oh, thank God! I'm locked in the stupid bathroom! I can't get out!"

"How the hell are you...? Oh, yeah, I see," he mutters on the other side of the door. "Oh boy. They're going to have to come fix this thing for sure now."

"Can you free me?" I choke out, pathetically resting one cheek against the bathroom door.

Mason shoves on the other side of the door, then kicks it. "*Umph*. It won't budge. Hang tight. I'll be right back."

As if I have any choice rather than to wait. I'm crawling out of my skin with anticipation.

Mason finally returns and slides a knife through the opening underneath the door. "Pop the door open by the hinges. Can you reach?"

Grabbing the knife, I climb onto the sink. With a sudden surge of energy, I jab and push until I'm able to force the bolt through the top from the upper hinge assembly. When it pops out, I breathe a sigh of relief, jump off the sink and pop the bottom hinge out as well. "I did it!"

Mason is able to remove the whole door a few moments later.

Rushing past Mason, I race to grab my shoes. "Whoa, what the hell happened to you?" He looks taken aback at the sight of my frazzled, swollen, raccoon-like appearance. "Were you crying?"

I ignore him, gather my purse and cram my feet into my shoes so I can run out the door.

"Hey, hey!" He grabs hold of my arm. "Calm down a minute, will you?"

I can't. I only have one thing on my mind and there's no time to lollygag and chit-chat.

"You might want to fix yourself before we head out." He frowns and takes a step closer, inspecting my face. "Wow, that stuff looks like it's really caked on there."

"I...I don't," I frantically stammer, "I don't have time to explain. The wedding—"

He grins, shaking his head. "Oh, we have plenty of time. The reception doesn't start for another forty minutes." Heading to the refrigerator, he opens the door and cracks open a Kalik.

A giant hand twists my gut. "R-reception?" I gasp. "What about the ceremony?"

"Oh, that's all over. Pictures done, too, thank God. That was a real zoo. It was so friggin' hot outside," he remarks, throwing his head back to take a long swig, heading over to the couch.

"All over," I repeat dully. I manage to trudge to the front bedroom, grab my makeup bag, and return to the bathroom. Standing for a moment in front of the mirror, I stare at the bag I just set beside the sink, in a complete fog. I don't know why I am standing here, or why I should bother re-doing my makeup. I'm just going to cry it all off again in a little while, right?

I splash my face with hot water, find soap and a fresh washcloth, and scrub away the dark, crusted splotches plastered to my skin, patting my puffy face dry with the towel draped over the wall hook.

I emerge from the bathroom and mumble, "Want to tell me about the ceremony?" I don't know if I truly want to hear the details, yet I can't help asking.

"It was pretty nice." Mason swigs more beer. "Sweated my ass off, though. Never seen JP so nervous. I finally found him in the Versailles Garden, by the way, standing behind the F.D.R. statue. He was mumbling some real crazy talk." He shrugs and shakes his head with raised eyebrows.

"What kind of crazy talk?"

"I couldn't understand most of it, but when I asked what he was waiting for, he just said, for a sign," Mason scoffs. "Then Evie showed up, had a quick chat with him, and he was fine." He looks at the damp wash cloth still clutched in my hand. "I'll let you finish getting ready."

I stare into his sharp blue eyes and nod, zombie-like. "Right."

Ten minutes later I'm looking as good as I will ever be under the current circumstances. When I step outside the fierce heat blasts my face. I may not have to worry about crying my makeup off. The heat will do a great job of melting it first.

* * *

We arrive at the Versailles Garden as champagne is being passed around. Mason introduces me to family member after family member and friend after friend. My anxiety is intense as I mumble the usual greetings over and over.

Where is Jared? I assume he and Liv are off taking pictures on the beach, or making a quick pit stop at their honeymoon suite. I shake my head, not wanting to think about that.

Though I don't feel hungry, I absently pop a few pieces of warm, half-melted cheese in my mouth from a tray carried by a thin young Bahamian waiter.

Aunt Tina approaches, thoroughly concerned about my bathroom captivity. "We'll get that door replaced in no time, dear. Don't fret about missing the ceremony. If you ask me, you were the lucky one. You didn't have to sweat your tits off out there. At least now there are tents set up and the sun will soon set. But sittin' there during the ceremony for over an hour," she bleats, "I perspired right through my clothes."

I manage to break away as Becky and Allie approach, begging for just a *teeny* glass of champagne.

Finally locating our assigned table in a far corner of the garden, I take a seat.

The deejay is now picking up the pace of the reception. "Ladies and gentleman," he booms into the microphone, "please rise to your feet and put hands together. It gives me great pleasure to introduce to you all, for the first time, Mr. and Mrs. JP Hartley!"

The wedding guests all rise, clapping, at the retro marital phrasing, dancing eagerly to the clubby pop music. I strain to catch a glimpse of Jared, on tiptoes trying to see above the heads of those standing in front of me. I swear, the man directly in my line of view has *got* to be a relative of Andre the Giant! I consider climbing onto my chair, but the moment I grab it the legs wobble and sink crookedly into the turf.

So I push through the seething crowd of wedding guests to reach an opening with a clear view of the dance floor.

I stop in my tracks the moment I set eyes on Jared and Liv, holding hands. Frozen with astonishment, I take in every bit of him. He still looks like my Jared, only older, more chiseled. Tall

*Dana Miller*

now, with broad shoulders, he looks fantastic in a pale linen suit. His short, wavy chestnut hair and a slight facial scruff create a rugged, sexy, mysterious air. And as I stare, I know that if I saw him walking down the street—even half a mile away—without a doubt, I would know it was Jared.

His bride's buttery blond hair is pulled into an up-do which spills in waves down one side of her head. She wears a flowing satin dress and looks blissfully happy. And why shouldn't she be?

I shift my eyes back to Jared. It's strange to see him grown into a man.

Just then Mason struts onto the dance floor, to Jared's side, and the first wedding dance comes to an end. They exchange a brotherly hug, then Jared smiles the same mesmeric smile I've kept locked away in the memory box in the back of my mind. Tears flood my eyes then, yet I still can't help but warmly smile. I'm staring at Jared right now. This isn't a dream. It's real. He's real.

Maybe on some level I've already accustomed myself to the idea that I will never get to see that genuinely perfect grin again.

"Okay, ladies and gentleman," the deejay blares, "time to have de best man give his toast to our lovely bride and groom." He hands Mason the microphone.

"Hello, everybody," Mason begins, "I want to start this thing off by saying congratulations to Liv and JP." He nervously looks down, then at Jared and Liv who seem to be anxiously awaiting his speech. "Some of you may not know this, but JP and I didn't exactly hit it off right away when we were younger. When Evie and my dad got married it took a little while before we became as close as we are now. Because we're very different."

Mason smiles out at the crowd of party guests, seeming more relaxed now. "All I wanted was to go surfing, since I was originally from California. But JP wanted to fish and go camping. I wanted to watch *Law and Order* on T.V. and he always had his head buried in books."

The wedding guests affectionately chuckle.

"But over time, I started to look up to him. It didn't matter that I was only a few months younger. I looked up to JP because he was the most genuine person I'd ever met. Smart and funny. Resourceful. Even though he was born in New York, he was more in his element in Pennsylvania. Let me just say, if a Zombie Apocalypse does ever happen, I want *this* guy at my side."

The guests howl with laughter.

"Liv," Mason says, turning to face her, "even though JP possesses all of these great qualities, I feel it's my duty to offer some pearls of wisdom about his quirks, too. First off, when JP loses his sunglasses, check the top of his head. Most likely they're sitting up there. Oh, and the keys? If they're missing, nine out of ten times he probably left them *in* the car."

Liv giggles and smiles up at JP. The guests hoot and cackle.

"Never let him close a pickle jar, or any jar for that matter. You will *never* get it open again."

Jared slaps a hand over his eyes, miming embarrassment, grinning and shaking his head.

"You can cover your eyes all you want, Bro. You're laughing because you know it's true."

Jared guiltily smirks and pumps a fist in the air, as if admitting to the crowd that his step-brother is only revealing the truth.

Mason pauses until the guests quiet down, then proceeds. "Liv, always wear closed shoes when he takes you dancing. Otherwise you *will* lose a toe. Sadly, he was not blessed with the ability to follow along with any rhythm. Oh, also, JP is known to be a pretty handy guy. He can fix just about anything, but keep in mind that about halfway through the project you might need to call a professional handyman, because JP will get bored with that project and start on something else."

The guests explode with amusement once again.

"I'm not kidding," Mason bellows. "Growing up with JP, anytime Evie or my dad would ask if homework or chores were done, his response was always, 'Eh, almost.' "

Liv cups a hand under Jared's chin and gives it a loving squeeze. He leans over and lightly kisses her lips. I have to look away.

Mason is still in high gear. "You know I love you, JP. You deserve nothing but a lifetime of happiness. You're the best guy I know. And Liv, JP will always put your happiness before his own. If my brother picked you, he thinks you're amazing. We may not know each other very well yet, but I'm looking forward to getting to know you better. I wish you both the best. Welcome to the family!" Mason raises his Champagne flute, and shouts, "Cheers."

The wedding guests follow suit, chanting it back to him. All except one: me.

The deejay takes the microphone just as Jared grabs his brother's arm, pulling him aside. As he speaks, Mason cracks up at whatever it is he's saying.

This isn't a dream. The wedding is real. *He's* real.

Turning away, I approach the bar closest to my table in the side garden. A lovely Bahamian woman, hair in complex plaits, is bartending.

"May I please have a ginger ale?" I ask.

She nods and grabs a glass tumbler to her left.

As I follow the gesture I see Evelyn standing off to one side, nearby. Our gazes meet. She cautiously stares, blinking rapidly, as if traumatized that I'm even here. She looks as though she may pounce on me if I make one wrong move. Well, I have news for her. I honestly have no energy left. I've already lost Jared. I don't know what she could possibly be so worried about now.

Mason appears at my side. He grabs an hors d'oeuvre from the lone tray of grilled pineapple and bacon sitting on the bar, chomping with his mouth open like a ruminating cow. I have to tense up in order not to cringe. "How'd I do?" he proudly asks.

"Like a pro," I reply automatically, and clink my ginger ale against his glass of champagne.

As the reception kicks into high gear I watch Jared from the sidelines. He and Liv take their time greeting each wedding guest, thanking them and making small talk. Liv beams as she soaks up the constant praise of her beautiful gown.

Most of the reception I spend alone, and I'm okay with that. I prefer to be by myself with my thoughts. Mason hangs with the other groomsmen, getting plastered out of his mind. It's best to keep my distance from that. I do find it amusing he has forgotten to even introduce me to the happy couple. I desperately want to go to Jared but can't decide when is the best time. I also have no idea what I will even say to him.

*Hey, old friend. Long time no see?*

Someone new swoops in and strikes up a conversation with him every time I buck up enough courage to rise from my seat.

At the table to my right, a scrawny bridesmaid with fiery auburn hair gets up and rushes over to another bridesmaid seated at the table adjacent to mine. "Connie! Connie! Oh my God, you won't believe this. I just had my fortune read!"

She plops down at a seat at that table and shakes Connie's arm just as she is taking a sip of her drink. It spills all over the place. But Connie, a real wedding trouper, hides her evident exasperation with a composed, artificial smile. Then grabs her napkin and dabs at her dress.

"Oops, sorry," the excited bridesmaid blurts out. "But you won't *believe* what she told me."

Connie sighs, glowering. "Let me guess, Amelia. Something to do with you getting laid." She sardonically raises one eyebrow.

Amelia looks momentarily stunned. "Well, not in those words, exactly. She said I'm going to meet the man of my dreams while I'm here on the island." She throws her head back and thrusts both fists in the air. "My search is over!"

Connie mockingly pats her shoulder and flashes a fake grin. "I'm very, very happy for you. So, which lucky guy is it? A groomsman?"

Instead of answering, Amelia roars, "You need to get *your fortune told!*"

"Pfft. I'm not into that stuff. It's such a crock." Connie flaps one hand, takes a sip of her drink, and turns away.

"It's not, I swear! She told me things there was no way for her to possibly have known. Just give it a try. She has a really cool name, too. It's Desti...no, Desta...hmm." Amelia thinks for a moment, then bounces excitedly in her seat when she finally does recall. "Desi Chase."

Wait. Not the woman from the bookstore?

My heart leaps in surprise. I scan the surrounding area in search of her table.

Amelia adds, "If you think about what her name actually means, it's so cool. Desi is obviously a variation on Destiny. So, flip both names around, and it means Chase Destiny. How awesome is that?"

*Chase Destiny?*

Without thinking twice, I rush to Amelia's side. "So sorry to interrupt, but I overheard you mention there's a fortuneteller here. Where can I find her?"

Amelia's face brightens as she provides precise directions. I thank her and dart off, finally spotting Desi at the opposite end of the garden, two levels down. She sits at a tiny, round café-sized table covered with a blue cloth. She's decked out in a bright orange Bahamian shift with a matching silk headband to hold all her long dark hair back as she does a tarot card reading. The customer is an attractive woman in her mid-fifties, with thick, light blond hair.

I stand in the rapidly growing line, impatiently waiting my turn, fiddling with Jared's Forget-Me-Not necklace.

As soon as Desi finishes with the blonde, her gaze falls on me. She actually smirks, as if she's been expecting me. That sends a shiver down my spine.

"Miss Laina, won't you please have a seat?" She extends a hand, inviting me to take the now-empty chair.

Dazed, I quickly settle in. "You remember me."

"Of course, I do," she replies, chortling, shaking her head as though I've just said the silliest thing she's ever heard. She reaches out and shuffles the tarot deck in front of her.

"How can you be here?" I ask, baffled.

"My dear." She smiles patiently. "Do you recall me telling you that I am often hired for parties? And more recently, I have been quite popular at weddings. Well, this is one I was hired to attend. I did say I have been blessed with opportunities to travel all over the world to share my gift. I go wherever fate takes me."

Maybe fate has brought her back into my life at this particular moment for a reason, then. What are the odds of her being at this wedding?

"The things you said to me," I blurt out, "have haunted me every single day. I can't wrap my head around what you said about my brother. About the signs I'd be receiving. It felt as if I was losing my mind. For a while I became obsessed, thinking everything and anything was a sign."

She peers at me intently, but her gaze is filled with disappointment. "My dear, that simply means you haven't been paying adequate attention, to be able to notice which signs were intended for you. When the universe and Tyler present you with signs they will be so clear, so undeniable, they will practically jump up and smack you in the face."

"Yeah, I get that now." I droop, despondent, tracing the still-growing lump on my forehead, courtesy of the STOP sign I encountered head first, earlier.

"Now, I assume you remember how this works?" she inquires. When I nod, she spreads the cards face down on the table, jumbling and stirring them into one untidy pile. She motions for me to proceed with the next step, so I assemble the cards, shuffle them, and set the deck in the middle of the table. Seeming pleased I remembered the process, she beams and fans the cards across the table in one fluid movement.

Taking a deep breath, I flutter my fingers over the cards, focusing intently on which three to choose. One by one I select them – past, present, and future – and turn them face-up in the center of the table.

Desi smiles, delighted, and scoops up the remaining cards, setting them to one side.

"Hmm…" she begins, tracing one finger over the top edge of the first one. "You have chosen the reversed Two of Cups as your first card."

The card shows a man and woman facing one another, holding goblets. Suspended over them is a winged lion's head. "The card representing your past is showing displeasure with your current relationship. I am sensing your romantic status has been veering down a bumpy and dead-end road for some time. It will not be very long until you reach that end."

As our eyes meet over the cards I flash her a look of alarm. It seems she is spot-on once again.

Moving on, she serenely taps on the center card. "You have chosen the Page of Cups for your present-day card."

I can't hide my shock upon seeing the image on this one. It portrays a man standing near the ocean, holding a cup with a fish inside.

"A love from your past will soon come back into your life." Scrunching up her face, she asks, "Is it possible your past and present cards have something to do with one another? I'm sensing some sort of relation there."

Could it be she's actually referring to Jared and Mason's status as brothers? And how is this even possible?

She adds, "I also sense you will soon be tangled in many love triangles."

"You sense . . . many." I scoot eagerly to the edge of my seat. "How many?"

"You're going to be a very busy woman. I'm also gathering from this card that while you won't feel necessarily romantically tied to all of these triangles, you will still have a severe effect on each of them in some way."

What in the world can she possibly mean by this? Could it maybe have to do with Preston and Jack? But how could that be?

Desi moves on to the final card. "Now, the future. The Ten of Swords," she informs me. "I'm afraid this is not what I had hoped you would choose as the card depicting your future."

"What! Why not? What does it mean?" I fretfully ask, practically falling entirely off my seat now as I peer at the horrifically morbid card before us. It shows a person lying face-down in the sand, with water in the background, and ten bloodied swords plunged into their back. It makes me think about the death of Julius Caesar, which was hardly a good thing, and I can't help but shudder. "This isn't . . . well, literal, right? The picture is just symbolic?"

Desi hurries to reassure me that I shouldn't be alarmed by the images on the cards because they all possess many different underlying meanings. "Miss Laina, I'm afraid this card is telling me fate will be sending quite a storm your way. You will soon be at the lowest point in your life."

I roll my eyes. "I'm pretty sure that storm hit today."

"No, I'm sorry." She sighs sympathetically. "And when it comes, it will test your strength." Her gaze softens. "You mustn't let it break your spirit. It will seem like giving up is the easiest path, but you must fight past it and persevere. I believe you possess adequate strength within you. Pull yourself out of the abyss! Be the person Tyler believes you to be."

Moving the three tarot cards to her left, she reaches across the table, grabs hold of my hands, and closes her eyes, just like she did at my first reading. "You've had a long, trying day. I can sense it in your energy. I wish there was something I could do to ease your spirit."

Oh, if she only knew what my day has entailed. Then again, perhaps she does.

"Oh my," she gasps. "It appears you may be forced to confront your worst fear very soon. It will be the last place you wish to be, yet, then again, the only place you wish to be."

I tilt my head. "Can you be a little bit more specific?"

She opens her eyes. "Let me ask, what is your worst fear?"

I pause for a moment. "I mean, I'm afraid of the water. And sharks. I almost drowned when I was young. But I don't have to worry about that. I wouldn't be caught dead in the water."

"Don't be too certain, Miss Laina."

I don't like the sound of that. She starts to close her eyes again, and move on, but I interrupt. "No, you don't understand. I'm pretty sure I had a close encounter with a shark the day I almost drowned. I would never get in the ocean again."

"As you say," she replies, still sounding highly skeptical.

The next woman in line for her turn at the table impatiently fidgets. Flustered, I say to Desi, "I, uh . . . I should let you get to all the others who're waiting."

As I rise from my seat, Desi grabs hold of my hand and tugs me back.

"Miss Laina, please remember this," she hisses. An intense, focused look comes over her. "After the rain there is always sunshine. You'll know what you must do when the time comes." She smiles then. Hope softens her expression.

"It's you! From the beach," a man exclaims behind me.

Desi glances over and looks delighted. "Ah, the nervous groom!"

My body goes rigid, my mouth dry as ash. I can't move, I can't even turn my head to look.

"You didn't take my advice, I see," she teases Jared.

"I apologize, but I'd already put the suit on," he jokes. "I had no idea you were working the wedding. I knew Liv hired a fortuneteller, but it's just strange it turned out to be you."

"I go wherever fate takes me," she smoothly declares, grinning. Still holding on to my hand with one of hers, she reaches for his with the other. As she grips it, her smile falters. Her gaze snaps away from him, back to me. "Oh my," she mutters.

"Should I come back later, or maybe schedule an appointment?" the impatient woman at the head of the line complains, tapping one foot on the grass.

"Sorry, I'm holding you up," Jared apologizes to Desi.

She lets go of both our hands simultaneously, looking uncharacteristically befuddled. That's...that's quite all right." She gives me what seems a regretful look as I quickly thank her and rise from my seat.

I'm now mere inches away from Jared, gripped by what feels like a fiery, magnetic pull fighting to bring us together. My heart thuds, my pulse races, my eyes burn. It's as if my body and the universe have been working overtime just to carry us to this point.

So close. Don't turn away. Don't chicken out, Laina! Grow a pair!

*Say something, stupid!*

My palms are drenched in sweat. I wipe them down the sides of my dress, but it doesn't help. I'm lightheaded when I get a whiff of Jared's fresh, lime and sage scented cologne.

*Holy shit, he smells good.*

Our eyes meet. He looks away, then quickly glances back, frowning a little. "Hello," he says, in grown-up Jared's deep, melodious voice.

I'm pretty sure I have a small orgasm at the mere sound of it.

"H-hello, Jared."

He blinks, taken aback. Probably he's no longer used to being called that. He gazes at me intently, attempting to piece the puzzle of my face together in his mind.

*Doesn't he recognize me? Do I look that different?*

His gaze lowers to my neck, and the Forget-Me-Not flower necklace he gave me so long ago. His eyes widen then, and he shakes his head.

He looks up once again, with a solemn, almost reverent gaze. I can almost hear the questions swirling in his mind.

He finally manages to mutter, "*Laina?*"

My face twitches into a faint, lackluster smile, though all I want to do is cry. All those things I wanted to tell him suddenly no longer seem important at all. Attempting to put on a brave face, I choke out the only appropriate thing I can say in a situation like this.

"Congratulations on your wedding."

Jared gasps. "How?" he begins, then starts over. "How can you be here?"

With impeccable timing, Liv rushes up. "JP! This is my favorite song. Come dance with me!" Grabbing his arm, she whisks him away toward the dance floor, where the speakers are belting out "I Want You Back" by NSYNC.

As she drags him down the cement steps he turns his head to stare back at me. His bewildered face makes me wonder if he is now feeling the way I did only a few hours ago.

Trapped.

# Chapter 9

# Just Norton

Later that night I lie wide awake on the tiny cot in the small bedroom I'm sharing with Becky and Allie. They're both snuggled into twin beds across from me. Mason is sleeping on the living room couch's pull-out mattress. The blurred cherry-red numbers on the nightstand alarm clock across the room is flashing *2:26 A.M.* The numerals' faint scarlet glow floats like a pesky ghost in the otherwise dark room.

Insects chirp and buzz outside our room's sliding glass doors, leading to the front patio. They seem to be mocking me with each comatose moment. I desperately want to sleep. I need rest. Instead I lie on my side strumming my fingers over the fluffy pillow beneath my head, my mind racing. The whole day feels like a strange, inescapable dream.

I need to walk. I need to do something – anything. I can't lie here until the sun rises. I peer at the alarm clock.

*2:26 a.m. 2:26 A.M.*

*Son of a bitch. Still?*

"Oh my God," I grumble, flinging the covers off. I step onto cool tile, sliding my feet around, trying to locate my flip-flops. Finally slipping them on, I pull my hair back, twirl it around one finger, and painfully thwack my free hand against the edge of the dresser top until I locate a large hair clip. I yank the lightweight quilt from the cot in one smooth motion and wrap it around me like a cape. Then, tiptoeing past Mason, who seems sound asleep in the living room, I slip out to the back patio through that room's sliding glass doors.

Small upturned lights at the base of each palm tree illuminate them and the grounds of the villa. The faint emerald glow from the leaves guides me along the path. The hushed whooshing of the ocean waves grows louder with each step, calling me forward. My flip-flops slap against my heels, the small sound seeming amplified, echoing into the night.

Crossing the sundeck, retreating down the stairs, I pass the back pool by the reef bar where two bright spotlights illuminate another set of stairs and lead me downward. The pool is lit as well, but with a bluish tint emanating from beneath the still water.

The heavy, painted white metal gate piercingly creaks when I thrust it open, then clangs shut. Down another set of wooden steps, I descend to the dark, secluded beach, abandoning my flip-flops on the landing. Then I step out and smother my toes in cool, powdery sand.

As I walk I replay the evening in my mind. I left the reception shortly after Jared and I came face to face. I couldn't stay and watch the merriment when all I felt was lost and miserable. So, I faked a migraine and told Mason I was retiring early. He was in full-on party mode, so this seemed of no consequence to him. I was free to go.

Back at the villa, I wallowed in self-pity until Mason and the rest of his family returned and filled me in on what I'd missed. I listened like a reluctant witness at the scene of an accident. But once the villa settled down for the night, I could not.

And now, I find myself peering down the long strip of beach in the direction of the One&Only Ocean Club, where Jared and Liv are lodging for their honeymoon. Inching closer to the water, I swing the quilt off my shoulders and set it down, careful not to get sand on top. I brush the soles of my feet clean, then sit.

For a while I watch the foaming edges of the waves subsiding on the shore before they slink back into the black ocean, then lie on my back and gaze up at the stars in the vast night sky. I recall Sebastian in *Twelfth Night*, when he says to Antonio, "My stars shine darkly over me." I, too, feel fate is working against me. My stars seem awfully dim tonight. After some time spent staring up, I get the sensation I'm floating among them.

Desi's voice whispers in my head, *I follow where fate takes me. I follow where fate takes me.*

My mind wanders off, and the hushing of the waves fades. I lie there wondering how tomorrow will play out, until a deep voice startles me. I sit up abruptly.

"What are you doing out of bed, Norton?"

*Norton.* Only one person ever called me that.

It takes every ounce of will to simply turn my head and look. When I do, Jared is standing a few feet away from my quilt. I take a deep breath. "Couldn't sleep?"

A huge sigh escapes from deep in his chest. He rushes to the edge of the quilt and drops there to his knees. Before I can think or move, he throws those strong, familiar arms around me. "I can't believe this," he cries.

I breathe him in and return the embrace, unsure if it's my heart that's beating so hard, or his, or a combination of the two. But the pounding feels so intense, so real, and so unbelievably perfect I don't ever want to let go.

"I don't understand." His voice trembles as he lets go and sits back to look at me. "How are you here?"

I sigh too, and fiddle with my necklace. "It's a long story."

Deep into the night I fill him in on everything that's happened, starting from the day he moved away, my parents divorcing, Tyler passing away, Preston and the bookstore, then how I met Mason, at a different wedding.

"So, you've just been living in Staten Island these last few years," he says with disbelief. "I guess that explains it."

"Explains what?"

He shakes his head. "Nothing. It's not important."

Sensing he wishes to change the topic, I say, "So I hear you're living in California with Liv. How do you like it out there?"

He wrinkles his nose. "Well, I'm teaching Literature at a local college. Liv teaches third grade. California is *okay*. I'm sure I'll like it more as time goes on."

It sounds as if he's trying to convince not only me, but himself, as well. "You hate it."

His gaze darts back to meet mine, and he blurts, "Damn, I have to practice being more convincing."

"Why? What's wrong with California?"

"It's the pace, I think. Everything moves so fast. Just like in New York, only I didn't realize it back then because I was a kid. Pennsylvania was more . . . relaxed."

"So why not live there?"

"California is where Liv is from. She wanted to be close to family, and I want her to be happy."

Then I have to change the subject. I thought I could handle this, but it turns out I'm far from ready to delve into their relationship. "Um, speaking of the past, a few weeks back I found the journal you gave me when we were sixteen."

His eyes widen. He chuckles. "Stop. Seriously? I can't believe you kept that thing!"

"Of course I did." I pull my legs to my chest and rest my chin on my knees. "It's filled with memories. I could never throw that away."

"Oh yeah." He grins. "Bet there are some real gems in there."

"You used to love to write."

"Still do," he says, smirking. "Even wrote a book." He stops himself. "Wait. Let me rephrase that. I *started* to write a book. Actually, a couple."

"Did you also build half of a library too?" I tease.

He throws his head back, chortling. "No, not yet. Maybe next year, after I finish all my half-books."

"So, Mason's best man speech was spot on, huh? How long have you been working on them?"

He looks as if he doesn't want to answer. "Seven years."

"Seven!" I exclaim. "What the hell has been taking so long to finish?"

"Oh, you know, every time I attempt to write a chapter, I bust out a whole paragraph."

I giggle, and he adds, "I don't know. Guess there's so much going on in my head, whenever I try to get it on paper it feels like I come up short."

I meet his stare. "That's shitty. Think that's probably why you're always forgetting your sunglasses are on top of your head?"

He grins, slightly embarrassed. "Yeah, I'm a half a head sometimes, too. I admit it."

"My roommate would say the same about me if he were here. No, actually, he might just argue that I'm lazy." I can envision Preston saying just that. "I don't remember you being a scatterbrain, though, growing up."

"Don't think I was, then." Leaning on an elbow, he jokes, "Yep, aging like a fine cheese."

"Don't you mean a fine wine?"

"Nope. Cheese is probably more accurate. Leave me to sit too long and I turn crusty."

"That's gross!" I giggle.

After a moment of silence, until I say, "So…JP…why were you wandering out here in the middle of the night?"

He cocks an eyebrow when I call him 'JP', then sighs. "Haven't been sleeping well. My mind races at night. I thought a walk would help."

"I've had some sleep issues lately, too." I suddenly wish I hadn't made that comment, in case it prompts a follow up "Why?". I have no desire to go into the whole debacle of my snoring habits, and what it's like sleeping with his stepbrother.

I'm relieved when he simply looks away and mumbles, "You called me 'JP'."

"Well, that is your name now, isn't it?"

"Just sounds weird when you say it."

"Doesn't anyone call you Jared anymore?"

He takes a moment to think. "Nope, only you."

"Well, to avoid causing any . . . um, issues . . . I'll try to refer to you as JP while we're here."

He nods. "And I'll try not to snicker every time I hear you say it."

We sit on the blanket for a while laughing over old stories. Gradually those years apart begin to feel as though they're fading away. I can't remember the last time someone made me laugh to the point of a stomach ache.

In the midst of a camping story, Jared lets slip he's a member of a Rod and Gun Club back in Pennsylvania. The club owns acres of lake-studded property where he's spent a great deal of time camping over the years, though he hasn't been back since he and Liv moved to California.

The first time he introduced Liv to his friends back home, he thought it would be fun to take her to the lake. It was summer, just before Labor Day. He got a fire going, did some night fishing, and cooked a nice meal. It all went extremely well until the sun set. Then bullfrogs moaned, crickets shrilly chirped, and Liv panicked. Turns out she has a crippling fear of most all wildlife, and here Jared had dragged her deep into the woods. She was petrified every bear and snake within a ten-mile radius had their gaze set on her. So, to get her mind off nature and show his romantic side, he took her out in a little rowboat to look at the stars. Suddenly, someone set off fireworks on the far shore, and the next thing he knew, Liv was clawing at the side of the boat. Taking the explosions for gunshots, she was ready to swim back to the dock.

Through chuckles, I manage to ask, "And what did your friends think?"

"That she was nuts, at first," he teases.

Even though the last thing I want to hear are stories of the two of them, I could listen to his voice for hours. As we lie back and listen to the ocean murmuring at our feet. I take a mental picture: the water, the feeling of Jared and I lying side by side, the sense of being the only two people in the world.

Apparently I am so relaxed I drift off to sleep. The next thing I know Jared is shaking my arm, trying to wake me. The sky has gone from jet black to muted blue, the shade that says the sun is about to peek over the horizon.

"Laina, I have to get back." He sounds hoarse and panicky.

"I can't believe I fell asleep," I say, rubbing my eyes.

"We both did."

One horrific thought creeps into my mind. "Did I? Um, I mean, I didn't..."

"What, snore?"

"Oh God!" I cry, mortified, closing my eyes. I can't bring myself to look him in the face.

He chortles, and tugs on my arm. "Laina, it's okay."

"No! I can't believe you heard that. This is so humiliating."

Rising to his feet, he says, "This may sound funny, but I think your snoring actually lulled me to sleep."

Unsure of how to respond to that, I simply stare, dumbfounded. No one ever likes my snoring.

He treks back down the beach. I watch him grow smaller and smaller, thinking how the last twenty-four hours seem like one big dream, and about how twisted my fate has truly become.

# Chapter 10

# Stay or Go

The banging of pots and pans, along with boisterous chatter from the other room, jolts me awake. I open my eyes to white walls, empty beds, and sheer blinding sunlight. I shoot up from the pillow. How late is it? I throw back the rumpled quilt, dislodging stray grains of sand, and collapse off the narrow cot, thudding to the hard tile floor.

I throw open the bedroom door. The aroma of eggs, bacon, and pancakes wafts in as I step out into the hallway. Bright tropical sunlight illuminates every corner of the villa. I see dirty plates on the dining room table and wonder if there are any leftover scraps for me.

"I don't care! I'm not going to some stupid pirate museum. I want to go to the beach!" Becky shouts. She's standing in the living room in her bathing suit, daintily applying suntan lotion to her already bronzed shoulders.

"It's our first real day here. This isn't fair," Allie agrees. She sets two beach towels on a chair and gathers her hair into a tall ponytail.

"Well, you don't have a choice. You're coming to the museum," Aunt Tina replies. She returns to the dining room and starts clearing the table.

"Tina!" Uncle Frank snaps from the kitchen counter, "Where's all the clean glasses?"

"Check the cabinet next to the stove."

"Already did. None in there."

"Well, wadda you want me to do, Frank? Take a dirty one out of the dishwasher and wash it!"

"You know I don't like touching other people's dirty dishes." He opens the dishwasher and glares inside, as though everything in there must be diseased.

"Then I don't know what to tell you, Frank. Suck on the tap! I'm busy cleaning."

He yanks open the refrigerator and proceeds to drink directly from the orange juice container.

"Frank, stop that," Aunt Tina screeches. "Now we'll be drinking your backwash!"

He throws his free hand up, looking disgusted. Mouth still full of orange juice, he shoves the container back in the refrigerator and slams the door.

*Note to self: Don't drink the OJ.*

There's a rap on the front door. Frank shuffles off to answer. It's Evelyn and Thomas. Her face is solemn as she enters the kitchen, greets the family, and finally turns to look at me. Thomas proceeds to the living room. Before Evie can follow, I call out, "Mrs. Gra . . .Hartley."

Stopping in her tracks, she turns to silently face me.

"Can we talk?"

She pauses, blinks, then shakes her head. "Not just yet, Laina."

"But, please. I –"

"Look." She takes a step closer, and whispers, "I understand you have a lot of questions. But I'm not ready to talk about the past just yet. I'm still trying to process this. Give me some time." She turns to walk away.

"How much time?"

"I'll find you when I'm ready. For now, it would be best if we didn't speak." She dashes off to join Thomas on the living room couch.

I don't know how much more of this I can take. But, if she insists on being difficult, I have no option but to play by her rules, or risk making a huge scene. So I'll leave her alone, for now. Give her the requested space. But one thing is certain – I will *not* leave this island without answers about the past.

Mason strolls in from the back patio as I'm washing out a dirty coffee cup. He announces, "So, I just spoke to Liv. She wants to get a bunch of us together to go snorkeling."

"Which bunch?" Becky excitedly chimes in.

"Sorry, but I think it's going to be just me, Laina, Liv, JP, and maybe the rest of the bridal party." He turns back to me. "I told her snorkeling isn't really your thing but…"

"I'll go," I blurt out, surprising even myself. I won't allow my conscience to talk me out of it. Jared's going, so I'm going too. I don't know how I'm going to pull off getting into the ocean without having a total panic attack, but I'll figure it out somehow.

"Seriously?" Mason asks, as if he thinks he didn't hear me correctly. He's peering at me, looking perplexed.

I gulp, and confirm it again, in a jittery voice. "Yeah, I . . . I want to go."

* * *

After everyone else departs for the pirate museum, Mason goes out to meet Liv and Jared, to sort out the snorkeling expedition details. I pick up my cell phone and head to the Breezeway for some privacy, so I can call Preston.

"Please pick up. Please pick up," I whisper as the other end rings over and over. "Don't go to voice mail."

"Laina! How's paradise?" Preston shouts.

"Eh. It could be better."

"Oh, honey," he says. "Can't you just enjoy yourself for a few days? What's wrong now?"

"Well," I manage to squeeze out, "Jared is JP. Jared is Mason's stepbrother."

"Jared . . . what? Shut the fuck up," he shouts so loudly I have to jerk the phone away from my ear. "You're screwin' with me, right? There's no way!"

"Oh, there's a way." I explain what Evie did.

"Oh. My. God. Sweetie, I'm so sorry. I really am. It's probably stupid to even ask, but are you okay?"

A colossal lump swells in my throat. "No, I'm not. But I am convinced that meeting Mason was fate, like you said. Otherwise I might never have been reunited with Jared."

"What happened? I need details."

"Well, I was going to try and stop the wedding but I accidentally locked myself in the bathroom. So it was too late. It was a nightmare. And before you lecture me, I do understand how awful it would be to do that to someone. I just felt desperate. I didn't know what else to do! Oh, and remember that fortuneteller I went to see a few months ago?"

"Oh yeah. The nutcase," he flatly answers.

"She was at the wedding yesterday too. Booked as entertainment for the reception. What are the odds of her, of all people, being here?"

Silence on the other end.

"Do you believe me now about the signs?"

"Laina, honey. I get that you wanna believe in fate, and signs, and that Tyler is watching over you. And yeah, it may have even been fated for you to be there. Maybe even for the nutty fortune-telling lady to be there, too. But it might have also been fate that you weren't able to stop Jared. Because he's *married* now. Did you ever stop to think that was his fate?"

"No," I grumble.

He sighs audibly on the other end. "Of course you didn't."

"He's only married now because I ignored Tyler's signs on the way back to the villa, in the first place. Before I got trapped in the bathroom."

"Hmm. That seems kinda selective as to what to choose to believe."

"I'm not being selective!" Well, not very.

"So, you're tellin' me," he raises his voice, "you believe that if you'd managed to get to Jared right before he tied the knot, he would've willingly walked away from his wife to be."

"Well, I . . . oh, you just don't understand how things were between us!" I cry.

"Honey, this is real life. You've got to stop living in a fantasy world! Could Jared's mind be that easily swayed? And if it could, what does that say about his character?"

"Ugh. I don't want to argue with you about this anymore."

The truth is, Preston is right. I know he is. Doubt creeps into my mind. Who's to say what would have happened if I'd gotten to Jared on time? Who's to say he *would* have left Liv, then and there, for me?

I slump, feeling defeated.

"Fine, then. When's the flight back?" Preston eagerly asks.

"I'm not coming home yet."

"But there's no reason to stay. You're not gonna stick it out with Mason after all this. Look, I'm proud of you for hanging on as long as you did. It led you to Jared, in the end. So there's that. Now you'll have some closure, be able to move on. But don't stay. It'll just make things harder in the end."

"I am staying," I declare. "I want to. We're going snorkeling today."

"Did . . . did you just say you're going . . . *snorkeling?*" He pauses a moment. "You, who won't set foot in a pet store in case they have baby sharks in the tanks all the way at the back of the store. You don't even like sprinklers, and now you're going swimmin' in the ocean, with sharks?"

"I don't care. Maybe I'm ready to face my fears."

I flash back to Desi's fortune for me, at the reception.

*. . . you may be forced to confront your worst fear very soon. It will be the last place you wish to be, yet, then again, the only place you wish to be.*

"Honey," Preston tries again. "It's game over. Clearly you must see that. Accept it and come home."

"Sorry, have to go, or I'll be late," I say quickly, annoyed he's still fighting me on this.

"Don't hang up on me. Don't you dare hang up the phone!"

"I'll...I'll call and talk to you later. I promise," I stammer, and abruptly hit END.

# Chapter 11

# On The Deep Blue Sea

Around noon, Mason and I head to the waterfront. Our Bahamian captain, Christopher, is at the dock, wearing a jaunty skipper's hat and supervising two guys loading diving gear for the expedition. The entire bridal party, Jared, and Liv are already on deck, waiting. As we climb aboard the thirty-five foot dive boat, Mason suddenly realizes he has yet to introduce me to Liv and JP.

Jared and I shake hands, as if we've never met prior to this moment.

Liv unexpectedly throws her arms around me, gushing, "Hi! I can't wait to get to know you!" Her warm, heartfelt welcome leaves a sinking, guilty feeling in the pit of my stomach. If only she knew I recently plotted to sabotage her wedding.

*I am a horrible human being.*

Christopher taps on an iPod and several strategically-placed wireless speakers pump out lively steel-drum island tunes. He passes around tiny white cups and fills them with rum punch, which I politely decline. It's crucial to steer clear of alcohol from this point on, even the smallest amounts. It won't be easy, but I will stay strong.

I begin to sweat as the boat's motor revs and we all put on our life vests. I cling to the gunwale as we roar out to the ocean, quickly leaving the shore behind. At the wheel, Christopher gives us an official rundown of safety procedures. Then he pulls the throttle back, the boat slows, and he shuts off the engine. We're officially in the middle of nowhere.

As we bob and roll on the swells I scan for shark fins.

Christopher instructs us to reach under our seats to retrieve flippers. The long rubber fins are heavy and feel clunky, as if I am an oversized duck about to offer myself as shark bait at the noon ocean buffet.

My stomach gurgles. Lightheaded, I try to focus on slow, deep breathing, but my life vest feels more and more like a straightjacket. This is nothing like riding on the Staten Island Ferry. One, half the time it doesn't even feel like I'm on the water at all because the ferry is so large. Two, in this rinky-dink bathtub toy, however, I can feel every ripple as the waves slam into us. And worst of all, I've never before had to consider jumping off a boat.

"All right! We. Are. Here! This is da prime spot to do tha' snorkel. Now everybody, reach under your benches for dose snorkels and put dem on," Christopher orders, as he lowers the anchor. The boat rocks from side to side as everyone moves around to get situated with his or her gear, preparing to descend into the water.

Mason stands, stepping sideways, edging over to the boat's ladder. Jared scoots into the seat beside me. "You okay?" He seems thoroughly concerned. "You're looking a little green."

I do my best to put on a brave face and squeeze out a smile.

He eyes me skeptically. "You can't fool me." He leans in close and whispers, "I know that look. It's your 'scared shitless' face." Adjusting his life vest, he adds, "I was surprised when Mason said you were coming. Didn't realize you had overcome your fear of the water after what happened at Point Pleasant."

"I didn't, but really, I'm fine." I try to push past a wave of nausea. "I'm great." I bob my head like a toy dashboard dog. "Yeah, I'll be just fine," I tack on through the next desperate exhalation.

His eyes widen and he leans slightly away. "Are you going to puke?"

"No," I whisper, and lift a finger to shush him so he doesn't mention that word again.

"You don't have to do this. Stay on the boat."

"What's wrong?" Mason abruptly chimes in.

Jared looks up at him. "Nothing. Laina was just looking a bit nervous so I said she could stay on the boat if she didn't feel up to going in."

"Ah, come on. That's ridiculous! I already paid for her ticket," Mason argues, then turns to me. "You came all the way out here, so at least give it a try. If you're nervous or whatever, just swim close to the boat."

"Or stay close to Mason," Liv suggests, as she tightens the strap on her face mask. "I'm sure he'll protect you."

"Yeah, but I'll be swimming around so you gotta keep up," he insists.

Ben, a baby-faced groomsman with curly auburn hair, approaches then. He and Mason high-five each other and Ben shouts, "Yeah! Let's go see some *fish!*"

Amelia the bridesmaid drops onto the bench beside me and pats my shoulder. "Don't worry," she coos, "this is my first time snorkeling too." She offers a few more kind words to try to soothe my nerves. And while it doesn't help much, I do appreciate the gesture.

One by one, our party jumps into the water until Jared and I are the last two swimmers left on the boat. "You sure about this?" he asks.

I nod, peering through goggles so tightly smashed against my face, I fear I'll be walking around with an oval indentation around my eyes and nose for weeks. Too bad. I need to make the jump and face my fears, no matter how scared I may be.

"Okay, Norton. I'll be nearby if you need me."

Jared's flawless smile makes my heart flutter. The thought of him being by my side does begin to soothe my frayed nerves. I climb slowly down the swaying metal dive ladder. Once my entire body is in the water, I gather enough guts to kick my flippers and take one hand off the ladder. Then the other.

At first, I flop around like a fish on a hook.

"Come on, Laina!" Mason shouts impatiently, somewhere in the distance.

I attempt to keep my head above the swells as I kick the heavy flippers beneath me. No matter how hard I thrust them back and forth, though, they only move in heavy, slow motion through the water.

"Hey, Liv, how is it?" Jared calls, as he helps Amelia fix her loosened swim goggles.

Liv's face is submerged under the water. She is apparently following after some rapidly-swimming fish, but she lifts an arm and flashes the thumbs-up sign. Finally, she raises her head, pulls the snorkel mouthpiece out, and gushes, "It's unbelievable!"

That doesn't sound bad. Perhaps I won't be so scared if I can actually see what's swimming beneath me. Unlike on the murky Jersey Shore, this is crystal-clear turquoise water. My first course of action should be to put my face in the water and do a quick panoramic scan of the beautiful underwater reef.

I lower my face into the water. At first I'm awed when I see about fifteen feet below a reef with various hues of coral, sea fans swaying gently in the current, and a school of striped tropical fish swimming through it without a care in the world. The scene, so calm, peaceful, and exquisite, eases my fears. I force my head entirely under, only to jerk it back up as I hear Amelia shouting in the distance, "Holy shit, you guys! You gotta see the size of this fish!"

Oh, just a fish, I tell myself. Relax. I'm about to go under once more when something bumps the back of my life vest. I twist to see which one of our party has clumsily knocked into me.

No one's there.

There is a slight splash on the other side. I twist back but don't see a thing. Now I figure someone is just messing with me.

"Laina. . . ." Jared slowly calls my name. I twist back to face him.

He is staring at me hard, eyes filled with intensity. "Now, stay calm. Everything is fine. I don't want you to panic."

"What're you talking about?" I nervously inquire. Again something brushes past my back. I look over one shoulder and see a gray fin cutting the surface about ten feet away.

I actually feel my entire nervous system shutting down with the realization of what's happening. Fearfully, I duck my face underwater again, praying the shark is now far away. But no, he's still here, circling beneath me.

I could swear I hear a symphony orchestra strike up the theme music to *Jaws* as I lift my head to the surface and gasp in air. I tell myself, *Swim!* But I cannot move a single muscle.

"Oh my God," I say, over and over, as if these are the only three words left in my vocabulary.

Christopher calls down from the boat, "Miss, please remain calm. No one has ever been eaten on one of my expeditions."

"There's a first time for everything!" I cry, surveying the water around me. Only then do I see Jared has paddled to my side and grabbed onto my life vest.

Off in the distance, Mason shouts, "Laina, just relax! It's not going to eat you!"

"Hey there," Jared says softly, as he grips one arm, pulling me close. "You're okay. I've got you. Give me your hand. I'm taking you back to the boat."

I cling to him, almost certain then that everything will be all right. We paddle together back to the dive boat.

Christopher holds out a hand as Jared boosts me up the ladder and onto the deck. Jared grabs a dry towel from the bench behind him and wraps it around my shoulders. "No more water adventures for you today," he teases.

"D-d-deal," I agree, through chattering teeth.

No matter how hard the searing sun beats down, I'm left uncontrollably shivering. I must be going into shock. It's impossible to keep recurring images of rigid, gray, leathery shark fins, of triangular razor-sharp teeth, of empty, cold, black-marble eyes from my thoughts. I just don't believe that whole theory about sharks being more afraid of us than we are of them. I also don't buy in the slightest that if I leave them alone, they won't bother me. I'm in their territory. I'm the trespasser. With my luck I'll come across the one shark in the area with an acquired taste for humans.

"You okay?" Jared sits beside me on the bench.

"F-f-f-fine." I shiver as if my jaw isn't attached to my face. "Thanks for helping, b-but you don't need to stay w-with me, you know. You should go b-back in and enjoy yourself." I say this, when in fact I desperately want him to stay.

"Come on, JP! She's back on the boat safe and sound," Mason exclaims, as he paddles around the boat. "Give her some Rum Punch and she'll be good as new."

Jared ignores him, looking only at me. "I'm not going to just leave you alone in this condition."

"I don't know what I was thinking." I shake my head as I stare into his entrancing hazel eyes. "This is my second close encounter with a shark. Clearly I'm not meant to be in the ocean with them. I'd hate to think if I went in another time, I might land my ass on an episode of Shark Week. Third time's a charm."

Jared chuckles at my comment. I stare off into the water again, half expecting to see the shark circling the boat again, taunting us, trying to lure me back in.

"Still thinking about it?" he asks.

I nod. How could I not be?

"Don't worry, I doubt Jaws is sniffing you out. But maybe we should take baby steps with getting you back into the water. This was obviously too much, too soon."

"Well, what would you suggest I do to overcome my fear?"

Pursing his lips, he peers off as if deep in thought. "You know that cove at the far end of the island?" I nod, and he continues, "I like to go down there early in the morning before anyone wakes. Been doing it for years. I usually bring a snorkel and some bread. You'd only have to wade out up to your knees in the water. And you wouldn't have to wear flippers."

"What's the bread for?"

"The fish. I get in the water, and within seconds they swim up and nibble it right from my fingers. I doubt anything traumatic will happen."

"It actually sounds like it could be fun." I can hardly bear to look away from his glimmering eyes.

"It is. Maybe the four of us can go over tomorrow morning. I'll talk to Liv and Mason about it."

Oh. Right.

"JP," Liv calls as she steps off the ladder and onto the deck. "Is Laina okay? She didn't get nipped or anything, did she?"

"Oh, no," he assures her, "she'll be fine. Just a bit shaken."

Squatting in front of me, Liv rests her slender dripping arms across my legs and peers into my face with lovely mint-green eyes. "Want me to stay with you?"

"No, no, really." I quickly shake my head. "I'll be okay. Hate to ruin snorkeling for you."

Shifting her gaze to Jared, she blurts out, "No offense, but your brother is being really insensitive to Laina. I might need to set him straight."

He shrugs. "Go for it."

Her eyes fill with concern again as her focus turns back to me. "I have a few tricks up my sleeve. Ones I like to use on my third graders when they act out." She pinches the base of her nose. "Wow, those swim masks are tight, huh?" She reaches out and gives my hand a squeeze. "Do you want to come back in at all?"

God, I wish she wasn't so nice. It's making it exceedingly hard for me to hate her, or to dislike her even a teensy bit. Her warm, inviting, and infectiously pleasant personality draws me in, and I feel compelled to be cordial in return. Her sweetness is not fake. It radiates through every word and action. Now, having met her, I can hardly bear to think about my own treacherous intentions from yesterday. Liv doesn't deserve to have some selfish stranger arrive on what is supposed to be the happiest day of her life, and blindside her with a huge betrayal. Now I genuinely want to get to know her, to see what it is about her that led to Jared deciding she's the one he wants to spend his life with.

"Back in the water? Most likely not." I chuckle. "There was this near-drowning experience, when I was young . . . I'm proud of myself for at least making the attempt. But I figure if I did jump in again, the shark would sniff me out and turn me into his mid-day snack."

Grinning, Liv rises to her feet. "You're funny. I like that. So will you be all right if we leave you for a bit?"

"Of course."

She reaches for Jared's hand, gazing at him with a twinkle in her eye. "You ready to jump in, honey?"

Nodding, he takes her hand and turns back to me. "Doing better?"

I flash a reassuring smile. "I am. Thanks."

"You got it," he says. And then the happy couple dons their snorkels and rejoins the rest of the wedding party.

# Chapter 12

# The Cove

Jared, Liv, Mason, and I arrange to meet bright and early the following morning at the metal gate that leads to the beach. We're all going to walk to the cove with bread, and bring the fish some breakfast.

My alarm sounds as the sun rises. Tiptoeing into the living room to wake Mason, I realize I'm actually excited about getting in the water again. I shake Mason repeatedly and call his name. The only response is a groan. He swats at me, then rolls over and resumes sleeping.

I make a few more attempts to wake him, until it's clear I am not going to make any progress. Unfortunately, I now have no option but to be the third wheel.

Awesome.

While trudging to the beach, I feel slightly unnerved again, not knowing how this experience will affect me. When I arrive at the gate, however, Jared is the only person waiting. A slight flutter of hope stirs at the thought of being alone with him, if only on this brief expedition.

I force a concerned look. "Oh. Where's Liv?"

"She decided to sleep in," he says. "What about my brother?"

"Couldn't get him up either."

Jared hoists a loaf of white bread still in the plastic wrapper. "Well, what do you say?"

"Sure you still want to go? I mean, just us?"

He laughs. "Well, yeah. I already told the fish we were coming."

Cracking a smile, I step onto the sand, leaving my flip-flops on the bottom landing of the deck. The tranquil beach in the early morning hours is filled only with the questing caws of a few seagulls, a long line of rollers crashing against the shore to wake the sand, and a soft swirl of morning breeze. As we pad barefoot up the beach toward the cove, neither of us speaks.

Not wanting to waste this time alone with him, I ask, "So, how does this work with the fish?"

"Well." He clears his throat as if about to present a formal lecture, which is adorable. "First there's a fish call I'll have to teach you how to make. It's top secret. And then, uh…well, then you have to perform a complex, rhythmic splashing dance once you get into the water. That way the fish will know breakfast is served."

I giggle, and the awkwardness dissipates. "How about I leave the rhythmic splashing performance to you? Dancing is not really my area of expertise."

"Same here. I was unfortunately born with two left feet, possibly of slightly different sizes. But I figure anyone born a bad dancer might as well embrace it." He flashes a thumbs-up. "In all seriousness, though, right after you wade in, the fish will almost instantly swim to you. It's as simple as that. I think at this point, since people have been coming here to feed them for years, they pretty much expect it. Once the sun comes up they know someone will be there with breakfast."

"Well then, we'll just see if you're right," I tease, glancing up at him through my lashes.

*Flirting, Laina? Really? You are still a terrible person.*

Along this strip of beach stand exquisite stucco beachfront mansions, each with its own unique style. The first big one is a cream colored, U-shaped home. Its ash-gray roof has a huge skylight in the center. The second is a powder-white home with a clay-tiled roof and tall windows that rise from floor to ceiling and curve all around the home. Each of the mansions has a porch with columns and arched entranceways, bringing some upscale elegance to the secluded beach.

Jared scoops a few shells from the sand. As we walk, he skims them one by one over the water. "So, tell me more about Viola's Hideaway."

I sigh, unsure of how far to delve into the way things have been. But this is Jared. It feels safe to bare my soul to him, still.

"Honestly? Business could be better. My partner, Preston, wants new ideas that will bring in more customers. It's difficult because we're competing against Amazon and Barnes & Noble. But we aren't trying to *be* them. Tyler and I originally saw Viola's Hideaway more as a living room, hang-out type of place. We wanted people to come not only to buy books, but to read on the couches, grab something to eat, and enjoy the art on the walls. Don't get me wrong; we do okay. It just, well . . . profits *could* be better."

"Ever think of having authors come in to read excerpts of their work and do book signings?"

"That's not a bad idea." I arch my eyebrows, watching my feet sink imprints into the sand which the waves immediately erase. "But I need to figure out a way to take it one step farther. Any bookstore can have authors come in for readings and signings. But it's harder to attract a crowd these days. To really draw a significant crowd, I need something even better, beyond that."

"Hmm. Well, why not make it bigger? Throw a large party, a celebration of a particular genre of book, maybe, and have two or three authors come together. Once a month, or every other month. Whatever you can swing. Let the fans mingle with the authors and get to know them without a table wedged between them. Serve food and champagne. Make each occasion a real event. Go nuts. I mean, you're the owner. You can do whatever the hell you want. Sky's the limit, right?"

Listening to Jared fervently offer suggestions rekindles an excitement in me that's been absent for quite some time. He's right. This is entirely up to me. I can push the boundaries as to how I run my own bookstore. I *can* and *should* take control.

"Thank you." I beam at him. "I really needed to hear that, not just be lectured by Preston about my duty. I mean, I don't think I ever realized brainstorming shouldn't have limits."

Of course, it wouldn't be cheap, especially if we made it a regular thing incorporated into our business. But I think I can manage to pull it off in a cost-effective way. We can start off small and build it up as time goes on.

"Speaking of authors," I continue, "think you'll ever finish your own books? Maybe one day they'll end up in my store."

He holds a hand up and crosses his fingers. "I think in order to finish, I'll regularly need a good, swift kick in the ass."

"No problem," I tease, "I can take care of that." I stop walking and lift a foot as if I'm going to boot him in the rear.

"Whoa, whoa," he shouts with a childish grin, holding out an arm to ward off my attack. "You might have to get tackled into the water."

Should I call his bluff? The idea of him tackling me, water or not, sends a bit of a thrill through me. We pause, staring at each other for a moment, as if wondering how this will play out.

Suddenly breaking the stare-off, Jared smirks and turns away, continuing the trek to the cove.

Major bummer.

We curve along the beach as it makes a backward C-shape, leading to an open patch of sand with tiny scattered pebbles and large heaps of drying ribbon-like seaweed. At the end is a lava-type rock formation. The ocean surrounds this strip of beach on both sides. At the neck of the clearing, a lone palm tree leans over nearby shrubbery. Across the stretch of water on the other side of the strip lies yet another shore. On it stand other mansions half-hidden behind stands of palm trees, like the world here goes on and on, in mirror images.

Stripping down to my bathing suit, I catch a glimpse of Jared's muscular chest as he removes his tank top, balls it up, and tosses it into the sand. I nearly drool on myself. Thus sidetracked, I get one foot tangled as I pull down my shorts and inelegantly topple onto the hot sand.

"Are you drunk this early?" Jared smirks at me as I lie pathetically on my side, still struggling to slip off my shorts.

I wish I could say that was the reason. I pretend to shield my eyes from the glare of the rising sun with the back of one hand. "Oh, you know me, just keeping it classy." I hope it's not too obvious that I'm actually taking a mental picture of every square inch of his body.

He holds out his free hand and pulls me to my feet, then opens the plastic bag and hands over two slices of bread. "Now we go into the water and wait."

"How far in?"

Jared takes a few steps into the ocean and turns back. "Wherever you feel comfortable. The fish will come to you."

I nod and follow him until the crystal-clear water reaches my knees.

Jared continues on until the water is up to his hips. "Here they come," he shouts.

"No way! Already?" I scan the surface. "I don't see any yet."

"You will. Give them a minute." He bends closer to the water, and calls, "Hey there, little buddies!" Jared wades back to my side just as I spot a whole school of tiny black, white, and yellow striped fish.

"Oh my gosh! Here they are!"

He nods. "Now roll up the bread into balls, and let them eat it off your fingers. Don't be nervous."

At first, I'm extremely squeamish. As soon as they get too close to my fingertips wiggling underneath the water, I screech and jump, and they hurriedly swim off.

"What's wrong?" Jared asks.

"I felt teeth," I say, gritting my own, slightly shaken.

Looking amused, he says, "Here, let me help. Just relax." He wads up a new piece of bread and hands it to me. Grabbing hold of that wrist, he lowers my arm into the water and keeps his hand there to hold me steady. "They aren't sharks. These fish definitely are more afraid of you than you are of them."

"Doubtful!" I jump once again as tiny teeth nip at the bread, but after a few moments I can allow myself to enjoy this moment. "Wow, this one fish just nabbed the whole piece."

Jared releases my arm and we turn toward each other, smiling. We stare at each other for a little too long, until he clears his throat, and abruptly looks away, back to the circling fish. He steps a few feet farther in. I submerge my arm to feed the fish that are too skittish to come to the surface. I know exactly how they feel.

"I want to do this every morning now." I glance at Jared.

He gives me a slow, sexy grin. "Come here, little guys," he calls in a lulling tone. "Look! See how they come racing back when they hear the bread hit the water." Balling up more tiny bits of bread, he tosses them in my direction. They plink into the water a few inches away. The fish race to nab the bread, some splashing fins and tails at the surface.

"Are you trying to get them to attack me?" I cry, shamelessly flirting. He chuckles, and I ball a piece of bread and throw it back at him. Just then, from behind me comes a gigantic splash, as if a small whale has breached the surface. I jump halfway out of the water. "Whoa! What was that?"

"Don't worry. Probably just a piranha."

"What!" I gape at him in alarm.

"Laina, I'm messing with you." He scans the water. "It was only a bigger fish that cruised on through looking for something to eat."

I burst out laughing, and Jared follows suit, seeming relieved I'm not running for the hills.

He sighs, and says, "At least it wasn't a shark."

Amen to that, brother.

# Chapter 13

# Beach Bonding

After the breakfast dishes are cleared, everyone buzzes around the villa getting their beach gear together. Mason and I are the first to sneak out and head to the still nearly-empty beach. There are about fifteen lounge chairs scattered on the sand in front of the Beach Club, all of which are empty. A twenty-something young man named Beni rushes to greet Mason and me at the bottom landing of the stairs that lead down to the beach. He helps us choose a prime spot with sufficient room for a large group to sprawl. We help him drag several chairs to that location. Afterward, Mason shakes his hand, slipping a ten-dollar bill into his palm.

The young man thanks us and scampers away over the sand toward another couple looking for chairs.

It's an extremely hot morning. I overhear one of the staff telling another guest today is supposed to be a scorcher. Fine by me. The hotter the better.

Not long after we arrive, so does the rest of the wedding party, then Evelyn with Thomas, and finally I spot Jared and Liv in the distance, hiking up the beach from the One&Only, seagulls squawking as they soar over their heads. The air is heavy with salt, and the sparkling, tranquil water is that beautiful gemlike shade of turquoise I love.

Amelia tramps up, dragging an oversized beach bag and a tote lined with double plastic bags filled to the brim with ice and beer. She plops down in the chair beside me.

As she does, Mason abruptly rolls up the *Men's Health* magazine he's been flipping through, announcing, "I'm gonna see what the other groomsmen are up to." As he stands, the beach towel draped over his chair becomes snagged on a button on his bathing suit shorts. It drops onto the sand at his feet, which he doesn't seem to notice. He tosses the magazine onto the chair, bends and snatches up the towel from the sand, wads it up, and drops it onto the beach chair as well, then traipses off to where the rest of the groomsmen lay.

Amelia digs through what I would call her never-ending beach bag, pulling out anything and everything under the sun: a towel, a collection of water bottles filled with booze, a stack of *Cosmo* magazines, a sandwich, sunglasses, a pair of goggles, snorkel gear, beach hat, a Frisbee, a complete makeup kit (mirror and all), a can of hairspray and about six hairbrushes. I'm honestly surprised when she doesn't produce a fishing pole, fish already hooked.

Once she locates tanning oil she takes an exorbitant amount of time liberally dousing every square inch of her body. She repeats this ritual about three times, going over spots she's already plastered, oil cascading over her as if it's a shower scene for an Herbal Essence commercial. But she's already so sunburned. In fact, borderline blistered. The oily sheen gives her the disturbing appearance of a scorched, glossy Barbie doll. This chick doesn't need more oil. What she needs is SPF 100 sunblock. Or better yet, a cool, dark room and gallons of Aloe Vera.

"Amelia, are you sure oil is the way to go today?" I ask, concerned, eyeing the unnatural redness of her skin.

"It's what I've been using since I arrived, and look at all the color I got," she replies, pausing to stare down with admiration. She appears pleased with her tomato-red complexion, though it looks thoroughly painful. It actually pains me to look directly at her. If she's not careful she's going to end up in the hospital for the rest of the trip.

"But doesn't it hurt? I mean, shouldn't you maybe cover up now so it doesn't blister and then peel? You could get sun poisoning, you know."

She shrugs one shoulder. "Yeah, it's a bit sore, but the way I look at it, I can't get much redder than this. It's got to start turning brown sooner or later."

"Um, I'm not sure that's how it works. Honestly, you should be careful." Rummaging through my own beach bag, I produce a freshly-opened bottle of sunblock, SPF 50, and beg her to use it.

Just then Connie strolls up, and asks in a mocking tone, "So, Amelia, any luck with finding your future husband?"

Amelia beams and coyly replies, "I can't say yes and I can't say no. But most importantly, I'm not saying no."

"Good for you, Amelia," Connie replies, but in a derisive way. I'm getting the sense she views her fellow bridesmaid as naive and boy crazy, and doesn't believe a thing she says. "Give me a hint," she adds. "Is it a groomsman?"

Amelia tosses her hair, seductively arches her back, and lifts one leg high before crossing it over the other, putting on the performance of her life. She glances toward the groomsmen to see if this act has drawn attention her way. Then settles back into the beach chair and purrs, "Well, obviously one of them had to give in to my charm sooner or later."

"So, then, which one is it?" Connie purses her lips, awaiting some fresh gossip.

"Classy girls don't kiss and tell, Connie." Amelia falls silent then, fingers nervously strumming the arm of the chair.

"Right." Connie looks doubtful. "Well, I'm gonna check out the water." She stalks toward the ocean as if she's on the Victoria's Secret runway, apparently unaware of the wedgie forming on her bikini bottom. It may in fact be intentional, since she makes an obvious detour in order to strut right past the groomsmen.

Beside me, Amelia sighs discontentedly, and reaches for a magazine.

"You okay?" I get a strong sense that Amelia fabricated her husband-hunting story.

Her lower lip creeps out. "I'm just tired of being the only one who can't seem to find a boyfriend."

"What about the groomsman you were talking about?"

"Oh, I made that up," she answers, frowning and looking ashamed. "I'm not really as smooth as I claim to be. Flirting sucks. I'm not good at it."

"You're being too hard on yourself. Do you think maybe you come on too strong?"

"I don't have a choice! It's the only way to get a guy to at least look my way. Half the time I can't get any attention at all unless I actually crash into someone. Sometimes not even then."

"But why do you need to try so hard to get a man's attention?"

She looks over at me in astonishment. "Have you seen all my friends? They're gorgeous. I was always the awkward one in the group, though Liv never made me feel that way. I just never had their self-confidence. I can't compare to them."

"I was never good at the whole dating scene either."

She blinks at me, clearly not buying it. "But you're dating *Mason*. Have you *seen* him? He's gorgeous."

"I was alone for a long time before he came around. And the night I met him, I was a complete disaster. Now that I think about it, I have no clue why he called me." I proceed to fill Amelia in on all the mortifying details. Her eyes gleam as I reveal every gritty, embarrassing detail.

"I appreciate you trying to cheer me up, Laina, but I think I'm a lost cause." She briskly flips the magazine pages as though searching for something specific.

"Amelia, I'm probably the last person who should be offering advice, but I'd like to help you gain some self-confidence."

"Really?" She stares in disbelief. "But why? You barely know me."

"Let's just say I know all too well how it feels to be alone."

She takes a moment to think, but finally nods.

"If you don't mind me asking, what did the fortuneteller predict for you at the wedding?"

Giggling, she shakes her head as if she's again contemplating Desi's reading. "That lady was *great*. She knew about my struggles with finding a boyfriend. She told me to open up, be my truest self, and dare to be vulnerable in the present. Still not sure what she meant by *that*," she squeaks. "Then she said I'd be forming new relationships while I'm here. That I'm fated to find my future husband here on the island."

Delighted, I say, "That's a great reading, Amelia. You should be happy!"

"But what if it doesn't happen?" she cries, again looking hopeless and dispirited.

"For a long time, I stopped believing in fate. That is, until I met Desi. We need to put more faith in her abilities." I sigh. "And we need to open our eyes more to everything around us. But also, I've come to realize our actions have an impact on our fate, too. If you sit back, don't open up to others, you turn away from being yourself. Then, like Desi said, you risk not having your future unfold the way she predicted."

"You're right." She grins. "You know, you're really great to talk to."

"Thanks. I feel the same about you."

Announcing she's going for a quick dip, Amelia rises from the beach chair, grabs the bottle of tanning oil from the base of the chair, and tosses it onto her towel. Unfortunately, she has neglected fasten the cap securely. The bottle bounces onto its side, and oil dribbles all over the towel. She walks off without noticing. I don't want to ruin her upbeat mood, so I lean over and close it.

Out in the water, Becky and Allie are diving for seashells, squealing with excitement as if they're recovering buried treasure. Each time they come up for air they each admire the other's loot.

Aunt Tina and Uncle Frank hobble quickly over the hot sand and stop at the shoreline.

"Come on in, Aunt Tina!" Becky calls, splashing wildly, swim goggles slung around her neck.

Allie surfaces like a porpoise, her goggles in place, spouting water like a fountain. "I got another one!" She hands a hefty conch shell to Becky.

Their uncle launches himself into the shallows as Aunt Tina fearfully shouts, "Frank, not too far! You swim like shit. Just floppin' around like a dyin' fish."

His bulk creates a huge splash as he crashes onto his back and tries to float, unsuccessfully. He stumbles when he lurches to his feet again. It seems Aunt Tina was right. He grabs hold of her outstretched hand, as they both wade deeper. When the waterline finally reaches their chests, a small wave washes mildly over them.

Aunt Tina screams, "Uh-oh, don't let go, Frank! I'll float away!"

"You're not going to float away," he counters, rolling his eyes.

But just then he loses his footing, and they both fall, sinking out of sight, legs flying over their heads.

Becky and Allie can hardly contain their laughter.

Aunt Tina surfaces, sputtering, and snaps, "Girls! I don't know why you think this is so funny! What you just saw was two people nearly drowning!"

A third wave arrives and knocks her over again as she tries to stand. Soaked and flustered, she trudges back onto the sand, Uncle Frank trailing in her wake. "All right, that's it. I'm wet enough. That's about all the beach I can handle for one week. There's about a pound and a half of sand in my crack." She hobbles to a beach chair, still puffing.

Jared and Liv finally arrive and greet everyone in chipper tones. Liv grabs two beach chairs near me and drapes emerald green beach towels over them. Pretending to doze behind my sunglasses, head resting against the back of the beach chair, I watch as Jared madly digs through their beach bag. He waves to catch Liv's attention.

She pulls her beach cover-up over her head, then asks, "Honey, what're you looking for?"

"Eh." He looks unhappy. "Think we forgot the suntan lotion."

She smirks. "You mean the same suntan lotion that's in your left hand?"

His eyes dart over to the bottle of suntan lotion in his grasp, then he closes his eyes as if he's thinking, 'Of course it's in my hand', and bops his head a few times before peering back at Liv, smirking. "That's the one."

Taking the lotion from his hand, she leans in for a kiss, and asks, "What would you ever do without me?"

"Oh, I'd probably still be here tonight, looking for the suntan lotion," he jests with a wide, goofy grin.

Their playful interaction gives me a sinking feeling deep in my gut. It's the way Jared and I used to flirt, way back. I ache to have that again.

When she asks him to put lotion on her back, suddenly needing some distance, I rise from my beach chair and head down to the ocean to dip my toes in the water to avoid witnessing any more PDA.

I know I have to accept what *is*, but it seems Preston was right. The prospect of walking away from Jared at the end of this trip is feeling harder and more painful with each passing moment.

# Chapter 14

# Neverland

Sneaking away to the Breezeway for privacy, I call Preston again from the Paradise Island Beach Club. I can't wait to fill him in on my day. I divulge every detail, anticipating some apprehension on his end. What I don't expect is the response I actually receive.

"Laina, when are you comin' home?" He sounds thoroughly exhausted. "There's a bad storm comin' and I really could use your help up here."

"Oh come on, Preston," I say soothingly. From what I've seen on the news, this is not such a bad hurricane. It might not even reach New York. "You know weather reports always blow these things out of proportion. Can't you manage alone for a couple more days? I have some great ideas for promotion when I get back, by the way, and —"

He cuts me off. "*Laina.* You're needed here. Not there. Don't you get it? There's nothing for you down there. The longer you stay, the more foolish and desperate you're gonna look."

I fidget, shifting nervously from foot to foot, biting my lip so as not to say something I'll end up wishing to take back.

"And you're right. There *is* a definite reason you've been sent there." His voice sounds unsteady now. "To see that it's time to leave Neverland. Time to grow up."

"I'm coming back in a few days on the flight Mason booked tickets for," I say stubbornly. "That's plenty of time to prepare for a storm. So stop pushing me to leave early."

His voice comes to me with a sort of forced calm now. "Oh, honey. You're too blind to see that you're at someone else's carnival. I can't keep holding your hand because you refuse to get off the carousel. I can't keep being the one to get you through every single *day*."

"What do you mean? Preston, I just–"

"Jack broke up with me," he suddenly bawls.

I'm flabbergasted. So taken aback I don't know how to respond. I'm heartbroken for Preston. Jack is the love of his life. He planned on a future with him.

"Do you want to know his reason for leaving? He told me it's you. Because I allow you to lean on me for every little thing. So I can't keep bein' your love guru, your therapist, your alarm clock, and the person who fixes things anytime your life takes a difficult turn."

"Preston, I'm...I'm so sorry! I had no idea you felt like this," I sob. His hurtful truths cut through me like a heated knife. I shrivel into a chair beside a potted palm.

"So I'm movin' out of the apartment. I won't be here by the time you get home. I'm sorry, honey, but this is for the best. We need some distance."

"No, please don't go! I'll call Jack! I'll talk to him. Convince him to get back with you. I'll tell him I know it's my fault, that he shouldn't blame you for the way I am. I swear! Please, just don't go!" I shout, my voice so garbled I might as well be speaking in tongues. Tears run down my cheeks unchecked. "Do you know *why* I lean on you for everything, Preston? Because you're my rock. Tyler died because of me. But you gave the comfort I needed to get through it. I can see now I've been selfish . . . and I'm so sorry. I can't change the past, and I despise myself for pushing you away. Without you, I have no one. You *are* my family. Please, don't go. I'll do better. I'll get on a plane and fix this!"

Voice low, all but stifled, he mumbles into the phone, "It's beyond fixing at this point. It's over. Good luck down there. Have a safe flight back."

"No, no! Preston?" I squeak, and let out a despairing cry as the other end of the line clicks off.

* * *

A few hours later, once I manage to pull myself together after the traumatic phone call, I sit listlessly at the dining room table attempting to bond with Becky, Allie, and Aunt Tina over books, movies, and music. Uncle Frank putts back and forth around the villa, drinking beer and stuffing his face with potato chips.

Mason and Liv enter through the sliding door in the back of the villa. He is carrying a heavy-looking plastic bag.

"Hey, party animals," he cheerily greets us. They head to the dining room and Mason plunks the plastic bag on the table. "Grabbed a bunch of sodas from the Mini Mart downstairs. Pretty much cleared the shelves. I figured you all might like something to drink."

Becky and Allie's eyes glimmer. "Thanks, Mason!" they chorus, and dive into the bag. They pull out cans and set them on the table.

"Don't drink too much soda, girls. I don't want you to ruin your supper," Aunt Tina warns. They pay no attention, gleefully popping tabs and swigging orange and grape soda.

"Do any of you know where JP is?" asks Liv.

"Oh, he'll turn up, dear. He always does," Aunt Tina blurts out. Once she realizes what she's just said, she claps a hand over her mouth, with a loud, attention-getting *whap*. She follows up with a nervous chuckle and tight-lipped smile, as her face darkens to a shade similar to the red on a Coca Cola can.

"Am I missing something?" Liv asks, surveys everyone's nervous faces.

Aunt Tina's eyes bulge like Rodney Dangerfield's. "No, no. Of course not, dear."

The back door slides open and Jared bursts through, grinning. Liv exclaims, "There you are! Where have you been?"

"Out securing a surprise for tonight." He reaches into the back pocket of his pale green safari shorts and pulls some tickets out. "The four of us are going to see *Twelfth Night!*"

Instantly, I perk up.

"Aw, man," Mason groans. "I don't want to see that. Besides, I had plans for later."

"What plans?" Jared says mockingly. "To get drunk and pass out on the beach?"

"Yes, exactly," Mason cries. "This puts a real blemish on my night."

Unsmiling, Jared says, "Dude, don't be an ass. We never see each other. You can spare one night. And that's just the first part of the surprise."

Mason sluggishly rolls his eyes, as if his eyelids weigh a thousand pounds. "I better start drinking immediately. Gonna need a serious pre-game session to get through this." He drags his feet across the floor, his flip-flops going *swish swoosh* as he wanders to the refrigerator to crack open a cold Kalik.

Jared turns to Liv and wraps his arms around her waist. "I know you're not a huge Shakespeare fan, but I thought this could be something fun and different for us to do." He gazes down, waiting for a reaction.

She lovingly sighs. "Of course it's okay, babe. This is your honeymoon too, and I know you enjoy those plays. Just please don't be offended if I have trouble following along."

"Deal," he replies, and lightly kisses her lips.

Not wanting to watch this public display of affection I reach across the table for a ginger ale. Jared reaches for one, as well. We simultaneously pop the tabs and turn them sideways—his to the left and mine to the right—just like we always did as kids. We instantly lock gazes and smile. Luckily, no one else seems to pick up on it.

# Chapter 15

# Twelfth Night

That night we have a scrumptious dinner of lobster and grilled conch at The Poop Deck in Nassau, which has a breathtaking view of Nassau Harbour. Then Jared, Mason, Liv, and I catch a cab to The Dundas Bahamas Historical Society to see *Twelfth Night*. I'm really looking forward to seeing a Caribbean take on my most beloved Shakespeare play.

As we sidle along the row and locate our seats, Mason makes a big stink over their location, not only because of how far back they are in the theater, but also about the fact that he's not seated near the aisle. "What if I need to take a piss?" he grumbles.

My attire this evening is actually one of the nicer dresses Preston urged me to bring. An emerald-green, knife-pleated sundress with a thin gold belt, worn with a pair of gold t-strap sandals. Thinking of Preston is so painful, though, I have to push down an urge to sneak out and call him again, to beg him to reconsider. When I get home, I *will* win my dearest friend back. Somehow. No matter what it takes.

Jared is in gray Bermuda shorts and a black polo shirt, Mason wears tan cargo shorts, a white V-neck t-shirt, and flip-flips. Yes, this is island-casual theatre attire, all right. Liv is the fanciest, in a white lace dress with sleeves that flare into graceful bells just past the elbows. Her hair is slicked into a perfect high ballerina bun, not a single strand out of place.

After we settle in our seats, she breaks the momentary silence. "So, Mason, when will you be popping the big question?"

*Excuse me, popping what?*

Jared and I snap our heads around to stare at her, then at Mason, in absolute horror.

He appears just as caught off guard, but quickly attempts to play it cool, leaning back in his seat and smirking. "Oh, I don't know." He rubs a hand up and down on my thigh—a bit too far up, I might add—making me highly uncomfortable. We're in a public place. To put an end to it I slide a hand over his and entwine our fingers, making him chastely hold my hand instead.

Luckily, he follows along. "We're still trying to get the sleeping arrangements down pat." He leans toward Liv, and stage-whispers, "Someone keeps me up all night, snoring."

I gape, then attempt to move past it, saying, "It's way too early to be thinking about marriage. We're just having fun for now."

Mason appears pleased with my summation and grins. "Works for me!" He settles back in his seat.

Leaning forward to extend an arm across Mason, Liv touches my arm. "Sorry if I made you feel uncomfortable, Laina. It's just, well, I heard the horror stories about some of Mason's ex-girlfriends."

"Hey!" he howls, cocking his head to better catch her comments.

"Oh please," she begins, flashing him a quelling side-eye glance. "Like you *don't* know." Turning back to me, she continues, "It's just that, from what I've seen so far, you're one of those rare girls any guy would love to bring home to meet the family."

She might mean well, but this all feels a bit too intrusive. "Even though I get blackout drunk and embarrass myself every fifteen seconds?"

"Every ten seconds," Mason chimes in.

Liv playfully slaps his arm. "Be nice, now." She rolls her eyes. "I always tell JP that I hope I'll have a sister-in-law I can become close with. And I hope I don't weird you out by saying this, but I sense you and I could have that kind of relationship."

Is this chick serious? Does she *have* to be this nice all the freaking time? She's making it way too difficult for me to dislike her. I feel awful every time she's kind and inclusive. I don't know whether to hug her or slap her. I don't know what the hell to do about *anything*. An urge to cry tightens the back of my throat.

Guilt is the worst feeling in the world. This insanely sweet woman has no idea that I'm in love with her husband.

The lights in the theater slowly go down. The few people still standing in the aisles scurry to find their seats, just as the curtain rises.

I smile at Liv, meeting her gaze in the darkening theater. "Thank you. That really means a lot," I choke out. Sitting back then, I control my breathing so the tears stay put instead of overflowing and too-obviously smearing my makeup.

The crazy thing is, in another time, place, or situation, she and I could be good friends. She's easy to get along with. Not catty at all. She goes out of her way to make everyone feel included.

I've never had a close girlfriend before – just Preston. But if I were to have a good female friend, I think it would be with someone like Liv. Unfortunately, under these circumstances, establishing a relationship with Liv is just not possible. It can't be, ever.

\* \* \*

*Twelfth Night* Bahamas-style turns out to be incredible.

With each production of the play I attend, I always eagerly anticipate two particular scenes, hoping the actors will do justice to their parts. Tonight the director has done a spectacular job of putting a modern spin on things, setting the play on the island, with present day props and costumes. The actors put their all into portraying the characters, and I cling to every word, immersed from the moment the curtain rises to reveal a beautifully-painted backdrop of a stormy sea, and onstage a real (though of course not full-sized) sailing yacht, to represent Viola and Sebastian's shipwreck.

During the final scene of the first Act, I'm literally on the edge of my seat, as the actress playing Olivia—clothed in a black cocktail dress and sheer black veil—mourns the losses of both father and brother. She is entertaining Viola—who is by then dressed as a young man, wearing a false mustache—who has been sent by the wealthy Duke Orsino to deliver a courting speech, professing his love for Olivia.

Olivia shows no interest in what Duke Orsino has to say. Instead she skeptically asks Viola, "*How* does he love me?"

Stepping toward Olivia with great purpose, Viola's voice deepens in a surge of passion. "With adorations, with fertile tears, with groans that thunder love, with *sighs of fire.*"

Chills race up and down my spine despite the tropical climate. I throw a quick glance left. Jared, too, is fixated on the stage, sitting forward, gripping Liv's hand. I sigh, and look away. Because Viola's lines perfectly describe the way I feel about Jared. My love for him has always been so strong, I wonder how I'll be able to contain it.

The other part I adore is when Viola finally puts Duke Orsino in his place in Act II, Scene IV. They're at his palace. The duke is babbling on about how no woman could ever love a man to the extremes that he loves Olivia.

As he drones on, the actress portraying Viola agitatedly presses thumb and forefinger against the fake mustache plastered to her face, as if she wishes to rip it off then and there, and reveal her true self to him.

At last it is *her* turn to speak. She heatedly responds to his pompous blathering about love. "We men may say more, swear more: but, indeed, our shows are more than will; for still we prove much in our vows, but little in our love."

What Orsino fails to see is that his words mean nothing with no action to back them up. If a man claims to passionately love a woman, he must show it. Viola also means to say, simply because a woman doesn't violently profess her love aloud doesn't mean she isn't feeling it deep within.

I feel crushed when the curtain finally comes down. I wouldn't mind an instant replay.

However, not everyone in our group felt the same, I discover, as we walk out onto the street.

Jared and I thoroughly enjoyed the performance, of course. But Liv shakes her head apologetically. "Wow, I'm afraid I really struggled to follow that story," she admits. "So many characters, all dressed like somebody else!"

Mason, on the other hand, fell asleep by the middle of Act Three. I don't even bother to ask what he thought.

The four of us pile into a cab. Jared asks the driver to take us to the Sunrise Beach Villas for yet another surprise.

"No more surprises," Mason begs. "No offense, but yours kind of suck."

"Thanks, man," Jared sarcastically replies. "The next one includes booze, so I figured you'd be cool with it. Assuming you're thirsty right about now."

Throwing his head back, Mason shouts, "Oh, thank God! I'm still getting sloppy tonight!"

He grips my hand so tight, I have to hide a wince, and realize I *am* looking forward to leaving here, in some ways. Back home I'll be able to end the charade of this relationship, without spoiling the wedding trip for the others.

The driver drops us off at the Sunrise Beach Villas. Just next-door is a lively restaurant and bar called Viola's. Again, really – *go figure*! High-top chairs surround the wrap-around bar and festive, colorful decorations hang from the arched wooden ceiling. One whole wall on the far side of the restaurant is natural stone, and a built-in swimming pool with an enclosed stone alcove sits just next to the restaurant for the pleasure of villa guests. During the day Viola's is a tranquil restaurant, but at night, it comes wildly alive with music and dancing.

As we head to the long bar, cheering and excited, drunken shouting drowns out the music momentarily. Everyone from the bridal party is in attendance already, and clearly a few drinks deep.

Jumping up and down, Liv shrieks, "This is *just* what I wanted! It's perfect, sweetie!" She leans in and kisses Jared, and then wraps one arm around his, leading him to the bar. Mason and I trail along behind.

"Whoa, one-dollar frozen margaritas! Sold!" Mason shouts. "My man," he calls to the bartender, "could we get five frozen margaritas when you get a chance?"

"Why five?" Liv asks, frowning.

Mason thinks for a moment. "Good point." He calls back to the bartender, "Better make it seven." He turns to us and hollers over the music, "Gotta play catch up. I'm gonna need a lot of alcohol to make up for that boring Shakespeare shit."

"Dude, you took a cat nap and missed most of it," Jared points out.

Liv chimes in, "Mason, the margaritas are going to be really watered down by the time you get to the second and third."

Jared grins and shakes his head. "No, honey. See, Mason has a system. He'll slam the first two right down the hatch."

Mason nods vigorously, as if Jared has predicted exactly what the plan is.

Horrified, Liv turns to him and cries, "But you'll get a brain freeze!"

Jared shakes his head once again. "Don't worry. He doesn't have the right equipment for a brain freeze."

"Ha-Ha! Screw you, man!" Mason playfully shoves Jared's arm off the tabletop.

I chuckle under my breath. In keeping with my new plan to not do anything stupid or alcohol-induced, I inform Mason, "Just ice water for me."

He shrugs and sings out, "Cool. More booze for me!"

Amelia is standing alone at the other end of the bar, arms folded tightly across her chest, clearly not enjoying herself.

I wave her over. "What's going on? Are you okay?"

"Not really." She heaves a sigh. "I tried talking to Ben, but he acted like he couldn't be bothered."

"Eww, screw him then!" I yell, curling my lip, flashing a scowl in his direction. "First of all, Amelia, you need to smile, even if you're not having fun yet. And don't cross your arms." I pull her arms gently to hang to her sides, then grab one hand and proper it on her hip, establishing her a splash of attitude. "There. Stand like that for a bit. It makes you appear more confident." Turning to Liv, who is intently following our interaction, I say matter-of-factly, "We need to get this girl some shots."

Liv beams and shouts, "I am *all* over that."

Connie shuffles to the bar and demands a shot as well. I tell Liv to make my shot Ginger Ale instead. No bad decisions for me tonight!

Liv returns and passes the shot glasses around, then stares at me, holding out her shot glass of tequila in my direction, as if anticipating I will be making the first toast. Amelia and Connie follow Liv's lead.

A sick feeling washes over me. Do I *really* have to toast to Liv and Jared, to their long-term happiness, right now? Unfortunately, I realize I do.

Holding out my ginger ale shot toward the group of women waiting for my toast, I force out, "To Liv and Jar…um." I catch myself. "And JP, as they begin their exciting journey through life together." I swallow the lump in the back of my throat. "And to meeting all of you wonderful women on this breathtaking island. Let's have a great night!"

"Cheers," they shout, and we all swig back the shots.

We weave through the crowd of people on the dance floor, and begin dancing. I am quickly drenched in sweat, as is everyone else in Viola's. As the songs keep coming, Amelia seems to loosen up. She even looks like she's beginning to enjoy herself. From the corner of one eye, I happen to catch sight of Adam, one of Jared's groomsmen, as he stares at Amelia and me dancing together. Quickly, I grab her hand and twirl her around the dance floor, which unfortunately causes her to trip over her feet, but she quickly catches herself and finds it hilarious. Adam must notice her laughing unselfconsciously at her own clumsiness, and genuinely having a good time without obsessing over what the groomsmen have been up to, because he sets down his drink and makes a beeline for her, through all the bobbing, gyrating bodies.

For me, the next part will be just like leaving the fishing line in the water after propping up the pole, and walking away. At some point, a fish is bound to bite. In Amelia's case, she unintentionally seems to have hooked the attention of someone she didn't even expect to respond.

Adam edges closer. Once he reaches us he lays a hand on Amelia's arm to get her attention. Slightly turning toward him, she leans in as if waiting for him to say something. With what sounds like disinterest, she says, "Yeah?"

"I'd like to buy you a drink," he shouts close to her ear.

She glances at me in surprise. I raise my eyebrows, then wink.

Turning back to him, she smiles, but only a little. "Okay. I'll meet you at the bar right after this song."

He looks slightly baffled at being sent to wait while the song comes to an end, but eagerly complies.

I'm proud of how Amelia is handling herself. When the song concludes, I wish her luck. She heads to the bar, but not *too* quickly.

The deejay suddenly switches over to slow dance music – a welcome, refreshing alternative, because I am severely overheated. The lights dim and Mason makes his way to my side. I drape my arms around his neck and we slowly sway to the music.

"Wow, you're drenched," he says.

"Uh, so are you," I joke in return. "You fall in the pool?"

Tipping his head forward, he shakes it, slinging his hair back and forth like a dog who's just had a bath. Drops of sweat fly from his hair, splattering my face and clothes.

With the back of one hand I wipe the wetness from my cheeks. "Ugh. Did you really have to do that?"

He only snorts and wraps his arms tighter around my waist. I lean back, still disgusted.

As we dance, I happen to glance over at Jared and Liv beside us. It pains me to watch him adoringly kiss her lips and the tip of her nose. She closes her eyes and smiles, happily taking it all in. I feel suddenly queasy, as if we're back on the snorkeling boat.

While the song comes to an end, the deejay picks up the mic and announces, "All dancing couples, switch partners with someone else, please!"

The four of us look at each other. Liv holds out a hand for Mason. "Looks like you're stuck with me, brother!"

"Appears so, sister." He releases me quickly and takes hold of her hand.

Turning to Jared, I see he's waiting to take mine. He twirls me once before laying his free hand on my back, pulling me close. Keeping the other hand wrapped around mine, he pulls it up against his chest, just over his heart.

"Sorry for all the sweat. You having fun?" he asks.

Grinning happily, I say, "Tonight's been great."

But the smile slips from my face when I think about how different life will be in just a few days. It takes me back to cruel reality and I feel suddenly lost. Jared studies my face, but I can't bring myself to meet his gaze.

He frowns in concern. "You okay?"

"Why wouldn't I be?" I gulp.

"You're shaking."

Horrified at how transparent I've become, I blurt, "Oh, I thought that was you."

"Not me, Norton," he says, and we burst out laughing. It takes a moment to compose ourselves.

"Are you not drinking tonight?"

"Actually, I'm giving it up altogether. I tend to make very poor choices when I drink."

"Oh." He raises a hand to scratch his chin with his thumb, still not letting go of my hand. "Does this have anything to do with the other night?"

"Yes, absolutely. The other night was the final straw. I never want to be in a situation like that again. I mean, not being in control of my actions. It's taken me way too long to realize I need to make a lifestyle change."

"I admire the choice."

Then an awkward silence descends. Finally I break it. "I can't believe there's a place down here actually called 'Viola's'. It's like *Twelfth Night* follows wherever I go."

"Maybe it does," he replies, just as we step on each other's feet. Wow, we are both such totally hideous dancers. After we apologize and laugh it off, I look off into the distance. This may be the last time we ever get a chance to smash each others' toes.

"You okay? You look upset." He squeezes my hand.

"Not at all." I force a grin. "Just taking everything in."

"I was thinking Liv and I should make a trip out to New York to visit you and Mason in a few months. What do you say?"

Oh dear. How to respond to that? Well, there is still time to figure out all the details. Politely nodding, flashing a hint of a smile, I say, "Sure. Sounds like a plan." Knowing full well this isn't going to transpire, since I plan on ending my relationship with Mason in the next few days. But my heart beats heavier in my chest contemplating the fact that I will most likely never see Jared again after this trip. I wish we could have more time. I feel cheated. Once again, I will soon find myself saying goodbye to a person who has always meant the world to me, and again this time for good. My breathing speeds up. As the thought settles deeper, I am gripped by the signs of an anxiety attack.

*Come on, Laina! You cannot have a meltdown right now!*

The song comes to an end. Mason weaves his way back to my side and drapes one sweaty arm over my shoulder. I'm actually grateful, this time, because it forces me to suck it up and pull myself together quickly.

"Thanks for the dance, JP," I whisper.

"This goofball didn't step on your feet more than three times, did he?" Mason chimes in.

"Only once. Only a little," I reply.

Mason frowns at Jared, who reassures him, "Don't worry, she got me back."

"That's my girl," Mason pats my shoulder so hard my head bobs.

"I hope you didn't dent my husband, Laina," Liv teases. "I need him in one piece when I get him back to our room later on." She wraps both arms around Jared's waist and buries her face in his neck. It takes every ounce of will power for me to push passed graphic images of Liv and Jared's entwined bodies out of my brain.

# Chapter 16

# Champagne in Solo Cups

On our return to the Paradise Island Beach Club, Jared makes a trip back to the villa room and asks everyone to meet him down at the beach. We traipse through the lit-up grounds of the Beach Club toward the dark, secluded water. Mason and Liv immediately jump into the ocean – Liv still in her dress, Mason in his boxers. Ben, Connie, Amelia, and Adam follow, leaving me to watch the merriment from the sand. I enjoy watching Amelia and Adam playfully flirting and splashing around in the water.

I want to warn them against night swimming, since this is exactly the scenario for the opening scene in *Jaws*. Finally I decide it's best to mind my own business. I don't want to be like the concerned, bossy, un-fun parent.

Jared finally greets us on the beach a few minutes later, equipped with two bottles of champagne, a can of Ginger Ale, and a stack of red solo cups.

"Great idea, man!" Mason stampedes out of the water.

"Grabbed them from the liquor store earlier today and stashed them in the back of the fridge," Jared says. "Figured this would be a nice way to finish off the night."

"Seriously, JP?" Connie jeers. "Champagne in red solo cups. Could you *be* any more of a country boy?"

"Hey," Liv sings, "leave my country boy alone." She retreats from the waves to help him hand out the solo cups.

"I figured you'd like this," he tells her as he un-twists the wire-caged cap over the champagne cork, then hands the other bottle to her to open.

"You can take the boy out of PA, but you can't take PA out of the boy!" she cries, as she pops the cork. Jared opens the can of ginger ale and pours the contents into one cup, for me.

Looking confused, Mason asks, "Uh, so what's with all the ginger ale, Laina?"

Taking the second bottle of champagne from Liv, Jared fills the remaining cups until the bottle is empty.

"Nothing, I just didn't feel like drinking tonight. Ginger ale is the only soda I like."

"Since when do you ever turn down alcohol?" Mason guffaws. "Come to think of it, you didn't have any Rum Punch on the boat today, either. And now that I think back, I don't remember you drinking at the wedding."

"It's not a big deal," I protest. "I just haven't been in the mood."

"Okay, come on; let's have a toast," Jared interrupts, raising his cup. "To making memories."

"To making memories," everyone repeats.

As the rest of us drink to that, Connie blurts out, "Laina, you're not pregnant, are you?"

Jared and Mason instantly, violently choke on their champagne.

I'm mortified. My eyes widen; my neck and cheeks flush with heat. I hope this is hidden by the darkness. "Oh my God!" I shout. "No! *No!*" Turning to Mason, I make my tone extremely severe and serious. "*Definitely* no."

He regains his composure then, and his voice. "What the hell, Connie! Why would you even say that?"

Bent over, still trying to catch his breath, Jared plants his half-full cup in the sand and props his hands on his knees, still coughing up champagne.

"I didn't know," Connie yells, "I was just asking. I swear I didn't mean anything bad by it."

As Jared's coughing gradually subsides, Liv pats him on the back. "You okay, sweetie?"

"Clearly I was mistaken," Connie huffs, and slugs back the remainder of her champagne. She icily informs us she's calling it a night, and stomps back to the villas.

Jared abruptly bolts into the water, until the ocean is up to his waist.

Turning to me, Liv apologizes. "I am *so* sorry, Laina. She should never have said anything like that, even if she suspected. It's not her place. She had a few too many tonight. Connie has no filter when she drinks too much. I promise to speak to her in the morning. I feel *so* bad."

"It's fine, really," I reassure her, over and over. But, of course, in the forefront of my mind, now I'm suddenly wondering if I actually do look pregnant.

Laying a hand on my back, Mason says a little shakily, "Okay, so, uh…think we're gonna call it a night too. I've had enough surprises and heart attacks for one day."

Not wanting to stick around either, I march back up the beach with him. "You all right?" I ask, since he still seems a bit spooked.

"I can't believe she actually said that," he gasps out, with a traumatized look, once we reach the illuminated back deck. "Even if she thought you were pregnant, she never should have said so. Scared me half to death. God almighty. She made me spit out good champagne!"

I begin to feel vaguely offended by his obvious and extreme horror at the mere idea.

"Well…" I tap the brim of my Solo cup to the one in Mason's hand, "Here's to making memories."

# Chapter 17

# Eavesdropping

The following morning, Connie appears at our villa suite and apologizes for her outburst the night before. Of course, I accept, promising we can move past it without any awkwardness.

But then, of course, after she leaves for the beach and I change into my bathing suit, I become fixated on the look of my body in the bedroom mirror. I try to determine if the very slight paunch in my lower abdomen, from years of pounding down beers, can indeed be misconstrued as a baby belly, not just a beer belly.

I spend an unnatural amount of time staring into the room's full length mirror, until Mason knocks on the door to see what could possibly be taking so long.

Liv's voice in the background scolds, "Stop rushing her!" Surprisingly, he quiets down without returning a comment in his defense.

Throwing on the first beach cover-up I dig out of my suitcase, I hurry so I can have more time with Jared. I bolt from the bedroom, and am suddenly startled when I nearly knock into him. He's kneeling in the hallway, fixing the broken doorknob on the bathroom door.

Our eyes instantly lock. We wish each other a good morning.

"Are you on the beach club's payroll now?" I joke.

Flashing a little smile, he returns unscrewing the cover plate of the knob. "Yeah, but only because they found out that I'm cheap labor."

"Good to know. Thanks for fixing the stupid door, by the way."

"Yeah, now I can finally pee in peace," Becky calls from the dining room, where she's fixing her long blond hair into a messy beach bun.

"No problem. Can't have people locking themselves in there anymore."

I freeze and stare at him, as his gaze briefly flickers to me, then back to the door. What could he mean by that?

Liv approaches, and I turn to greet her.

She gives me a warm but still unwelcome hug. "Did Connie come to see you yet?"

Even after explaining she did, and that everything is fine, Liv still apologizes again for what happened the previous night.

Mason interrupts, asking if I'm ready to go in the most antsy tone possible. "We need to get down there to secure the best spot. Plus lots of chairs," he insists.

"I need to use the bathroom before we leave."

He rolls his eyes. "Use the one in the other bedroom."

Aunt Tina informs him, "Its occupied. Frank is in there. He most likely won't be out anytime soon."

Yikes.

Mason huffs, then suggests he and Liv get a head start down to the beach to grab chairs. Jared and I can follow once the doorknob is fixed and I'm ready to go, which I agree to without a speck of hesitation.

During our trek to the beach, Jared and I laugh over old stories from childhood, such as the imaginary swordfights he and Tyler used to have at Belvedere Castle. I recall always wanting to play along and not be excluded from the swordfights—acted out with no swords, I might add—so I constantly chased after the pair of them, hoping they would let me in on at least one make-believe duel.

This had often annoyed Tyler, who felt I consistently interfered with their games. That's why he branded me with the nickname 'Scutch' – his imaginative way of calling me a pain in the ass. As we got older the nickname became more a term of endearment.

Jared mentions the time he, Tyler, and I told ghost stories, when we were hanging out at his old apartment in Manhattan. There was a blackout from one of the frequent summer thunderstorms. With only a few candles lit and one extremely dim flashlight, the three of us concocted scary stories to tell, to see who'd be the first to scream. Of course, as we sat in Jared's dark living room watching our own creepy shadows writhe on the walls, I squealed almost immediately. Tyler knew exactly what to say to freak me out.

We finally catch up to the rest of the party on the beach, and must go our separate ways. It's so hot I can actually feel my skin pulsating from the sun's intense rays, so hot that, every so often, I head willingly into the ocean—only to my shins—to cool my overheated body with splashes of lukewarm seawater.

Evelyn and Thomas have set beach chairs at the farthest front right corner of the group. I'm situated close to the back left side. Evie doesn't look in my direction the entire morning – not even when I wander down to the ocean to cool off. She stares fixedly at the waves or keeps her nose buried in a Jude Deveraux novel. However, later in the afternoon, on one of my many treks to the water, I spot her dipping her toes in about twenty feet away from where I'm standing.

"Hello, Mrs. Hartley," I call, crouching to splash water over my shoulders and arms.

She's in a sleek black one-piece, a wide-brimmed straw hat, and big black sunglasses perched halfway down her nose. She slightly turns her head, and without looking at me says flatly, "Laina."

"So, do you think . . ." I begin.

In one smooth motion she turns toward me, readjusts her sunglasses, and cuts me off. "Laina, please. Now is not the time. I've already told you that. I'll discuss this when I'm ready."

I nod, afraid to push too hard, in case she changes her mind about talking to me altogether.

A couple of hours later, Mason, Jared, Liv, and I are at the Reef Bar, getting something to eat. After perusing the menu, Liv and I both order the Blackened Conch Wrap, then head to the ladies room just behind the bar. There's no air conditioning, so the restroom feels hot and sticky, and the air inside is thick.

"I'm glad we have a minute to chat." Liv sets her sunglasses on the edge of the sink. She pulls the rubber band from her hair, and tries to comb out some of the beach-induced tangles with her fingers. "I noticed a couple of things about you and Mason, and thought it might be good for you to get an outsider's view."

Oh, great. Relationship advice for a relationship that's about to no longer be one. But I can't say that. So I raise my eyebrows and stare blankly at her in the mirror while readjusting my beach cover-up. "What do you mean?"

"I haven't really known Mason long. But from what I can see, he's kind of got you wrapped around his finger."

"Uhh, well. . . . " I say in a doubtful tone, "I'm not so sure about that."

"Does he always get his way?"

"Well, I guess so, yeah." I scratch at a white haze of dried salt on my forehead.

"And you always give in?"

"It's just easier." I shrug, shaking a bit of trapped sand from my bikini bottoms.

Liv shakes her head, lips pursed disapprovingly. "I can tell he's the kind who needs a woman to call him out on his bullshit. If he thinks he can always get his way, that's what he'll expect. It's what my third graders do. He needs someone to be firm, to keep him in check."

I think back to all the nights I slept on the couch rather than in my own bed so my snoring didn't disturb his sleep.

"Like this morning," she continues. "He was really pushing you to hurry up, even though you obviously weren't ready. That's why I said something. I hope you didn't get upset that I told him to knock it off."

"No," I say, though my voice is a bit too high-pitched to sound sincere. "I actually appreciated it. Sometimes he can be overbearing."

"Well, don't let him walk all over you! Now, I just wanted to let you know," she continues, turning on the faucet and slicking her hair back with water, "that I said something to him as we headed down to the beach this morning. I might've embarrassed him. He said he didn't realize he comes off that way. I don't think he was happy to find out that this is the impression I have of him. I tried to smooth things over, but he might be upset with me now. That's fine. It doesn't bother me. He needed to hear it."

In that moment, I feel grateful to Liv for sticking up for me, annoyed she is butting in, and that I am a terrible person, all at the same time. I wish I didn't still have such strong feelings for Jared. The wrongness in this situation . . . it leaves me feeling sick to my stomach that this insanely nice woman has no clue about my history with her husband.

"I appreciate you speaking up, actually. I don't enjoy confrontation, so I try to avoid it with him as much as possible. That's not always a good thing, I know."

"Oh." She stares at me thoughtfully, in deep contemplation.

"What?" I ask, slightly baffled.

"Oh . . . nothing." She shrugs and sets her sunglasses atop her head. "It just seems a little odd that you try to avoid confrontation at all costs, but you've chosen to date an attorney. Someone who argues for a living."

I gape, utterly flabbergasted. She's right! Why didn't I realize this myself? Even worse, how have I let it go on as long as it has? Of course, if I hadn't, then I wouldn't be standing here right now. Still, a normal person would have picked up on the fact that Mason and I are polar opposites. No wonder it's been such a struggle to make things work. He and I aren't *meant* to work!

"If I wasn't so gross and sticky I'd hug you right now," I admit.

Looking amused, she turns with open arms and gives me a quick hug. "We girls have to look out for each other."

Emerging from the bathroom, Liv trailing a few steps behind, I stumble upon Jared and Mason standing at the bar, deep in conversation.

Jared's look is intense, his lips set in a grim line. One hand tightly grips the edge of the bar. As we approach I hear him say, "She's a nice person, Mason. Trust me, you don't want to screw it up."

Swallowing a slug of beer, Mason slams the bottle on the bartop, and retorts, "First of all, my relationship is none of your business. And second, why do you care so much?"

Jared shakes his head and takes a step back.

"What's going on?" I say. Both flinch. Mason takes a long pull on his beer, still glowering at Jared. To avoid aggravating the already obvious tension I let it go, and turn to Gracie, the bartender, who's blending a frozen cocktail behind the bar. "May I have an iced tea?"

"Of course," she says smoothly, "and your lunch order will be out in a few moments."

I smile and thank her, then take a seat beside Mason. Liv scoots over and nuzzles Jared's neck.

Lunch is spent mostly in concentrated chewing and uncomfortable silence. When Liv remarks on the awkward atmosphere, Mason blames it on too much island sun making us sleepy.

"Then we better take a nap when we get back to the beach chairs!" Liv orders.

I wish mere sleepiness was the issue. All I can do now is hope the brotherly tension eases a bit so the rest of the day isn't spoiled, since we have plans to go to the Atlantis later on in the evening.

# Chapter 18

# Atlantis Found

That evening, during a wonderful dinner at Luciano's of Chicago, we witness a magnificent, stunning sunset. The restaurant is located on the water, overlooking the Atlantis, so we have front row seats to the sky's best work of art. After dinner, our taxi driver drops Jared, Liv, Mason, Amelia, Connie, Adam, Ben, and me off at the Atlantis for some late-night shenanigans. The entranceway is lined with stores like Cartier and Versace – too high-end for me to dare set foot in.

We pass a huge, clear crystal statue in the center of the lobby, right outside the casino's entrance. We step in, into a blast of frosty air conditioning. Soon Amelia's teeth start to chatter. "Oh, why'd I leave my sweater back at the villa?" she moans.

Taking pity on the ferociously shivering girl, I loan her my favorite chartreuse cardigan, making her promise to take good care of it and not to forget to give it back. She repeatedly thanks me, and quickly puts it on, sighing as if it provides instant warmth.

The group scatters to give generous donations to the various gambling stations. Slot machines jingle and twinkle around the spacious room. It's alive with hundreds of hopeful gamblers, itching to win a million. Mason, Jared, Liv, and I head over to a Roulette table to play a few rounds.

After making our own donations to the casino, we descend a marble double staircase with a black metal railing. It leads to a fountain at the bottom with pearly, shell-shaped statues and a giant marble ball in the center. Behind it, large glass tanks run floor to ceiling, a multitude of different fish swimming inside. We veer right, toward a dark tunnel-like entrance, which is the start of an underwater labyrinth inspired by the Lost City of Atlantis.

"Who's up for the aquarium?" Mason asks, jittering with excitement.

I peer into the tunnel of darkness, worrying I may freak out if I come face to face with one of my gray, leathery friends.

Mason urges, "Ah, come on, Laina."

I just can't. It would be like voluntarily walking into a passage of doom where my worst fears lurk around every corner, waiting to traumatize me yet again. For me, the aquarium has a *Legends of the Hidden Temple* vibe.

"So, are you in?" Mason asks.

"Uh, well . . ." But clearly the terrified look on my face says it all.

He rolls his eyes. "If you want, you can wait here by the fountain until we come out."

"Ease up on her," Liv says, "because I'm having reservations about walking in there, too."

"Want me to go in first, Liv?" Jared asks.

"What's the matter?" Mason asks her, suddenly sounding concerned.

"It's not that I don't *want* to go in."

Liv cuts me off. "See, I get claustrophobic sometimes. I just don't know if I can do it." She flits to my side. I thought she was putting it on for my benefit, but she does look a bit pale.

"Well," I suggest, "what if we go in and stick together? That way if one of us can't handle it, we'll have the other to guide us out."

Smiling, as if this plan eases her nerves a bit, she links arms with me and grips my hand.

"Oh, great." Mason snorts. "It's gonna be like the blind leading the blind in there."

I feel determined now to not reveal how scared I actually am. I refuse to hesitate when Liv and I reach the entrance. Instead, we march straight in without a millisecond of hesitation, so there's no time to convince myself to turn back around. Once inside the dimly lit aquarium, I stare wide-eyed at the tall glass walls. There is also glass on certain parts of the ceiling where lobsters are visible crawling overhead. On the other side of the glass are thousands of tropical fish, as well as manta rays and stingrays, all gliding around in their indoor oasis.

The tanks are designed to give the illusion you're at the bottom of the ocean, where ships have sunk and fallen apart or rusted over time. In smaller tanks are other varieties of fish, mostly kept with their own kind. One holds electric yellow and pink jellyfish, clownfish, seahorses, eels, lobsters, and other funky species I can't identify.

The maze isn't as closed in as Liv originally expected, so we don't get freaked out, even when I see a few smaller sharks up close. I keep telling myself they can't scent me behind that thick wall of glass. Gradually we both begin to relax and happily bounce from room to room. We eventually make it to the other end of the maze, outside of which are waterfalls and a man-made lake. I breathe a sigh of relief then. I made it through to the other side, unscathed.

Mason offers Liv a congratulatory high five for not having a claustrophobic attack. Jared stares at me, and I desperately wish to know what thoughts are running through his mind. Then he nods and gives me a crooked smile, as if to say, *I knew you could do it.*

My cheeks flush as I return the smile and coyly look away.

I'm proud of myself for facing my fears head-on. Perhaps this *is* the beginning of a new me – a *stronger* me.

Now, when I return home, being alone is still inevitable. But at least I can tell myself that with more baby steps progress will come. That maybe, just maybe there is a better fate waiting for me, after all.

\* \* \*

The entire bridal party returns with us to the villa, and a downpour starts as we reach the front gate. We rush through the grounds and pile into the air conditioned villa. I'm soaked and chilly, so I excuse myself to change into a pair of flannel PJ pants and a dry t-shirt.

In the living room, Becky and Allie are flipping through the channels until they decide that they want to rent the movie *Six Days, Seven Nights*. Becky tosses the remote at Jared, leaving him to figure out how to get the movie rental going and retreat to the kitchen to pop every bag of microwave popcorn in the cabinets.

The villa is slightly chaotic now, with more people in the main living area than usual, but the vibe is fun. Mason squeezes into the kitchen between Becky and Allie to whip up a pitcher of margaritas while everyone else settles onto the couch or floor to finish the night with a movie. Becky and Allie beg Mason to concoct a batch of virgin margaritas. And out in the living room things are getting louder.

"Are you seriously too scared," Adam is playfully shouting at Amelia, "to go down that slide?"

"Are you kidding?" she cries. "Of course I am. It's just *way* too steep a slide. What if I get hurt? I mean it's all up to gravity at that point."

He gives her a toothy grin. "How come I never realized 'til now how funny you are?"

She smirks. "Oh, I only let really cool people see my awesomeness. Guess you just made the cut."

"Lucky me," he answers, wrapping his arms around her waist.

I smile and head off to the kitchen to give Becky and Allie a hand. Jared asks if one of them will stick some popcorn in a solo cup for him, since he's not hungry enough for a whole bowl. I tell the girls I'll take over the popcorn duties. They agree, then become overjoyed when Mason agrees to make them their own alcohol-free margaritas.

Mason whispers under his breath, "If you girls swear not to rat me out to Aunt Tina, a few drops of Tequila might accidentally spill into your batch."

They nod, and squeal with delight.

I prepare bowls of popcorn to be passed around, then grab two solo cups and sift through, searching for half-popped kernels – Jared's favorite. I locate a few in each bowl and toss them into one solo cup. I then take the empty solo cup and slide it inside the half-popped cup, and fill the top cup with fully-popped kernels.

"This is the perfect end to a great night. I'm glad we decided to come back here." Liv rises from the couch and plants a kiss on Jared. "Be right back. Just running to the bathroom. You can start the movie. I'll only be a second."

She weaves around people sitting on the floor and disappears into the bathroom.

"All right, girls," Jared says, as the opening credits play, "you're good to go!"

Becky and Allie shout "Woo hoo!" from the kitchen, as Mason hands them their drinks.

I pass around popcorn and the crowd settles down, Mason's blankets are spread out among the group. I hand a bowl to Amelia, who's seated on the couch, just as Jared slips in beside her. I hand him the Solo cup and he thanks me.

I whisper, "Check the bottom cup."

"Huh?" He peers up at me, looking confused.

"Bottom cup," I repeat, smiling. I scamper away, and sit on a cushion on the floor at the other end of the couch.

He slides the top cup up and peers into the bottom one. After a pause, he looks over at me and grins. *Thank you*, he mouths.

I whisper, "You're welcome," just as Liv returns to the living room, and sits on Jared's lap.

Allie flicks off the lights, takes a big gulp of her maybe-virgin margarita, and takes a seat beside me on the floor.

In the dark living room, with only the television screen for light, I swear I keep catching Jared's gaze aimed in my direction. I can't stop staring at him, either. I'm probably reading way too much into it. I constantly remind myself that he's married.

He and Liv hold hands in the dark. She leans back, kisses his temple, and caresses the side of his face.

I wonder then if at some point in my life I will meet someone I can love as much as I have loved Jared. Will I ever be that enraptured by another man, so I can finally move on?

It's hard to imagine, but I have to believe this could possibly be my fate.

# Chapter 19

## Sun Showers

The following morning, while everyone flocks to the beach. I have other plans. In the bedroom mirror I notice my skin has a sun-kissed, pink glow from the last few days in the sun. I comb my fingers through my damp hair, which feels softer than usual, probably due to all the salt water. I want to explore the grounds around the Paradise Island Beach Club, and figure this is the best time to head out.

The villa staff have mentioned there is a pond a little way past the One&Only Ocean Club, stocked with turtles and leaping fish. I'll check that out first.

As I stroll along the sidewalk, across the street both the Cloisters and the Versailles Garden appear empty and serene. I cross toward the Cloisters, halting at the top of the stone steps overlooking the gazebo where Liv and Jared exchanged their vows. I hesitate there, wondering if I should turn back. Maybe this isn't a good idea.

Even though I've been doing unexpectedly well lately with facing my fears and phobias, as well as facing reality, I just don't know if I have it in me to go down there again. A wave of sadness washes over me as I stand listening to the faint rattle of palm fronds swishing in the wind.

Down there all traces of the wedding have been cleared, as if the wedding never happened at all. Not one flower petal is left behind. If I'd come here before Liv and Jared were married, this place would have only felt magical to me, with its historical ruins, the statues, the sparkling turquoise water, and the tall, regal palms – the way Shakespeare Garden feels for me again, back home. But now this place is a symbol of their promises to each other – promises I wish Jared and I could have made instead.

While on this island I've already confronted the ocean and sharks. I've proved to myself and others I can forego alcohol and avoid being a foolish, immature drunk. I know I can't keep running away from other things I'm afraid of, or things that may cause me pain. I want to take charge of my life and stop feeling like a disappointment to myself, and to Preston.

Feeling a surge of gumption, a compulsion to knock down the invisible wall I've put up around this alluring place, I start down the steps to the gazebo. No turning back! I'm going to see this through, and stand where they stood. Then I feel certain I can let him go, once I leave this island.

I have to live the rest of my life never truly knowing what transpired all those years ago – why Jared never came to look for me, why his mother suddenly whisked them both away, and how he could have so easily forgotten what we meant to each other, growing up. Fate has steered us in opposite directions, for good this time, and I have to live with that.

It's strange how some things that at first seem meant to be simply don't work out. Were Jared and I supposed to end up together, had other forces not kept us apart? Life now seems almost like a never-ending tug of war between fate and chance.

Finally, I reach the ground level of the Cloisters. The stone gazebo has six intricately-carved pillars propped beneath a rounded roof. Standing just in the center of them, I admire the way sunlight filters through the dainty, wrought-iron vines overhead. The moment is so serene, instead of feeling sad I'm suddenly only grateful for the chance to see such a magnificent bit of history, close up.

After a few minutes I turn back toward the street and continue on to the pond, and the One&Only Ocean Club, hooking a right onto Lakeview Drive. I nearly miss the pond on my left entirely  because there are no signs or any other indication it's there. A small clearing leads to a wooden deck overlooking the water. I descend the steps of the deck and gaze down at hundreds of fish and turtles swimming below. One large fish leaps out of the water, so close the splash it makes falling back into the pond showers me with droplets. Turtles of all sizes clumsily climb on each other's backs to take in a bit of sun. Others glide around the pond, or dive for food. All around us is a wall of greenery. Some trees even grow up from the pond's floor, to rise and flourish above the water.

"Mind if I join you?"

Evelyn's low, husky voice startles me. Without answering, I watch her descend the wooden stairs and walk to my side. We stand there a moment in silence before she speaks.

"I want you to understand something, Laina. Everything I did for my son was done out of love. The choice to leave New York was mine to make. To benefit both our futures."

Staring into her eyes, which finally don't try to evade mine, I figure there is no better time than now to attempt a little Q&A session. "Like the decision to change his last name?"

She sighs and slowly nods. "If you'd ever endured the hurt I had to, you would understand why I did that. I am curious, though, and have to ask, why *are* you still here?"

*If I ever endured hurt?* This woman is either clueless, or intentionally cruel.

I snap, "The wedding is over. Jared and Liv are married. Do you seriously still think I pose some sort of threat?"

"That's not what I'm saying," she calmly answers. "I see the way you look at Mason. I also see the way you look at my son. You're only hurting yourself by staying, Laina."

Dropping my head, I choke out, "I'm not ready to say goodbye again, yet."

"Saying goodbye is part of life. It wasn't easy for us to leave New York, Laina. I want you to know that. It was my home for a long time. But too many memories would have haunted me around every corner. It also hasn't been easy seeing you here."

"So you've been avoiding me. What did I ever do to you? I was sixteen. What could I have possibly done wrong?"

"It was not *you*, Laina. Never you." She shakes her head and looks down at the wooden deck, running her fingers lightly over an infinity symbol etched into a railing post beside her. "You were always a sweet, precious little thing. I watched you grow from the time you and Jared were in kindergarten until you started high school. I saw you grow up loving my son. But then I experienced loss in a way I hope you never have to understand."

"Oh, I've had my own share of losses, Evelyn. Don't assume you know anything about my life anymore."

"Fair enough." She narrows her eyes, frowning. "You really don't know what happened, do you?"

I hotly retort, "I have no idea what you're talking about. How can I? You never answered my questions."

Sighing, she pats me gingerly on the shoulder. "If you want to know the truth, then it's about time you and your mother had a little heart to heart talk."

She turns away, back toward the street.

"Wait!" I call after her, perplexed. "Are you saying my *mother* is the reason you and Jared left New York?"

"I know you want the truth, Laina, but you shouldn't hear it from me. It wouldn't be right. Speak to her. It might quell some of the resentment you feel against me for taking Jared away. And if not, well, at least you will finally know the truth."

Evelyn ascends the wooden steps, leaving me speechless, wondering what the hell could have happened all those years ago. After staring at the pond with nothing but confusion and wild thoughts to keep me company, I decide to take a walk around the Versailles Garden, to try to clear my head.

As I descend the old stone steps there, the sun blindingly emerges from behind a cloud, making everything in the garden glow with color. But then a single raindrop lands daintily on my cheek. Then another one, this time on my arm. Then another, and another.

In a flash the rain picks up momentum, darkening the old stone steps with gray splotches. The droplets make a crystalline plinking sound against the stones. I jog deeper into the garden, passing the statue of Zeus in the lily pond and ducking behind the giant bronze statue of Franklin Delano Roosevelt. Seeking cover from the rain, I dart beyond a large stone wall.

As I do, a strong hand grabs one arm, pulling me behind a palm tree.

I let out the loudest, most bloodcurdling scream of my life. Then yank my arm free, whirl to confront my attacker, and come face to face with Jared.

He gapes back at me, wide-eyed, as if horrified a sound of that magnitude could force its way from my body.

The heavens open then. A monsoon ensues.

Even underneath a dense stand of palms, we are pelted with what feels like golf ball-sized rain drops smacking down on us. And yet I'm smiling. This came at the perfect moment. I've never been so happy to see rain in my entire life!

Hanging from the branches above us are green dreadlock-looking plants with purple gum-ball shaped berries. The water cascades along the surface of the trees like a series of wall fountains. Even as it pours rays of sun shine through the gaps between fronds, casting streaky patches of light and shadow.

"Holy shit, do have a set of lungs," he finally says, laughing.

"What the hell are you doing back here?" I gasp, heart thumping so hard it hurts my chest.

"It just so happens that this is *my* hiding spot."

"So this is where Mason found you before the wedding."

He avoids my gaze, shifting uneasily. "I'm just going to pretend I don't know what you're talking about." Tiny droplets stick to his lashes. Up close, his honeyed hazel irises gleam. "What about you? What are you doing here?"

We are thoroughly soaked at this point. The mixture of the sun, heat, rain, palm trees, and a secret, hidden location make this spot feel indescribably beautiful. The potential of this moment feels incredibly romantic.

No, wait, what am I saying? I shake that idea out of my head, glancing at the gold band on Jared's left hand. That's a real jolt back to reality.

"I was just looking to take cover until the rain stopped."

He gazes down at me, one hand braced on the closest palm trunk. I feel mesmerized by the closeness of his wet, glistening body.

*Snap out of it, Laina!*

I realize then that his gaze is riveted on the Forget-Me-Not necklace, as if he's carefully inspecting its condition.

He looks up at me, his expression incredibly serious. "I can't believe you still have that."

"I wear it every day," I reply, as we continue to stare into each other's eyes. Then, slowly, carefully, we turn away from each other, shifting our focus to the rain as it resplendently waters the garden.

I wonder why in movies everyone always gets the fairytale ending. What happens to the people in real life who don't? What about me? It's a grandiose notion, I know, but just then I feel as if I'm in the final scene of one of Shakespeare's tragedies.

But any remaining time I have with Jared is precious and limited. So I finally buck up enough courage to blurt out, "Why didn't you ever try to find me?"

He turns his head only slightly in my direction, frowning, but doesn't say a word.

I press on. "Maybe it was just me over-thinking everything back then. Or misreading our feelings for each other, growing up. But I know what you meant to me and . . . and I thought I meant something to you, too."

He turns then and studies my face, then says in a stern tone, "Laina, I *did*."

"You did *what?*" I bark, feeling my hands tremble.

"Oh, Laina, come on. Don't do this."

"I have to. I need to get this stuff off my chest. It might be the only way to move on." My chin quivers, and I manage to force out, "*Please*, Jared."

He sighs uneasily. "For years I tried to find you. Phone books, letters, calls. But . . . nothing. And then I did, sort of." He closes his eyes as if he needs a moment to compose himself. He runs a hand over his forehead, down his face, and under his chin, sluicing away rainwater. "Look, I know you said you haven't spoken to your mom in a long time, so this might come as news to you, but I came to New York about two years ago. Now that I know what happened to Tyler, I realize it must have been just after he died. I managed to track down your mother's address on the internet. She was *not* happy to see me. I had no idea at the time you weren't speaking. She made it perfectly clear you wanted nothing to do with me anymore."

"*What?*" I shout, my shrill voice echoing through the trees. My blood boils, my head aches, as though my eyes are going to burst out of my head from the sheer fury of betrayal. How could my own mother do such a thing? I feel like rushing to the airport, jumping on the next flight out, driving to Manhattan, kicking my mother's door down, and shouting and cursing at her until I have no voice left.

Jared sighs. "She told me you had moved out and were living with your boyfriend. From her tone, I got the sense she wasn't a big fan. I couldn't understand why you wouldn't want to see me, but . . . I also didn't want to cause a problem between you and him."

Woozy now, I press one hand over my stomach and the other against the tree for support. "So, what . . . that was it? You just gave up after that? Man, Mason is right. You really *are* shitty with follow through!"

"Laina, come on. At the time I thought *I* was crazy to figure you still held the same feelings for me as when we were teenagers. Regardless of how I still felt for you. I kept telling myself to forget it, that we were just kids, and it was insane to expect that things would stay the same. After seeing your mom, well, that confirmed it all for me. I was being ridiculous and needed to let the past lie. You were with someone else. For all I knew, *he* was the guy you were always supposed to be with. Not me. I didn't want to be *that* asshole. The one who shows up out of nowhere after an eternity and causes a ruckus, for nothing. We were kids, Laina!"

"What is that supposed to mean? Just because we were teenagers, then it wasn't real?"

"No, no. But after I found your mom, she sat me down and made me realize just how crazy I was acting, to think you and I could just pick up where we left off. It took me a while to come to terms with the fact that you might not be the same girl I remembered, because I sure as hell wasn't the same sixteen-year-old boy you remember."

"But you are! Nothing ever changed for me," I cry.

"No, I'm not the same. Yes, I still love camping and Shakespeare, but that's only one piece of who I am. I've grown up. There are things I've done at this point in my life that I'm not necessarily proud of. I've made mistakes just like everyone else. I've had my heart broken many times and I've broken them, too. I'm *far* from perfect. I don't know why you need to hear me say all this because it doesn't change where we are right now. I'm married, and you're dating my brother. You clearly moved on, Laina, and so have I."

I can't take it anymore. I break down. Tears gush down my face, mixing with the rain, and I don't even try to hold back.

"Laina, please . . . the last thing I want to do is hurt or upset you." Looking distressed, he rakes his fingers through his dripping hair, and circles me nervously.

"Was it really that easy for you," I gasp out through sobs, "to forget about me and move on?"

"No, of course it wasn't!" After a moment he adds, "But then I met Liv."

I hold my breath, trying to gain control over the sobs. My eyelashes feel heavy, sodden with raindrops and tears. I wipe my eyes on one soaked sleeve and make myself stand taller, intent on shaking the weight of grief off my shoulders.

"Well, what about you?" Jared urges.

"What *about* me?"

"Why am I the only one getting the third degree here? Didn't you ever try to find me at all?"

"Ha!" I shout. "Oh wait, I'm sorry: Jared Grant. No, wait. My mistake. I mean JP Hartley. I have no idea why I didn't think to dig up the Pennsylvania White Pages and search for a name I'd never heard of in my entire life!"

"Okay, you win!" he holds both hands up in defeat. "So, are we done now?"

"Oh yeah, we're done. I'm so glad we had this little chat and cleared things up. I think I needed to hear this. I've been clinging to the hope of being with you far too long. Maybe things would've turned out differently if you'd searched me out anyhow, after seeing my mother, just to be sure. Then again, maybe not. But these last few days, being around you, I felt alive in a way that I haven't experienced for so long. Or maybe it's this place creating an illusion."

"Laina..." he cuts in, forehead furrowed, as if deep in thought.

But my speech is not quite over. ". . . or maybe the chemistry I was sensing between us was all in my head, a leftover from the past, and it was just me, refusing to let the fairytale end. But I have to. You love Liv now. And believe me, I hate myself for even feeling this way, especially since she has been nothing but kind to me from the minute we met." I do pause then, taking a breath, before adding, "I don't really have any girlfriends, but if I did they would be like Liv. I see now why you chose her."

"Laina..." he tries again.

I hold up a hand. "Wait! I'm almost done. So, I'm sorry. It was selfish to force you to have this talk. But I needed some answers if I'm ever going to be able to move on. Also I want you to know, if it wasn't meant to work out for us, I'm glad you found someone as wonderful as Liv to share your life. I mean that sincerely. Even though it might not look like it at this moment, I am happy you finally found your soul mate."

Jared stares at me somewhat despondently now. The rain has subsided to a light drizzle, the sun has brightened even more. The timing of this dramatic sun shower was almost too perfect to be real.

With a long last look at Jared's face, I add, "Well, guess that's my cue." I turn away and rush through the Versailles Garden, back toward the villa, not once ever allowing myself to look back.

# Chapter 20

# Farewell

B ack at the villa the living room television is on the Weather
    Channel, volume blaring. I call out and dart from room to
    room, searching, but there is no one to be found. As I dig
around in the couch cushions for the missing remote control, the
meteorologist on the screen begins an update on the hurricane
that's about to make its way up the East Coast. He's predicting it
will be a bad storm – in fact, one for the record books.

"So brace yourselves for the impact expected from Hurricane
Tyler," he announces just then.

My knees give way and I sink onto the nearest couch cushion.
*Tyler? Did he seriously just call it 'Hurricane Tyler'?*

I recall Desi's last reading about my future. *Miss Laina, I'm
afraid what this card is telling me is that fate will be sending quite a storm
your way. You will soon be at the lowest point in your life.*

Could she have meant a *literal* storm? Is it possible Hurricane
Tyler is about to blow through and create even more chaos in my
life? Or was that a warning about its impact on the bookstore, days
from now?

I also remember her saying, *You will know what you must do when
the time comes.*

Well, hello. If that's not clear enough. I need to get off this
island!

Madly dashing through the sliding glass doors, I take the back
stairs two at a time, almost losing my footing and falling down the
steps. I have to find Mason. I must talk to him immediately.

Figuring he's somewhere on the beach, I jog along the white cement path, but stop in my tracks when I hear his familiar sly chuckle coming from the Reef Bar. Nearly tripping over my feet, I whirl and spot Mason and Liv at the bar, sharing conch bites and laughing as the bartender sets freshly-blended frozen drinks in front of them.

Slowing my steps, taking deep breaths, I approach the bar. When I catch Liv's eye, at first she smiles and greets me, but her look switches to concern when she takes in my sodden clothes and strained expression. "Is everything okay?" she asks.

"What's up?" Mason leans back on his tall bar chair, popping an entire conch bite into his mouth.

"Mason, I need to talk to you," I reply, in a low tone. "Right now."

Taking a leisurely pull on his straw, he gulps a mouthful of frozen drink, then cringes, muttering, "Brain freeze." Wincing, he rises from his seat, turns to Liv and says, "I'll be back. Now don't eat all those yourself."

She chuckles, "Can't promise anything."

I lead Mason to the villa through the back doors, though he trails a few steps behind me the entire way. Once the door swings shut behind us, I ask him to take a seat on the couch. He does, eyeing me strangely. I wonder if he senses what is coming.

I stand in front of him, shifting from one foot to the other, my fingers twisting together. "Mason, I have to go home."

He stares with one raised eyebrow, silent, one side of his jaw working as if he's using his tongue to dislodge something stuck in between his teeth. "What're you talking about?" he finally says. "We have two whole days left."

"I know." I hang my head and bite my lower lip.

"Wait a second," he mutters, and scoots to the edge of the couch. "You're ending this."

"Mason, look," I begin.

His expression twists into a glower and his narrowed eyes sweep around the villa as if he's looking for something to throw at me.

"I can't tell you how much I appreciate you bringing me here to meet your family, and enjoy the island. But deep down, you must know by now we just aren't right for each other."

His eyes dart back to meet mine. His voice is croaky yet firm. "Laina, don't do this."

"Mason, you're a smart, funny, wonderful man, and I want you to find happiness. I don't want to waste any more of your time. And I'm so sorry to do this here, but it just didn't feel right to let it slide until we got home. You're probably really angry now, and you have every right to be. I haven't been honest about my feelings. As much as I like you, as great as you are, I still know the way I feel isn't what it should be. I hate to cause hurt to anyone. I'm so sorry, Mason."

He exhales a long, deep breath and drags both hands anxiously down his face, as if trying to wake himself up.

I wait, staring at him, mystified. *Is* he mad? Is he going to yell? Try to convince me to change my mind?

His gaze is on the glass coffee table in the center of the room. His eyes glaze over, as if he's gone into a trance. Deeply sighing once more, he slaps both hands against his thighs and abruptly rises from the couch. Taking three steps toward me, until he is standing only a few inches away, he pulls me into a long, tight hug, kisses my forehead, and whispers, "It's okay."

Then he releases me and strides off through the villa, closing the front door softly but firmly behind him.

*Wait. What just happened?*

Unsure about whether he is taking a detour before heading back to the Reef Bar, and his drink with Liv, I rush through the back door hoping to beat him there. His seat is still empty when I arrive. Liv is swirling her semi-frozen drink with her straw. She doesn't see me approach the bar this time, so I call her name.

Slightly startled, she spins on her tall bar chair and reaches out for my arm. "Is everything okay?"

"I just came to tell you g-goodbye," I say, my voice splintering as the words pass my lips.

Her face falls. "You're leaving now?" She glances behind me, frowning in confusion. "But . . . where's Mason? Did something happen?"

"We aren't together anymore. As great as he is, we just aren't right for each other. I'm sorry to do this now but . . . I can't stay."

She gapes at me, then wraps both arms around my shoulders. "Oh honey, I completely understand."

As we end the embrace I say, "I just want you to know I'm so glad I had a chance to get to know you. You're delightful. I hope that you and Jared have an amazing life together."

"Ehk, what?" She gives out a light chuckle, and tilts her head, looking puzzled. "Did you just say Jared?" She snorts. "No one ever calls him that."

*Fuck.*

Pinching my lips shut, I nod, then nervously cackle. All I can muster is, "Yep. Right."

Luckily, she doesn't seem fazed, just offers another hug and wishes me a safe flight home.

*Phew!*

Slightly jittery on the trek back to the room, I can't help but think of all the ways my stupid name slip could have been so much worse.

I enter the bedroom to pack my belongings. Skimming through the printed checklist Preston prepared, to make sure I don't leave anything behind, I realize I can't locate my favorite green cardigan anywhere. I peruse the entire villa, but no green sweater in sight. Then it hits me: I loaned it to Amelia last night, when she was cold.

I head out the back doors of the villa just as Becky whizzes in, drinking a big strawberry smoothie.

"Hey, you haven't seen Amelia, have you?" I ask.

"Yeah, actually. She went into her room a little while ago. Not sure if she's still in there, but you can check."

"Great, thanks." I slip out the back, close the door behind me, and descend the back stairs to villa room twenty-three. I knock on the back door to Amelia's villa, the closest entrance when taking the back stairs. I wait for a moment, then knock again. No answer.

I slide the glass door open a crack and yell in, "Hey, Amelia, it's Laina. You in here?"

"Come in!" she yells.

I enter, figuring she's in the front bedroom, where music is being played. The bedroom door is closed so I knock. I hear her say, "Come in," over the music.

"Hey, it's Laina. I was wondering if you have my…"

My mind goes blank. I can't formulate more words to finish my sentence, because right in front of me, Amelia is lying naked on the bed, beneath Adam. To top it off, the sleeve of my green cardigan is sticking out from underneath her back.

"Oh my God!" I shriek, horrified yet unable to peel my eyes away. I realize I must not have heard accurately when I thought she said to come in. Clapping a hand over my eyes, I shout, "Oh, God, I'm so sorry! Best of luck to you both! Keep the sweater."

I rush to close the door and sprint back to the villa, head invaded with sweaty, tangled, naked images of Amelia and Adam. With superhuman speed, I finish packing and speed off to the reception desk to arrange for a cab to take me straight to the airport.

# Chapter 21

# Hurricane Season

The airport is jammed with people hauling suitcases, carrying crying children, waiting in queues to check in. It's complete madness, but at least there's air conditioning. I wait in line for over an hour before I get to speak to a ticket agent. There is no way I can keep my original booking and have to sit next to Mason on the flight back to Newark. It's unimaginable to comprehend how awkward that trip would be.

A young Bahamian woman in her early thirties, whose name tag reads *Jodi*, greets me with a soft smile. Her thick black hair is pulled back in a braided ponytail, her wide brown eyes look sympathetic.

She is about my age, so I attempt to gain some sympathy by explaining my current state of affairs.

The ticket agent is apologetic. "I'm sorry, miss, but all flights are full. People trying to get back to de states before de storm hits."

"Are you sure there's nothing at all?"

Yes, Miss. I can truly appreciate your situation but there are no available seats on any departing flights today. I can put you on standby, but who knows how long a wait you will have," she says. "Are you sure you don't want to keep your existing flight?"

"I'm positive. I'd rather wait for another. Thank you."

I numbly stroll around the airport until I find a seat tucked out of the way of all the people weaving back and forth, calling to each other, and talking on cell phones. It appears I may be here for a while so I might as well try to get comfortable. Luckily there are televisions scattered throughout the airport, each displaying a different news station, so I can track the storm.

The ticker scrolling at the bottom of one of the news channels reads: *HURRICANE TYLER PUMMELS EAST COAST*. It shows images of trees in Georgia violently swaying in an intense wind. It appears forceful enough to wrench them straight out of the ground. The torrential rain is so severe, the blurry gray landscape shown on the large flatscreen bolted to the wall is barely discernible.

To avoid becoming even more obsessed and anxious, I turn away from the televisions. Slumping in my seat, I wish I had a book to distract me. I don't even want to look at my phone, in case anyone has texted to chew me out, though only Mason has my number. At last I reach for an abandoned magazine on the seat beside mine, and peruse every inch of every page.

When I come to the end I look up and realize just how slowly time is passing. I sigh and flip back to page one.

* * *

The hours pass with excruciating slowness. Gradually the clouds that are visible through the big plate glass windows darken. A while later it begins to drizzle. I drift in and out of sleep in my hard plastic airport seat throughout the night. Each time my eyelids flicker open, I check the Weather Channel or CNN, whatever is up on the TV, and each time, I'm fearful of what I may see on the screen. By the middle of the night, the hurricane has officially struck New York City. Newscasters drone on about how the mayor has ordered an immediate, mandatory evacuation.

The next morning nearly every flight out to the upper eastern coast is cancelled. I watch footage of Hurricane Tyler's aftermath, feeling utterly helpless, recalling with shame how I blew off Preston's concerns, telling him they always blow these storms out of proportion.

Not this time.

I attempt to call him numerous times but the towers must be down. All my calls go immediately to voice mail.

I'm sickened by the clips of Staten Island's immense destruction shown on the screen. The streets are inundated with murky, grimy water. Huge trees lie at crazy angles, uprooted and tossed around as if they were Mother Nature's playthings. Some homes are entirely destroyed, blown to the foundations. And most chilling of all, the rising death toll. It's unbearable to watch my own beloved island being torn apart by nature's wrath.

I should have listened to Preston. I should have left the Bahamas when he insisted. I've let him down once again, for my own selfish reasons.

After waiting on standby for a day and a half I'm called to the ticket desk and handed a new ticket to go home. At this point, I haven't showered in two days, my clothes are rumpled and creased, I'm sore, bleary, and exhausted.

At last I board and take my seat by the window, peering out at the airport as the plane sits idling on the tarmac. I'm suddenly hit with an overpowering, unsettling realization that absolutely everything is over – any possibility of a Happily Ever After with Jared, no more cherished friendship with Preston, my mistaken relationship with Mason, the whole trip to the Bahamas that reunited Jared and me, and, finally, Hurricane Tyler.

The storm has passed and I'm returning home, but who knows what I will find? What horrors will I see once I arrive at my front door? Clearly the life I had before this trip no longer exists. Like Staten Island, I will no longer be the same.

I wonder if I'm even strong enough to get through it alone. Even as this fearful thought sinks in, I realize the truth: Whether or not I believe I'm strong enough to handle what lies ahead, all on my own, I simply must do it. And then and there, I resolve that I will.

* * *

I call a Lyft to take me home from the airport in Newark. The sky is cloudy but at least the rain has ceased. Harry, the driver, is a chatty father of four in his mid-fifties with thick gray hair and a kind yet exhausted expression. He gives me a blow by blow of the storm and what he has been faced with over the last couple of days. Fortunately his family members and their homes haven't been affected too badly, aside from some flood damage.

But, he informs me, "Lots of folks I know were not so lucky." It's almost unbearable to hear some of his stories of innocent lives taken, entire families losing their homes, and their pets and possessions.

The drive through Staten Island after crossing the Goethals Bridge is a bit like meandering through a mythical labyrinth. Many streets are blocked off with yellow caution tape. Police officers, the National Guard, and firemen patrol the area. Massive trees are yanked from the ground, roots and all, just like I saw on the news. Many others have fallen on lawns and driveways, or across streets, blocking the way. Some are hopelessly snarled in downed telephone wires.

One place I pass on Tysens Lane has been so unfortunate as to have a big tree in their front lawn fall right onto the roof of the house, causing the entire second story of the home to cave in. Sidewalks are cracked and lifted as if by an earthquake. Street signs lean crookedly out of the ground. Mounds of debris, ruined furniture and clothing, and piles of scattered garbage cover the sidewalks, as people somberly clear their homes. Down every street stand literal walls of debris left on the curb.

There are many people who appear to be just wandering the streets, some no doubt looking to help neighbors in need. Help stations have been set up for donations to assist those who have lost everything. Some gas stations are also closed off with yellow caution tape, while at others—the ones still functioning—a long line of people stand equipped with gas cans, patiently waiting, no doubt praying they will be able to reach the front of the line and not be turned away because the station has run out of gasoline. Some of these lines are several blocks long.

"This might sound weird," says Harry, glancing at me in the rearview, "but it's times like this that make me proud to be a New Yorker."

"Not weird at all," I assure him.

Because I know exactly what he means. No matter how bad things may seem, it's a beautiful thing to see the community pulling together as a whole to survive and recover. During times like this, it doesn't matter if two people are strangers. At the end of the day, they will have bonded and have helped each other through one of the most difficult times in their lives.

Harry manages to get me about two streets away from my apartment. I wish him the best, tap out a big tip on my phone, and grab my luggage from the trunk. Wheeling my suitcase along, only a block from my apartment I'm stopped by a police officer.

He looks stressed, the puffy, dark circles under his eyes indicating he probably hasn't slept in days. "I'm sorry, Miss, but I can't let you pass. The next block over is a flood zone. It hasn't been secured yet."

"But that's where I live," I gasp.

"Sorry, about that. You'll have to find somewhere else to stay. Maybe a parent or a friend's home," he remarks.

I don't answer. My bleak expression probably says it all. I'm alone.

He smiles apologetically, and starts to turn away, to halt someone else.

"Can I. . . ." I try not to cry. Instead I take a slow breath to calm myself. "Do you happen to know if I can get through to the Hylan Plaza?"

"Yeah, there you can get through. I'd stay clear of the back roads, though. They're such a mess I honestly can't say which are closed off at this point. Stick to Hylan Boulevard."

I thank him and decamp on the longer trek to Viola's Hideaway, dragging my suitcase over bumpy, broken sidewalks and newly-opened potholes. As I enter the Hylan Plaza, at first glance the bookstore appears unscathed.

I hold my breath as I march through the vast parking lot to the front door of the bookstore.

*Please, let everything be all right.*

My hand trembles as I take hold of the door handle. I turn the knob. It's unlocked. I'm unsure if that's a good thing or a bad thing. I pull the door open, leaving my suitcase on the sidewalk by the door.

I cautiously step onto the top landing of the bookstore. To my right is the wheelchair ramp. Directly in front of me, the three steps down to the main level. I hear an ominous sound, one any bookstore owner dreads: a faint, continuous trickle of water.

Those three steps are mostly submerged beneath dark, murky, stinking water. Books have toppled off shelves into the flood. Loose papers and other debris float like doleful little boats on a black sea of despair. The nice, comfy furniture is submerged and destroyed. A few side windows are broken.

Stunned, feeling trapped in a bad dream, I unsteadily wade down the steps through the bitterly cold water, which at the bottom reaches the tops of my thighs.

As I take another step I kick something. A trade paperback copy of *Twelfth Night* lies sodden and swollen, half submerged. My breathing accelerates. I feel lightheaded, unable to hold my grief in any longer.

I don't cry this time, though. I scream. Long and loudly, forcing out of my body all the misery I feel now, all that I have felt over the past week.

Finally I stop, out of breath, unable to even pull in enough air to fuel another wail. Unable to stay upright any longer, I drop onto the middle steps, not even caring that it puts me chest deep in stagnant, unpleasantly pungent water.

My entire world has truly crumbled in the last few days. Desi was right yet again. She warned me this was coming. I think back to the wedding. What else did she say about the storm?

In a flash, I recall her face, her tone, pretty much the exact words.

*Whatever you do, don't let it break your spirit. It will seem like giving up is the easiest path, but you must fight past it and persevere. I believe you possess the strength within you. Pull yourself out of the abyss. Be the person Tyler believes you to be."*

Just then comes a crash, followed by a loud splashing from the back.

I abruptly stand, water streaming off me, attempting to compose myself. It must be Preston.

A moment later, he wades from his office, soaked and filthy in a pair of sodden sweat pants and the 'I love Mr. Darcy' t-shirt I bought for his birthday last year.

"Oh, it's just you," he mutters in a monotone. "I thought some crazy person broke in and started screamin'."

We stare at each other for a moment before wildly sloshing through the water, pushing through any debris in our way, to grab hold and cling to each other.

I sob, "I'm sorry! I'm so sorry!" Then incoherently wail, clawing and clutching at the back of his shirt.

"Okay, okay, let it all out," he urges. "That is exactly how I felt when I first set eyes on this mess."

Once I calm down, Preston holds me at arm's length, though close enough to allow me to still cling to his shirt. "Laina, honey, yah look like shit and yah smell like Hell."

I snigger. "Yeah, well, you don't exactly smell like attar of roses, either."

He wipes the tears from my face. I tell him how happy I am to see him. Then I start to apologize for what happened with Jack, all over again.

He holds up a hand to stop me. "Later. We have bigger things to worry about right now."

"R-right." I try hard to paste a brave face back on. "Well, get me a damned mop and a freaking bucket. It's time for me to help clean up this mess."

# Chapter 22

# Aftermath

Preston and I run to five different stores to buy surgical masks and elbow-length rubber gloves. Who knows what the hell is actually in the sullied water swallowing Viola's Hideaway? We don't need toxic crud splashing into our eyes, up our noses, or into our mouths. First we have to tackle draining as much water as possible from the bookstore.

The second we get back we dive right in, so to speak. Luckily Preston is prepared. He has his parents' pump, a generator, and their fifty-foot garden hose – a relief, since I'd been under the assumption we were going to have to form a bucket-brigade to manually bail it out, Jack-and-Jill style. It's a huge relief that this, in fact, is not the case. It still takes many hours to pump the water out, along with clumps of dirt and wet leaves that have somehow managed to get inside the building.

After the standing water is gone, it's easier to assess the damage. Unfortunately, the place doesn't look good. Preston and I keep on, and don't stop until eight o'clock that night. Even so, it looks as though we have a week of heavy work ahead, just to haul out debris, mud, waterlogged books, never mind cleaning and renovation.

Preston groans, "I could go for a deep-tissue massage right about now." He hunches over a couch and rubs his back.

Sluggishly, I mosey over to the purple velvet couch adjacent. Just as I slink onto one cushion, he warns, "I wouldn't sit there."

Too late. The cushion gives off a deep, ominous *squish*, followed by an outpouring of at least a gallon of frigid, stagnant water.

He sighs and mutters, "Never mind." But he droops with sheer exhaustion, staring at the fresh puddle on the floor. "Let that spot air dry. I'm not wipin' it up. I have no energy left at all."

"I know. I turned into a prune about six hours ago. Guess a little more water won't make much difference." I shiver and settle deeper, resting my feet on the coffee table in front of me, looking around at our abominable bookstore. It's hardly recognizable anymore. I'm living in a nightmare – an exceptionally cold, soggy one.

I actually pinch my own arm just in case this *is* a terrible dream I'm trapped inside. But no, I don't bolt upright in bed, saved. Clearly I am awake.

On the table beside me lies a broken picture frame which I accidentally stepped on while inspecting my demolished office. Behind the spider web of cracked glass is a photo of Jared, Tyler, and me taken on a childhood camping trip. We posed with freshly made S'mores, widely grinning, mouths smeared with melted chocolate and marshmallow.

"This has been the day from Hell." Preston shakes his head and looks around. "I sure hope we can bounce back from this."

"We?" I ask, taken aback.

His looks surprised. "Yeah, why?"

"I guess . . . well, I kind of assumed you didn't want to have anything to do with me anymore. Not after what happened with Jack, and all."

"If that were true, would I be here right now? Let's not mention it anymore, okay?" He sighs. "We should probably call it a night."

"So, did you find a new place then?" I ask, half-hoping he's going to say that he didn't move after all.

"Yeah. A little small, but I like it. On Nelson Avenue." He shakes his head as if he's just realized something. "Sorry, I forgot to ask how the apartment came through. Did you check it yet?"

"No. The street was blocked off when I got there. If it's flooded I'll run out to Walgreens and see if they have a blow-up raft I can sleep in," I joke.

Preston shakes his head. "Absolutely not. I won't allow that. You can crash on my couch."

Before I have a chance to respond, I hear footsteps tapping closer, out on the sidewalk. My gaze shifts to the open front door. I do a double-take because I could swear Desi Chase is breezing past, holding a young girl's hand. But on second look I see my eyes are playing tricks. It's just some anonymous mother and daughter, no one I know. Good thing I realized it, or would have made a mad dash for the front door, only to be embarrassed by a case of mistaken identity.

I shake my head, smile, and turn my attention back to Preston. "Thanks for offering, but I think I'll be okay."

"Well I can't let you sleep on a raft in your flooded living room. What are you gonna do if you need to use the bathroom? You gonna buy a paddle too?"

"First of all, you know I'm not going to actually sleep on a raft." I snort. "And I can't tell you how much it means, you offering to take me in for the night, but I'm going to pass."

"But is the street opened up yet? What if you aren't able to get back to the apartment?"

"I don't think I'm going back there tonight, whether or not the street is secure."

"I don't understand." He peers at me intently. "Where else are you gonna go?"

# Chapter 23

# The Murray Hill Project

For at least fifteen minutes I stand solemnly outside the door to my mother's apartment in Murray Hill.

Not ringing the bell or knocking. Just staring.

I'm unsure of how I'm going to handle this, and of how she's going to react when she sees me there. Will I yell? Will I cry? This exhausted, I have no idea how I'll respond. I may simply slither to the floor, curl in a fetal position, and take a nap. It feels like ages since we've seen each other. We barely spoke at the cemetery. She might slam the door in my face, for all I know.

A few neighbors see me standing outside her door — some pass me more than once. I don't recognize any of them. They must be relatively new neighbors. I'm pretty sure, though, they all think I'm a crazy person who wandered into the building. Even though I greet them with a tired "Hello", I still receive wary side-eye glances. I should buck up enough courage to knock on my mother's door before someone calls the cops on the dirty, wet, crazy lady lurking in the hallway.

My first knock is so faint I can hardly hear it myself. Little by little I urge myself to keep on, knocking harder each time. Suddenly, the front door swings open with some force, catching me by surprise. My mother stands in the foyer, wearing a pair of light pink pajama pants and a white tank top. Her straight brown hair is tied loosely into a ponytail. She and I look so much alike, now that I'm getting older. For one thing, she's kept herself in fantastic shape. It's almost like looking into the face of my future — at least I hope it is. Her mouth falls open. She is clearly amazed to see me standing in her hallway. I figure it's also due to seeing me in such a filthy state. It probably looks as if I've been living on the street the last few months.

I'm feeling so many emotions right now that I don't seem to know how to act or what to say. If this were a couple of days ago I'd be screaming my head off right now.

"Can I come in?" I flatly ask.

She takes a deep breath. Her chin quivers. Then she throws both arms around me and pulls me inside.

"You probably shouldn't have hugged me. I'm pretty gross right now."

She laughs and shakes her head. I explain about the bookstore clean up.

Even though it does seem slightly awkward being around her after all this time, she tries her best to make me feel at home. She grabs a towel from the linen closet and insists I shower while she orders Chinese takeout.

My stomach growls with great appreciation.

The hot shower rejuvenates me, even though the sodden skin on my fingers and feet feels as though it is shriveling away to nothing. I blow-dry my hair and put on a clean pair of pajamas still in my suitcase from the Bahamas.

I feel like a new person then. In a way, I suppose I am. Opening the bathroom door, I glance across the hall at Tyler's closed bedroom door. I step out and lay a hand on the doorknob, hesitant at first, but curious as to whether the room has been kept the same. I open the door, flick on the light, and smile.

Not a single thing has been taken out or moved. The faded jungle-green walls and gray down comforter feel like home. I run my fingers over his writing desk. It's surprisingly dust free. Upon closer inspection I notice his entire bedroom is impeccably clean. It looks freshly vacuumed, in fact.

My mother clears her throat from behind, and I spin to look at her, feeling guilty. "Sorry, I, um, I just…"

She shakes her head and closes her eyes, then shrugs as though me being here is no big deal. "Perfectly fine."

There's a fraught silence after that. Then she attempts to change the subject. "I just put fresh sheets on your bed."

*Wow, I still have a bed!*

"Thank you" I sweep a hand over Tyler's comforter.

"Unless you'd like to sleep in here?"

I take a quick peep back at her. "Would that be okay?"

"Of course." She nods.

Just then there's a knock at the front door. She perks up. "Ah! Our Chinese food is here. I have to grab my wallet." She scurries off.

Dropping onto the edge of Tyler's bed, I recall the first time I slept in here, right after we'd moved in. It wasn't long after Jared and Evelyn moved away and my father had left my mom. We were only living here for about a month when I woke drenched in sweat from a terrible nightmare.

In the dream, I was all by myself at the beach and, for some reason, it was the middle of the night. I was stranded, swimming frantically, way out in a black ocean, and no one was around. The beach was deserted, too. No matter how hard I kicked my legs and propelled my tiny arms through the water, I couldn't get any closer to shore. The ocean kept pulling me out deeper and deeper. Soon numerous tall gray, leathery shark fins surfaced all around. They circled me, and no matter how hard I tried to choke out a scream, no sound escaped.

My bedroom was just down the hall from Tyler's, so I'd sprinted as fast as I could and scrambled into bed with him. Most big brothers probably would have rolled their eyes and told their kid sister to go back to their own bed. Not Tyler. He let me sleep beside him the whole night, telling me repeatedly that everything would be okay.

My mother calls me to join her in the living room for dinner. Slowly, reluctantly, I leave Tyler's bedroom to join her.

She tells me to have a seat on her new cocoa leather couch. "Can I get you anything to drink?"

"Just water, thanks." I sit back, making myself comfortable. She returns with a glass of water with ice, then darts back into the kitchen. I tap my foot lightly on the floor and take a swig of water, then set it on the coffee table near the takeout bag.

She returns, carefully carrying two cups of steaming green tea and sets them on coasters on the table. "Now it's a real Chinese meal," she says.

The large flatscreen mounted on the wall above a dark mahogany cabinet shows more news footage of Hurricane Tyler's aftermath. I wonder if Mom finds the hurricane's name ironic, considering our current situation, but I don't quite have the nerve to ask.

As she removes several white cardboard take-out containers from the oil-stained brown paper bag, I thank her for letting me stay the night.

She shrugs slightly. "Of course. You're my daughter."

I pick up my chopsticks, then set them down again. I follow with the one question that's burned inside me for the last two years, ever since my brother died. "Mom, do you resent me for what happened to Tyler?" It's all I can do to force the words out. My pulse quickens as I anxiously await her response.

She stops opening food containers and looks over, pain in her eyes. She takes a moment as if trying to figure out the best possible way to answer my question. "At one point I did. But then the resentment faded a bit. I was still angry, though." She shrugs again. "Suppose I still am, a little. It was a very tough time, Laina. But, no, I don't resent you anymore. No matter what, you're my daughter and I love you very much." She follows this with a gentle smile, then digs into a container of beef and broccoli.

I wonder why she keeps repeating "you're my daughter", as if we could both somehow forget. Maybe she's just trying to remind herself she actually *has* a daughter. Or perhaps even still trying to fling some guilt my way for staying away so long.

"Okay, then . . . why'd you turn Jared away when he came looking for me, after Tyler died?"

I know the question startles her because the piece of broccoli pinched between her chopsticks slips and plops into her lap. She fumbles to scoop it up as she snatches her napkin from the coffee table. She dips the napkin into my water glass, trickling drops onto the carpet, then wildly, unsuccessfully attempts to wipe her pants clean of brown sauce.

"How . . . how did you…" Then it hits her. "You *saw* him?" Her tone as incredulous as if I'd just told her I hitched a ride in a canoe with The Jersey Devil across the Hudson River.

I silently regard her, patiently waiting for an answer.

"I…I only did what I thought was best."

*Oh, really?*

"For yourself," I hiss. "Because of what happened between you and Evelyn."

Clutching her chest, she gasps. "You know about that?"

"I have a hunch. But I want to hear the whole story from you. And I want the truth."

She looks dazed, staring at the gray rug at our feet. She suddenly stands, excuses herself, and leaves the room. I wait as patiently as I can for her to return.

When she does, she takes a seat next to me and holds out her hand, clutching a small stack of discolored white envelopes rubber-banded together.

Reaching for them, I ask, "What's this?"

"Love letters…from William."

*William.* This is what I was afraid of. My own mother is the reason Jared was taken away from me. To hear it confirmed, though, is another feeling entirely. I can't believe it, but it seems to be true. Jared's father and my mother had an affair.

"It began around the time you graduated from middle school. William and I truly loved each other, Laina. Then he got sick."

She pauses, looking stricken, as if all of this just happened last week.

"After he passed away, Evelyn found the letters I wrote to him while she was going through his things. She confronted me. Well, I could hardly deny it. And then, within a few days, she and Jared were gone. Your father and I tried our best to move past it, but he felt he couldn't trust me after that, so I didn't blame him for leaving. I know I should've told you sooner, but . . . I was so ashamed. I didn't want you to look at me the way you are right now. I knew how much you cared about Jared, and I didn't want you to hate me, so I hid everything. I lied. I wanted the truth to disappear. That's why we moved into this apartment after your father left."

She hangs her head for a moment, before meeting my gaze again.

"So then why did you send him away?" I ask again, bitterness hardening my voice.

"When I saw Jared standing at the front door, I panicked. I was afraid Evelyn had told him what I'd done. Then, if he found you, what would stop him from telling you everything? I know an apology probably doesn't mean much now, but I'm so, so sorry. I hope someday you can find a way to forgive me. I know I ruined your childhood and Tyler's because of my own weakness. I'm the reason our family was torn apart, and I've had to learn to live with that."

She drops her head again. "Well, now that you know everything, there's nothing preventing you from reconnecting with him. I guess I shouldn't be surprised he still tracked you down."

I shake my head. "He didn't. A few months back I began dating someone. His name's Mason. We aren't together anymore, but, I was invited to his stepbrother JP's wedding."

She looks at me, frowning. "Um . . . JP?"

"Short for Jared Parker." I clear my throat. "Mason is Evelyn's stepson."

My mom looks utterly baffled. She stares at me as blankly as if I've been speaking Latin and she's wracking her brain trying to translate.

"I can't even express how angry I was when I found out you came between us. You're my mother! No matter how upset you were with me, or how ashamed of yourself, you still kept us apart. I can't pretend things are okay now, because I'm still trying to process everything that happened. Jared was all I ever wanted, and now he's married to someone else. Gone! No matter what happens next, it won't change the past, though. And I don't want to be angry at you anymore."

I do want to forgive her, just like she's trying hard to forgive me for my part in what happened to Tyler. I can no longer harp on all the things I'm unable to change. I must accept what is. So I can either hold this against her for the rest of my life, or take the high road and learn to forgive. And, hopefully, over time, rebuild a relationship with her. I know it's what Tyler would have wanted.

Taking her hand, I croak, "Mom, I need you to swear there won't be any more secrets from here on out."

"I swear. I swear!" she cries, squeezing my hand as her tears fall onto it. Her chin quivers but she forces a smile. "I can do that."

# Chapter 24

# After the Rain There Is Always Sunshine

As I settle into bed in Tyler's room, my mother knocks on the door and enters to say goodnight. It's like I'm a kid all over again, Mom tucking me in before I fall asleep.

She takes a seat on the edge of the bed, clasping her hands, her face contemplative.

"Honey..." she begins, but then pauses, gets up and steps over to Tyler's old desk. She opens the middle drawer, pulls something out, and returns to me. "Every couple of weeks I clean both of your old bedrooms. I've gone through his drawers hundreds of times. But the other day when I was in here I came across something I never saw before. It's funny you're here now, after I just found this."

She holds out a small white envelope with my name written on it in Tyler's familiar, chicken-scratchy handwriting.

Stunned, I ask, "Did you read it?"

"No. See? It's still sealed."

My hand shakes as I take the envelope and stare at my name written on it in blue ink. What kind of letter would he have written to me, and why? How strange . . . how eerie that, after two whole years, she just came across it now.

She rubs my arm affectionately, then leans in and kisses my forehead before heading off to bed.

Carefully, I slide a finger under the flap so I can open the envelope without tearing it. Then I begin to read, hearing his voice in my head as if he's saying the words to me at this moment, and I can't help but tenderly smile.

*Hey Scutch,*

*If you're reading this, it's probably because I'm no longer here. Either that, or you're snooping in my desk again. Either way, I can explain.*

*I couldn't sleep tonight. I kept thinking about when we were kids. Remember that day at Point Pleasant beach? I know you do. I still don't believe you saw an actual shark, by the way…but when your head didn't pop up out of the water I really thought we'd lost you.*

*Anyhow, tonight I started thinking about what would happen if that ever actually did happen.*

*You and I are so different when it comes to dealing with disappointment. I always take things as they come. But I know how sensitive you are. Things haven't always been easy for you. Well…for both of us. But you seem to be affected so much more. You hold onto everything, carrying every bit of heartache on your shoulders.*

*So if something were to happen to me—knock on wood—I just wanted you to know this: No matter what, no matter where fate leads you, even if it's not where you expect, even if you don't end up with the person you hope to (you know who I mean), please let yourself be open to still being happy. You can spend your whole life searching unsuccessfully, or choose to be happy every single day.*

*Never stop smiling that same loser smile, and never stop seeing the beauty in things. Lately I kind of feel like you're slipping away from me.*

*Life will always find ways to try and drag you down. Don't let it. You're stronger than that. You're stronger than you know, even if you don't think so. Show the world what an amazingly annoying pain in the ass you truly are.*

*And please, never stop believing in fate. Anything is possible.*

*I love you. I will always love you.*

*Tyler.*

*P.S. Just remember, after the rain there is always sunshine.*

# Chapter 25

# Brighter Than the Sun

I never fall into a deep sleep during the night. I can't help but think about the past, about everything I've gone through the last two years. Although my body is exhausted, my brain refuses to settle down. So, when I hear birds chirping outside Tyler's bedroom window, and the garbage trucks coming to pick up trash left out on the curb from the night before, I figure it's a decent enough hour to grab the day by its balls.

To start the morning off, I whip up eggs and toast for my mother and me. Once the coffee brews, she emerges from her bedroom, as if following its tempting scent. For a moment she stares as though she's forgotten I stayed last night. But as we chat and eat breakfast, gradually things feel more normal, as though it *is* getting better between the two of us. And for the first time in a long time, I'm at peace. After breakfast I thank her, kiss her goodbye, and promise to call next week and meet for dinner.

When I arrive at Viola's Hideaway the front door is unlocked again. It's quiet inside, and the bookstore smells dank and musty. The old oak floor will unquestionably need to be ripped up. A fresh roll of colossal black commercial garbage bags lies on the checkout counter.

Preston strolls out of his office wearing a pair of dark drawstring pants and a t-shirt that says, *Gay and Fabulous*. He practically jumps out of his skin when he sees me, pouncing backward like a startled cat. "What the fuck are yah doin' here so early?" he shouts, gripping his chest, eyes bulging in alarm. "Fuckin' scared me!"

"Sorry. I was up insanely early. Figured I might as well get started on the cleaning."

"Oh. Okay. Wow." He appears pleased. "Good, that's great. Just make sure you make more noise when you come in next time. I don't normally carry around a change of underwear."

"Sure thing. Nice shirt, by the way."

He glances down and shrugs. "Yeah, it's been sittin' in my drawer for years. Thought I'd dig it out. Comfy is my new way of life."

"Does this have anything to do with Jack?" I pose, pulling a garbage bag from the roll.

"Could we not talk about that?" He sulks for a minute behind the checkout counter, then grabs two fresh surgical masks and hands me one. "Anyhow, I'm fine." He puts his mask on. "So where did you end up crashing last night?"

"Mom's apartment." I pull the mask up over my nose and mouth.

"Whoa. That's seriously the last thing I expected to come out of your mouth. How did it go?"

I give a full recounting of last night with my mother. Of course, he's stunned to learn of the love affair, and the appearance of a secret letter from Tyler.

At around ten o'clock in the morning, as I'm cleaning out the supply room in the back, I come across my old boom box and a stack of CDs. Amazingly, the boom box doesn't appear to have any water damage. I carry it all to the checkout counter. After scrounging for a working outlet to plug it into, I click the ON button and am pleased to see it still works. At first, I flip the radio to *Z100* and crank the volume. Preston and I dance around belting out tunes as we sort and mop and scrub and fill garbage bag after garbage bag, dragging them out to sit at the curb.

On about the fifteenth trip we stop and take a moment to rest.

"As much as this sucks, at least it's nice outside," he says, wiping a slick of sweat from his forehead, and drying his damp arm on the side of his t-shirt. Just then, a few drops of rain fall. In a panic, he yanks his surgical mask off and peers despairingly up at the sun. He balls one hand into a fist and propels that arm into the air as if he's John Bender at the end of *The Breakfast Club*, shouting, "Really? Are you friggin' kidding me?" He glares at me. "Son of a bitch! As if we haven't had *enough* rain!"

Even as it falls, the sun holds up its vibrant head, creating a shimmer on the wet pavement. I recall Desi telling my fortune, and the sun shower in the Bahamas with Jared. Then it hits me: The final words on Tyler's letter.

*P.S. Just remember, after the rain there is always sunshine.*

Preston stares at me, looking baffled. Then shouts, "Why the *hell* are you smiling like a complete friggin' idiot?" Then he shouts at the sky again, "We don't need more water! Everything is soggy enough!"

"I'm smiling because it's a sun shower. Everything will be okay."

He lets his upraised fist drop to his side with a dull slap. "Yeah, how so?"

I say matter of factly, "After the rain there is always sunshine."

Preston screws up his face as if he smells something awful. "You're delusional. Your brain has gone mushy from all the damp!"

The rain abruptly stops, and the sun beats down even more brightly. I whirl to grin at Preston. "Told you so."

He squints as if he can't comprehend me at all. "Since when did you become such an optimist?"

"When did you stop?" I retort.

He looks as though he's not sure how to answer, nor does he want to.

"Come on," I urge, tugging on his arm. "Let's get back to work."

He trails along behind me. "And since when did you get so gung-ho about workin'?"

I laugh and turn back to him. "If you give me a chance, I think you'll find plenty of new surprises."

"Has an alien taken over your body?"

"Why, because I'm starting to take control of my life?" I pose like a model, pleased with myself.

"Yeah . . . it's like I don't even know who you are. Don't get me wrong, it's terrific. Just...strange."

"Maybe I'm growing up. Better late than never! I may not have the happily ever after I used to believe in, but I won't let that stop me from being happy. Anyhow, everything will work out the way it's supposed to."

We have reached the front door to the store by then. Preston grabs my arm. "When did you come across this whole new outlook? A visit from your Fairy Godmother?"

He looks so funny, I have to laugh. "No, a more gradual realization. But something also happened last night that gave me that one final kick in the pants. It's actually what I think I've been needing all along."

"Hmm." He looks thoughtful. "And what might that be? Did you get rip-roarin' drunk?"

"I don't do that anymore. I don't need to." I rummage through my purse, pull out the letter from Tyler, and allow Preston to read it. Once he's finished he hands it back to me. All he manages to utter is, "Wow."

We go back inside to resume clean up. Flipping through the mountain of CDs, I come across a burned Colbie Caillat one.

*Score!*

I pop it in, switch the setting to 'CD', and hit play. The first song is "Brighter than the Sun". Perfect for this moment. I dance around the bookstore chanting the lyrics.

Preston stands in the middle of the room, staring, as if I've lost my mind. Maybe I have, but it no longer matters, because deep down I truly believe in fate. There isn't anything except sunshine in store for me now.

# Chapter 26

# Home Sweet Home

At the end of a long and sweaty day I decide to return to my apartment, for the first time since getting back from the Bahamas. To be honest, I'm exhausted from the many hours of cleanup. Yet, even though I'm not saying it aloud, I feel a glimmer of hope that everything will be okay when I get there.

My street is finally clear. It seems a good omen. As I plod down the block, though, I encounter mounds of garbage in front of every single home—most at least five feet tall—lining the sidewalks as far as the eye can see.

Dragging my suitcase behind me over cracks and potholes, I try to maintain a positive attitude. Desperate for a shower in my own bathroom and to sit on my own couch in comfortable pajamas while sipping a nice, hot cup of Chamomile tea, I all but run down the street.

Finally, at the door to my apartment I slide the key into the lock. As I open it I pray a river of water won't come pouring out and sweep me away, carrying me down my street on a flood tide of my own ruined furniture.

Before I turn on the light I close my eyes and quietly chant, "Oh please, oh please, oh please."

At first glance, nothing appears damaged. No standing water is visible. Everything looks just the way I left it.

Well, almost. Some of the items in the apartment either came with Preston when he moved in, or he bought them while he was living here. Those, of course, have been relocated to his new apartment. That includes the living room TV, the big clay jar of cooking spoons, and the kitchen wall clock. These are just the few I notice of right off the bat. It's no big deal, though. I can carry the television from my bedroom to the living room, and plastic cooking spoons are what, five dollars? Everything will turn out fine.

I drop my keys on the kitchen table and wander through the apartment, opening the doors to different rooms, holding my breath as I do, praying for no surprise damage. Miraculously, the entire place seems unscathed. My bed looks cozy and welcoming. Yes, my room does look like high winds blew through it. My clothes are all over the floor in jumbled piles. But that's how I left it. I can hardly expect shirts and shorts to walk into my closet and fold themselves.

I scurry about, throwing all the dirty clothes in the hamper, tossing the clean ones on my bed to be folded or hung up. I then empty my suitcase, deciding to re-wash everything, and drop every piece of clothing in the hamper. Whirling around the room like a tornado, I tidy my bedroom until it's supremely spotless. Preston would surely be proud.

At last I take Tyler's letter from my purse, kiss it, slip it inside my journal, and tuck it away in the nightstand. Now I need to do one last, life altering thing. Sitting on the far-right corner of my triple-dresser is a mahogany three-tiered jewelry box. I gently side open the bottom drawer. In order to truly let Jared go, I have to stop wearing the necklace he gave me so long ago. Carefully, I unclasp the thin gold chain, then lift the Forget-Me-Not charm necklace from around my neck, and set it safely in the drawer. It's time I finally let him go.

When I go down the hall and open the door to Preston's empty bedroom, I feel a sense of gloom. I decide to keep the suitcase from the Bahamas in there. Every room should have a purpose for something, even if that purpose is only to store my empty luggage. I haul it in, open the closet door, and tuck it away for the next trip.

To my surprise, inside there is one thing left behind – the suit Preston wore to Fran's wedding, the one he ruined tackling me into the pool to douse the flames. Dry-cleaner plastic is draped over the suit, but clearly there's no need for it. The suit looks rumpled, stained, possibly even shrunken, though it's clear Preston has already taken it to be cleaned.

Add that to the list of things I need to make up for.

After a hot shower, I defrost a container of Preston's frozen homemade sauce, boil some pasta, situate my television at the far end of the living room, and flip through channels until I land on an episode of *Friends*. I pick up a fork and happily settle into the new version of my life.

# Chapter 27

# Gotta Have Friends

As the weeks pass and autumn is all but upon us, Preston and I discuss plans for the renovation of Viola's Hideaway. We hire a crew of workers to help us clear out the larger pieces of destroyed furniture and bookcases, and gut the walls and floors.

Preston, however, doesn't seem to be doing so great dealing with the breakup with Jack. To help cheer him up, I visit just about every dry-cleaner in the surrounding area to see if anyone might be able to improve the condition of his poor ruined suit.

Finally, I find one willing to take a stab at it. They actually do a phenomenal job. The following night, before leaving the bookstore, I hang the suit in Preston's office with a note pinned to the plastic that simply reads, *I'm sorry*!

Feeling pretty good about reuniting Preston and his Armani, I turn back to my own personal progress, jotting down two full pages of ideas for the bookstore renovation and grand re-opening. At the rate we're going, we're confident we'll be able to re-open the first of July.

At around eight o'clock, as I sit avidly watching an episode of the renovation show "This Old House", someone knocks on my front door.

It's Preston. He hugs me, and thanks me for rejuvenating his suit, nearly in tears.

I'm becoming increasingly concerned. He seems to be on a downward spiral when it comes to appearance, no longer the same sprightly Preston who used to roust me from bed in the morning. Oddly, somehow our roles have become reversed.

I show up at Viola's Hideaway each morning prepared to tackle the day's work, discuss the renovation process with the contractor, review design plans with the interior designer, and keep track of our budget.

Then I call Preston, letting it ring and ring. When he finally does answer, he sounds groggy and muffled, reluctant to get out of bed. Hours later, he wearily trudges into work wearing the same sweats and t-shirt from the previous few days, plus fingerprint-smudged sunglasses. He sports that edgy, unwashed, un-brushed, looks-right-out-of-bed hairstyle. Except his actually *is* unwashed, un-brushed, and straight from bed.

On top of it all, each day he carries in a large Dunkin' Donuts coffee – fixed the same way Jack drinks it. But Preston has always loathed Dunkin' Donuts coffee. So naturally, I find his behavior troubling. No matter how delicately or forcefully I attempt to broach the subject, he shuts down and refuses to talk. I know I'm to blame for what he's going through. He's only like this because he desperately misses Jack. And hey, I get it. I'm no stranger to heartache.

So now I invite Preston to have a seat as he wearily trudges into the apartment. How strange to be inviting him in, when this place was once his home. I offer a drink. He asks for a Tanqueray on the rocks with lime. I recall this as Jack's favorite drink, not Preston's. Without questioning his choice, though, I make one. He's taken a comfortable spot the couch. I join him, lift my recently brewed cup of Chamomile from the coffee table, and take a sip.

"What are you drinkin'?" He cocks an eyebrow at me.

"Tea," I reply. It seems a silly question, what with the obvious steam rising, and the string from the tea bag draped over the side of the mug.

"But it's only eight o'clock. Is there booze in there?"

"Why would I put booze in tea?" I chuckle.

"I dunno, to make it Irish? I've only ever known you to drink tea in the middle of the night, if you can't sleep. You always had a cocktail before going to bed."

"I stopped drinking, remember?" I take another sip.

He stares at me, seeming mystified.

"I realized I fall asleep a lot faster if I have a cup of tea instead. And I don't wake up every morning with a booming headache. I've been sleeping much better. I actually wake up a lot easier, too. As soon as the alarm goes off, I'm up. No snooze button for me."

Looking impressed, he asks, "So what else have you been doin'?"

"Oh, that reminds me!" I cry. Setting the tea down, I pop up from the couch. "There's something I want to show you, actually." I dash to the bedroom and grab the spiral notebook I've been filling with all my ideas for the bookstore.

Preston's footsteps behind me are so light, I don't realize he's trailing behind me until I turn and see him in the doorway.

"Oh my Gawd!" he screams, clutching his chest, scanning my room with alarm. "Did someone break in? Were yah robbed?" Drink in hand, he steps in and paces around, mouth agape, staring at my bare floor in wide-eyed horror.

I laugh. "No, silly, I cleaned up. Did all the laundry. Put everything away. You proud?"

He asks in a jocular tone, "When did you get carpet put in?"

"Preston, I've always had carpet."

"Nuh-uh," he protests. Amused, I hand him the spiral book open to the page containing my list, and he asks, "What's this?"

"Thoughts on how we might bring in more customers. I've been looking at the numbers from last year. You were right about needing to do something drastic. I didn't realize how close we were to losing everything. I can't tell you how sorry I am for putting that all on you. It wasn't right. I promise, it won't be like that anymore." I lay a hand on his arm.

He nods, accepting my apology.

"So what do you think?"

He scans the first page. "I love this idea." He points to the third bulleted item. "Hold author's readings and book signings every other month, with casual meet-and-greet party, serving champagne and finger food." He glances up at me. "It might be difficult at first. Definitely gonna be a lot of work. We'll need contacts, marketing…"

"I understand that," I cut him off, not wanting just then to feel a negative vibe about my ideas. "But for the first time in years I'm confident I can handle it. I want our bookstore to be more about readers and authors connecting on a more intimate level. I envision turning Viola's Hideaway into a place of entertainment. Every other month at first, then more often if it goes well. Not just with traditional readings or book signings. We can hire bands to play after those finish. I want people to be excited about our bookstore, because *I'm* so excited about all the cool things we can do to revamp our image. We have a second chance to make the Hideaway even more wonderful and unique."

Preston's mouth slowly stretches into a smile. A big one. "I love it. Let's get this going." He takes a sip of his drink. "So, how you doin' with everything else?"

"Well, oddly enough, I actually spoke with Mason earlier today."

Nearly spitting out his drink, he gasps, "Wait, what?" Waving a hand to urge me to spill, he says, "Details, lady! I need details."

"Well, it came about over the last couple weeks." I take a seat on my bed, to get comfortable for the long haul. "He left a couple messages on the answering machine. I was a little hesitant to call back, thinking maybe he was going to push for a chance at round two. But, that wasn't the case at all."

Preston doesn't utter a word. He simply stares avidly at me, a rapt audience waiting to get on with the story.

"He asked how I was doing. Said he was great. He wanted to let me know there were no hard feelings about the breakup. Which seemed believable, since he hadn't said anything besides 'It's okay' before he rushed out of the villa. I told him it was fine, that I was sorry again it didn't work out."

"And that's it?"

"Well, no. He asked if we could stay friends."

"Wait," he interrupts, frowning with suspicion. "Does he want to be friends, or *friends*?" He bounces his eyebrows.

*Yikes.* "Definitely just friends!" I say quickly and firmly.

"And what about Jared?"

I sigh then, picking at a peeling flake of polish on my thumbnail. "What about him?"

"Are you okay? I know it was all rough on you."

"The Jared phase of my life is officially over. I've left Neverland," I quip, quoting Preston from our telephone call when I was still in the Bahamas. "So, back to you. How're you holding up with the whole Jack situation?"

Slumping next to me on the bed, he shuts his eyes, looking exhausted. "I'm miserable. He won't return my calls. I can't sleep. I have no energy. I even started drinkin' Dunkin' Donuts because I miss him so much." He grimaces. "I hate Dunkin' Donuts."

"I'm so sorry, Preston. It crushes me to see your hurting like this."

"It's just gonna take some time to get over him. This is the worst breakup I've ever had. I know you're not used to hearin' me say shit like this, but I actually do believe he's my soul mate. I finally understand why you were so hung up on Jared all those years."

Inching closer, I throw an arm around his shoulders, trying to provide a smidgen of comfort. "Gosh, I had no idea you felt that way."

"I never quite understood your obsession with fate, and with Jared. I think because I'd never experienced anything like that before. Until Jack." He sighs deeply and rakes his fingers through his disheveled hair. "You find that one person who means everything. Then all of a sudden that's it. Game over. I wish I could go back in time. Do things differently." He flashes me a sad half-smile.

"I wish I could make this better. I'm here for you, Preston. No matter what. Anything you need."

He reaches for my hand and gives it a gentle squeeze.

We return to the living room and hang out until two in the morning, talking and laughing. To be honest, I think it's what we both needed tonight, to feel even briefly that things had returned to the way they used to be between us, back to when we were in college.

Just like old times.

# Chapter 28

# Relentless

Over the next couple of months, I repeatedly call Jack, hoping he'll agree to meet with me. Of course, Preston knows nothing of this. I leave Jack countless voicemails begging him to please call back. I want to apologize in person for creating a wedge between them, which led to their breakup. I desperately want to make amends but need to be given the chance to do it, first.

As the weeks roll by with no return call from Jack, I go through different stages of grief. First, intense guilt and remorse, followed by a phase where I blow up his phone with at least ten voicemails a day. Then, I reach anger.

*Why won't he call me back? How insensitive can a person be?*

Finally, one day, just as I hang up the bookstore office phone after arranging the first author's appearance and party at the bookstore, the phone rings. It's Jack.

At first, I fumble for the right words—for *any* words—that will keep him on the line.

His deep voice floods the earpiece, cutting me off. "Laina, you have to stop calling. I don't want to have to block your number."

"No, no! Please, I just want to talk," I cry. "Will you please meet me for dinner tonight?"

A lengthy span of silence leads me to fear he's already hung up. Just as a string of obscenities rise from my lips, he says, sounding reluctant yet curious, "Fine. Where and when?"

I decide I'd better make a reservation at an especially nice restaurant. "A new bistro that just opened on New Dorp Lane. It's supposed to be fantastic."

Practically hanging off the edge of my seat, I grip the phone like a limpet, afraid to move a single muscle for fear I may somehow break the connection.

"Yeah, I've passed by it. I know which one you mean." He pauses. "Okay, I'll meet you there. Seven work for you?"

"Yes! Seven is perfect! Thank you. I'll call now to make the reservation." As soon as we end the call, I breathe a giant sigh of relief.

Finally. Progress! Weeks of being a horrific pest have finally paid off. It's about damn time, too. Soon I would have implemented Plan B and made a surprise appearance at his front door, which probably wouldn't have gone over well at all. The last thing a respectable business owner needs is a restraining order against her.

\* \* \*

Jack meets me at *Destino Bistro* on New Dorp Lane, a few blocks from the Hylan Plaza. The new bistro's ambiance mimics having a candlelight dinner under the night sky. Tiny votives glow on each table and a mural of a starry sky adorns the ceiling. The twinkling stars are actually lights, constantly dimming then glowing brighter, just like stars, which is truly captivating. Royal blue tablecloths and matching upholstered chairs enhance the galaxy ambiance.

At dinner, I apologize, for everything.

"For years Preston was my only family. I came to rely too much on his help and friendship. I didn't realize I was pulling him deeper and deeper into my own issues, at his expense. I see that now."

Jack raises an eyebrow sardonically. "Oh, really?"

"I don't blame you for disliking me while you two were together. I wouldn't have wanted to be around me either, in your situation. But I've changed the last few months. I've grown to be a more independent person."

He doesn't look convinced, however. Suppose I can't blame him. He hasn't known me for long. He's only seen Codependent Laina.

So I try a different tack. "But the point isn't to make excuses for myself. Preston has been in a bottomless depression ever since the breakup. Since it's because of my careless actions, I will do anything I can to make amends."

He looks faintly interested then. "Anything?"

I ignore that for now, and explain how much Preston still loves him, how deeply the breakup has hurt him, and how I don't even recognize Preston any more.

"In retrospect, look how much happiness you brought to each other. I know what it's like when one person brings out the very best in you and then someone comes along and destroys that. What you and Preston were to each other . . . well, that can never be replaced."

"Look, I see what you're trying to do," Jack says. "But our breakup took everything out of me as well. I'm only now starting to get my life back on track. Preston is the only man I ever fell head over heels in love with. He made everything beautiful with his energy and charm. Once you started dating Mason, you suddenly made Preston your relationship guru. No, your crutch! He practically became a parent. You were too blind and self-involved to see it then. He was so fixated on keeping you and Mason together he neglected our relationship. My wishes didn't matter. How do I know it won't happen again? I can't go back to that." He clenches his jaw, then hangs his head, obviously upset.

I reach across the table and gently lay a hand on his arm. He doesn't pull away, which seems like a good sign. I wait to speak until he finally looks up and meets my gaze.

"I know nothing I say can change the things I've done, but *I'm trying my hardest here*, baring my soul. Not just because I feel guilty, but because Preston is like a brother. I love him so much, I want to see him happy. And *you* are his happiness. The last few months forced me to grow up. Mason and I aren't together anymore. I no longer need a 'crutch' or a 'love guru'. I realize I have to take care of myself, and take responsibility for my past mistakes. So punish me for what went wrong, if you want. Hate me, too, if that helps. But please don't punish Preston. Don't let my mistakes keep you two apart."

He sighs after my long speech. We sit in silence for a while, staring at each other across the table. Eventually he glances around the restaurant, frowning as if trying to gather his thoughts. "I appreciate what you're trying to do here, but . . . we fought constantly because of you. I don't hate you. I hate how much damage you caused between us. As much as I love him, I have to walk away." He takes his napkin from his lap, drops it beside his plate, and rises. Sliding his coat off the chair, he slips it on and wraps a scarf around his neck.

I stand as well. "I understand feeling like you do. But if anyone deserves happiness, it's Preston."

As he heads toward the door I take hold of his arm to tug him back. "Wait!" I cry, as half the patrons in the restaurant stop and stare.

Jack turns back. Tears have pooled in his eyes.

"I'm having a New Year's Eve party at my apartment. Preston will be there, along with a bunch of our friends. I would love it if you could come, too."

"I can't. I'm sorry. I appreciate what you've tried to do, but please don't call me anymore, okay? Thanks for a nice dinner." He lowers his head and leaves the restaurant.

I'm left standing there, deflated. With no hope of Jack relenting, clearly I'm going to have to kick my efforts into high gear to get Preston back to his old, wonderful, happy self again.

# Chapter 29

# Countdown

Before I know it, along comes New Year's.

But not just any old New Year's Eve. Today is also my thirtieth birthday. Some people may want to hide in their closets until the dreaded thirtieth milestone ends. Not me. I've decided to embrace it. The new me is mature, after all.

I can hardly wait to begin decorating my apartment for the night's festivities, and I've officially decided to go overboard: streamers, enormous balloons with the new year bedazzled across the foil, signs, hats, noise makers, confetti, flashing lights. You name it, I've most likely bought, borrowed, or made it.

On top of everything else to celebrate, my mother will be in attendance. I only hope I can cheer Preston up enough to actually enjoy himself, just a teensy bit.

I'm eagerly anticipating the year ahead. I love fresh beginnings now. And, with the bookstore re-opening, I have a gut instinct even greater things will follow. I firmly believe fate will finally be on my side in the coming year. I simply need to keep renewing my weekly pass on the positivity train.

I go all-out on my fashion choice for the evening, too. Preston will be extremely proud. My maroon, sequined minidress has long sleeves and a long ribbon that ties into a tiny bow at the nape of my neck. Beyond that point—all the way down to my tailbone—the dress is entirely backless. The bodice, however, rises to my collarbone. I pair the dress with the sexiest pair of black heels I own.

As my party guests begin to arrive, I adorn each with New Year's crowns, hats, and gaudy necklaces. Flipping the cable channel to footage of Times Square, I also turn on some background tunes to get the party revved.

My mom arrives, surprising me with a homemade cake and candles, so we can sing "Happy Birthday" just before the ball drops.

Drawn like a moth to a flame, Preston greets me by grabbing at my new pixie haircut, running his fingers through it, shouting, "What've you done? It's so short! I love it! Oh, you look *just* like Audrey Hepburn!"

"That was the idea! Figured I'd start the New Year with a new look."

Throwing his head back, he squeals, "Honey, it's totally you. You're stunning. So bold and daring." Closing his eyes, he leans in for a hug, which lingers a bit. I finish off with a kiss on his cheek.

But Preston has made no effort to spiff himself up for this occasion. New Year's Eve used to be one of his biggest suit-up nights. Usually he's the best dressed person at any party, in fact. But tonight, when he takes off his overcoat, he has on faded jeans, black sneakers, and a t-shirt that reads *I've Already Given Up on My New Year's Resolution* beneath an unzipped hoodie.

I groan when I catch sight of his outfit. "How could you show up wearing that?"

"What? I bought this specifically for tonight."

I flash him a *that's-pretty-pathetic* face.

Arms folded defensively, he cries, "Well, I like it."

Each time my front door opens and someone walks in, I anxiously turn toward it, fingers crossed, hoping Jack has changed his mind. But as the hours roll by and midnight creeps nearer I start to lose hope.

Most of the party Preston sulks on my couch, drinking Tanqueray on the rocks with a slice of lime. I try my best to get him talking to people, but he clearly has no interest. Each time I find him back on the couch in the exact same seat, gazing blankly at the television screen.

After the birthday cake and song, with midnight closing in, I fill flutes with pink champagne. Then pass them around to the guests, making sure to fill a few extras in case I forget anyone, or if someone happens to want seconds, or if someone prematurely downs their official midnight champagne.

I hand Preston a flute, and he thanks me, flashing the most pitiful attempt at a smile.

Plopping beside him on the couch, I slide one arm through his in attempt to make him relax. "Can you at least pretend to enjoy yourself for my sake? It's breaking my heart to see you like this. It's New Year's Eve. It's my birthday. We should be celebrating!"

"Sorry, sweetie. I don't feel very festive tonight. Sorry to disappoint you." He slumps deeper into the couch.

"Well, I need you to snap out of it for at least the next two minutes." I rise from the couch, turn to face him, and extend a hand.

Looking exhausted, he counters, "And why's that?"

"Because I need someone to kiss at midnight, and I think it should be my best friend in the whole world." I grin, bat my eyelashes, and tilt my head, hoping he accepts.

Smirking halfheartedly, he finally takes my hand. I heave him up from the couch and onto his feet. Swiping the remote control from the coffee table, I turn the TV volume all the way up. "One minute, everybody!" I scream, as party guests eagerly gather in the living room, our attention riveted on the Times Square bash onscreen.

"Ten, nine...eight," we chant.

I glance at Preston to my left. He's stuck in a stupor. He's not even counting! I grab his hand and give it a squeeze. He looks at me, flashes a forced smile, then returns his frowny gaze to the television.

"Seven...six...five!"

Just then, someone taps my right shoulder. I turn my head to look. My mouth drops open.

It's Jack!

"Four . . . three!"

He grins and pats my shoulder. I wildly beam back, then release Preston's hand and scoot out of the way so Jack can slip into my place.

"Two . . . one! Happy New Year!"

Preston turns toward Jack, who is now at his side, and does a double take. He looks beyond stunned. Maybe he thinks he's dreaming.

"Happy New Year!" Jack leans in and whispers in his ear. Preston bursts into tears, throws his arms around Jack, and closes his eyes.

A blissful grin spreads across Jack's face, as if holding Preston is the best feeling in the world. "I've...I've missed you so *much*," he sputters.

I ball up a fist and jam it in my mouth, to stifle the squeal building there. Tears leak from the corners of my eyes, though I quickly wipe them away, careful not to smudge my eye makeup. Jack opens his eyes again and glances over. He mouths, *Thank you*, and extends a hand to me while still clinging to Preston. I take it, and he tenderly gives it a squeeze.

Just then my mother scoots to my side. "Happy New Year, honey. And Happy Birthday!" She gives me a kiss on the cheek.

All in all, who could ask for a better start to the New Year?

# Chapter 30

# The Truth in My Stars

With a fresh year, fresh style, and a fresh outlook, I decide it would be nice to visit an old friend. A bit of snow's expected later in the day, so I dash out just before eight to drive to St. George on an overcast, twelve-degree day. The whipping wind cuts at my face, until my eyes tear up from the cold. It's insane to leave my apartment on a day like today. Still, what would I do instead but sit at home watching television and polishing off an entire box of Swiss Miss?

The worst part is, I have to park farther away than last time. Just after New Year's Day we were hit with a nasty blizzard, and dirty snow mounds still remain, taking up quite a few spaces. I finally find a spot and get out, bundled head to toe, trekking through slushy, dirt-covered snow straight to Desi's shop. My body goes rigid whenever a strong gust whistles down the street, bracing against the bitter cold air, waiting miserably for it to dissipate.

Finally, relieved to see Desi's lights illuminated in the front window, I make a mad dash across the street and into the store.

I sigh with pleasure at the immense warmth inside the fortune tellers shop. My body defrosts almost instantly, as I jerk off my gloves and hat, unwrap my wool scarf, and unzip my coat to let some of that toasty air get in. The scent of woodsy evergreen incense helps, too.

"Hello?" I shout.

"Miss Laina?" Desi calls from the back.

I freeze for a moment, spooked. How on earth did she know it was me? "Uh, yes. Hello."

Pushing through the red curtain dividing the front and back room, Desi appears, her face lighting up as she spots me standing there. "I'm so very glad to see you again," she says in honeyed tones. "You are my first official customer of the new year. Please, come in." She ushers me to the same back table. "I will take your coat. Let's get you warm."

"Thank you," I say, handing over my belongings.

Desi hangs it all on wall hooks just above a radiator.

"How have you been?" I ask.

She seems caught off guard, as though she doesn't get asked this very often. "I'm...I'm quite well, thank you." She smiles sweetly and nods. "Your new haircut is lovely."

"Oh, thanks." I brush a hand over the nape of my neck. "I've never gone this short before. First winter in my life I ever needed to buy a wool scarf to keep my neck warm."

"Your face is not hidden, as before. Your face also seems brighter." She takes the seat across from me and reaches for the stack of cards on the table. "Would you like to begin?"

"Yes, please do." I inch closer to the table.

Desi fans the cards across the table, arbitrarily slides them around, then piles and stirs them into one disorderly heap. Sitting back in her seat, she stares pointedly at me, as if to say, *Continue.*

I gather up the cards, thoroughly shuffle them, and set the deck back on the table between us.

Once again, she swoops them across the table, then waits patiently as I make my selections.

I flurry my fingers above them and select three, flipping them over, placing them in the center of the table.

Desi sweeps the remaining cards off to one side, then rubs her hands as if she's keeping them warm. "For your past card, you have selected the reversed Three of Swords." She sighs, sounding a bit relieved. The card shows a heart stabbed by three swords. "This represents a great deal of healing in both personal and work life. While you are mending broken or strained relationships, though, a tiny piece of you still clings to your past."

"I . . . I don't want to," I stammer.

"Whether or not you desire that, Miss Laina, it is who you are." She pats the top of my hand, then gazes down at the next card. "You have chosen The Star to represent your present."

The card shows a naked woman beneath a night sky. She is pouring water from one jug into a pond, and water from another onto land.

"You've finally reached a point in life where you can let yourself be happy. You feel content, inspired, even loved. This is a very promising card. From the first time I met you until now, I have seen your life transform in drastic ways. It brings my heart joy to see this now."

"I've been through a lot the last couple of years, but I think I've grown even more over the past few months."

"And it pleases me," she continues, matter of factly. "Let's see about your future now. The reversed Four of Cups is what you have selected for the future." She taps her index finger lightly on the card. It shows a man sitting beneath a tree, arms crossed, staring at three cups set before him. An outstretched hand has popped through a hovering cloud to offer him a fourth cup.

"Your life is still unfolding. Hold onto the faith that things will all work out. Also, you must always remember to keep that beautiful heart open." She reaches across the table for my hands, then closes her eyes. "Your story is still being written, my dear, but the pen is in your hand this time. You have the power to create your own fate. Seize that power."

As I gather my belongings and thank her for the reading, I say, "Our bookstore will be hosting our first author event in July. I'd be thrilled if you could attend. Someone's designing a website right now. We'll have the event details on it by next week."

Desi promises to attend. Then she calls me back just as I reach the front door. "By the way, Miss Laina, this was your final reading."

"Yes, I think so," I sheepishly reply, reluctant to give the impression I'm ungrateful for everything she has done. She's the reason I believe in fate again. She opened my eyes, exposed my flaws, and forced me to reexamine my life. If I never met her, I might not be where I am today.

As she holds my gaze, her gentle smile reappears. She steps toward me, takes both my hands, and whispers, "Good. You are finally ready to find your fate."

# Chapter 31

# Gotta Have Faith

Preston and Jack have picked up their relationship right where they left off. Seeing them together, witnessing the love between them fills me an overwhelming sense of fulfillment. To think I was able to bring them back together!

In the second week of June, one month before the grand re-opening of Viola's Hideaway, Preston comes in wearing a new light-gray suit. The top two buttons on his white shirt are left casually undone. It's great to see the old, dashing Preston back in action.

The renovation of the bookstore is nearly complete, ahead of schedule. True, my bank account is scraping bottom, as no doubt is Preston's. But I have to admit the place looks even better than before. We included an entire second level with exquisite wrought-iron balconies that would look right at home on stage in a production of Shakespeare's *Romeo and Juliet*. These have been furnished as seating areas for our customers to gather and read or look down on special events.

The walls are re-painted with new murals of *Twelfth Night*, and they're even more elaborate and colorful than before.

Off to the side of the bookstore, through antique French doors, is a new addition. We turned an empty alley into a large, custom-designed outdoor garden where our customers can go to be served lunch on café tables. The seating area is bordered with raised beds which contain all the herbs and flowers mentioned in Shakespeare's plays.

Much of my inspiration for the design was the Shakespeare Garden in Central Park. Glass walls surround our outdoor café as does a glass greenhouse ceiling and etched-glass doors. These can be kept open during beautiful weather, allowing the breeze to flow in. The room will be functional year-round, rain or shine, heated during the winter months. It's an oasis filled with small shrubs, flowering plants, marble statues, and wide benches. I want my customers to feel as if they've transitioned not only into a different place, but a different time as well.

Preston comes into my office, taking a seat in one of the chairs facing my desk. "What are you workin' on?" He sounds quite chipper.

"Oh, just calendaring the author appearances into the computer."

"These events you've planned will be amazing. I want you to know I'm proud of all the work you've done. I sometimes can't believe how you've morphed into, like, a completely different person, overnight. Tyler would be extremely proud, too. Just look at the place!"

I lean forward and lay a hand on top of his. "Thank you, Preston. It means everything to hear you say that."

\* \* \*

A few days prior to the grand reopening, I make reservations at Kismet, my favorite dinner spot on the Upper West Side, so Mom and I can catch up. Spending time with my mother has become a frequent event. Our relationship is now closer than it ever was before.

Mom and I eat dinner at a tiny, two-seat table next to the second-floor window as I fill her in on the last few weeks: finalizing the first author event, planning the after party, the joys of being engulfed in a whole new bookstore.

At first, she listens intently, as she digs into her Bourbon Honey Chicken. She allows me to gush about every detail, not once interrupting. But she doesn't make eye contact, even after I tilt my head low, trying to catch her eye.

"Well, that's all really wonderful, sweetie," she eventually says, dabbing her mouth with a napkin, then taking a long sip of water.

"What is it?" I scoot to the edge of my chair and lean forward, giving her my full attention. I frown, fearing I'm about to be scolded for something. Though what, I can't even imagine yet.

"First off, I want you to know how proud I am you're finally making something wonderful happen for yourself. I know how much time the remodeling has taken, and your complete devotion to the bookstore. I know it hasn't been easy the last few years, without Tyler there to help run things. So I'm grateful to Preston for stepping in. From what you've told me, he's one reason the bookstore lasted this long." She shakes her head. "I know it's still early on in your career and the reopening is just around the corner, but may I offer a bit of advice?" Leaning back, she gazes out the window beside her, as if looking into the distance will help collect her thoughts.

I set my fork on my plate and fold my hands on the tabletop. "Yeah, of course it is."

"Being successful in a career is extremely important, but I don't want you to think it's the *only* thing that is. A career is only one piece of your life. Once everything is back up and running, I hope you take time for some other joys."

"You mean a relationship," I flatly reply.

"Well, yes." She sighs. "I don't want you to end up like me. Before we reconnected, all I really had was my job. And while I enjoy what I do, I know I'm missing out on other things. There's no one to come home to, to share dinner with or stories of my day. There's no one to laugh with during a movie, or go on walks with. I've made a lot of mistakes, and I've punished myself for them. I was convinced I didn't deserve that kind of happiness, because I had my chance and only caused heartache and pain for others. So, I stayed alone."

She leans forward and puts a hand over mine. Her voice grows softer. "But I want to see you live the fullest life you can have."

It's quite a lecture, though a good one. "I'll make sure to keep this all in mind. I promise."

"You haven't heard from Jared, have you?"

"No. Why would I?"

She shrugs. "Just wondering, is all. The only other advice I can give in that area is, the next time you have love right in front of you, hold on to it. You've already shown the world you've grown up. Let fate take it from here."

I nod, flashing a halfhearted smile. "That's proven difficult. Fate and I always seemed to have a love/hate relationship. I just hope it's on my side now."

"It is, more than you realize. I believe that's been proven to you in more ways than one. You just have to have a little faith."

Learning to be happy with myself was an important step, and a necessary one, I think, before having a serious relationship with anyone else. But as time rolls on, I haven't taken the time to figure out if I'm already there. Have I proven I can be happy on my own? All I can say for sure is that now I can stand on my own, without always relying on Preston—or anyone—to make every single decision for me.

After we finish our incredibly tasty dinner, and Mom takes a Lyft home, I decide to go into Central Park. It's the first time I've visited the Shakespeare Garden since I wrote that long letter to Tyler in my journal.

I take a seat on my favorite bench, rummage through my purse and pop a mint in my mouth. I get in the mood for something sweet after dinner, but am now so full there was no room left for dessert.

As I lean back, enjoying the view, a girl of about five climbs the stone steps, with a woman—a tired looking brunette in her mid-thirties—I assume is her mother. With them is a boy, possibly the girl's brother.

The first time I ever climbed those stairs as a child, they seemed gigantic. The long flight made me feel like a princess, though, making a grand entrance on my way to an enchanted forest. Back then, this garden seemed filled with love, magic, endless dreams, and unlimited possibilities. I make a wish now for it to feel that way once again.

Maybe it's just turning thirty, but lately I find myself furiously hoping everything in my life will eventually work out, that every decision I make will be the correct one. If I were to write Tyler another letter, would I continue to receive signs? Perhaps everything I've experienced ever since I met Desi Chase only occurred because I was in need of my brother's guidance, and therefore, I received it. Now I don't so much *need* as *want* it.

I admire the butterflies peacefully flitting by, landing on flowers, then winging off amid the greenery. Closing my eyes, I listen to the hum of the garden, hoping for just one more sign to know everything *will* be all right. I allow that feeling to fill me, and try to hold onto it as long as possible.

When I open my eyes again, the little boy is standing near me. He's maybe six or seven, with dark brown hair and light brown eyes. He admires the bed of flowers beside my bench, then reaches out and picks a tiny, light blue flower. He gently brushes specks of dirt from the stem and dawdles around the bench, kicking at the grass, finally stopping to stand in front of me.

One thin little arm rises and holds out the dainty blue flower, offering it to me.

"For me?" I ask, taken aback, so moved by his action it chokes me up. I stare at the delicate flower. It's a Forget-Me-Not. What are the odds that this little stranger would hand me this exact flower?

"Did you know this is called a Forget-Me-Not? I have a necklace just like it at home. It's my favorite kind of flower, and this is the most beautiful one I've ever seen."

He bashfully smiles, swaying from foot to foot. "Why don't you wear the necklace if it's your favorite?"

I lower my head to smell the sweet bloom. "That's a very good question."

He opens his mouth and announces, "I'm going to see Shakesteer in the Park."

"Really? Oh, you're going to have such a good time. Who are you going with, your mom?"

He excitedly nods back. "And my sister. I'm older."

"I used to go to see those plays with my mom and brother when I was about your age. I haven't gone in a very long time, though."

"You *should* go!" he enthusiastically advises.

"Maybe I should." I giggle at his adorable enthusiasm.

"Tyler! Tyler, where are you?"

*Tyler.*

The woman I saw him with earlier darts around one of the stone walkways. She rushes toward the little boy and grabs hold of his arm, turning him toward her. "Tyler, what did I tell you about wandering off? Come on, we're leaving," she scolds. She glances at me apologetically. "I'm sorry if my son was bothering you."

"Oh, not at all! We were just talking. He's very sweet."

"Come on, honey. We're going to get something to eat before the play, okay?" She looks less anxious now, bending so she is eye-level with him.

He frowns and shakes his head, lips compressed, clearly upset at having irritated his mother.

"Never mind," she says, and smiles. She takes his hand and leads him away.

Before they disappear, he twists around and looks back at me, waving goodbye.

I return the gesture and whisper, as tears fill my eyes, "Goodbye, Tyler."

It's difficult to believe this has simply been a coincidence. Now I suddenly feel compelled to start going to see Shakespeare in the Park again. I can't ignore the signs when they practically jump out at me. I'm not going to wait for a big red STOP sign to smack me in the face this time.

Exiting the park, I catch sight of a cheery woman handing out bulletins with *Shakespeare* in large letters on the paper.

I approach and receive a flyer.

*Shakespeare in the Park Presents*
*TWELFTH NIGHT*
*July 17-August 19*
*At the Delacorte Theater in Central Park*
*Two free tickets are available per person at the Delacorte Theater.*
*Don't miss out!*

I dig out my cell phone to call Preston.

His rings and goes to voice mail. But I repeatedly call until he answers, sounding panicked and out of breath. "What's wrong? Is everything okay?"

"Yes, of course." I laugh. "Just wanted to ask if you'd go see Shakespeare in the Park with me on Sunday?"

"Really? You called me twelve times for that? Hmm. Sure you want to do this with the reopening coming up?"

"Yes, I do. We close early on Sundays anyway. Shakespeare in the Park is showing *Twelfth Night* and I want you to come."

I wait for a response, but there is none. "Come on, I haven't gone to one of these plays in the Park since I was a kid. Besides, it's *Twelfth Night*. Hello? We can't pass this up." There is more silence. "Did you hang up on me?"

"No, I'm just thinking." He pauses once again.

"Think faster," I urge, "I need to pee."

"Oh, good God, woman! You and your tiny bladder. Give me a second here"

"Okay, fine! What about Sunday?" I press.

He sighs, exasperated. "Okay, fine. Get the bloody tickets."

"*Yes!*" I squeal, so loudly several alarmed pigeons take flight nearby. I shake my ass joyfully as I strut across Central Park West. Some onlookers passing by flash puzzled glances. Others pretend they don't notice my awful dance moves. Either way, I don't care, because at that moment I'm filled with so much excitement I could swim back to Staten Island from South Ferry.

I impatiently wait on the corner for the streetlight to change. Closing my eyes, I whisper, "Thanks, Tyler, for popping up just one last time."

# Chapter 32

# The Stranger

The day before the grand reopening, Preston barges into my office while I'm finishing up a telephone call with one of our book jobbers. He paces the office, looking ready to burst. So I fear something is wrong.

The moment I hang up, he begins jabbering about Milliana Smith, the author booked for tomorrow's reading and book signing party.

Luckily, nothing is wrong – he's just *that* excited.

The rest of the day I endeavor to stay busy, but as the hours tick on I can't conceal my excitement either. By late afternoon I feel as if I'm about to crawl out of my own skin, just thinking about the thrill of what tomorrow will bring.

At home that evening, I sort through clothes, intent on choosing the perfect outfit for tomorrow. I lay out three different dresses to try on, to decide which one feels right. I shower and look in the fridge for something to eat, but I'm too anxious to cook or even feed myself. Instead, I have Sushi delivered and turn on Netflix.

Most of the night I lie tossing and turning, unable to shut off my brain, imagining what tomorrow will be like, wondering if it will turn out well. It feels like more than just a promotional event, to me.

* * *

The night of the grand re-opening of Viola's Hideaway has finally arrived. After weeks of advertising and getting the word out on social media about our new image, we are ready open our brand-new doors to the book-loving public. I arrive at work bright and early—about an hour before Preston—and scamper throughout the bookstore checking everything to ensure the place is spotless.

When Preston finally arrives, he takes in my long, black, sleeveless dress with a wide side slit that reveals a good portion of upper thigh, and my gold strappy heels. He stops in his tracks. "Whoa, you look . . . whoa! Just . . . insanely gorgeous. You know you're not meetin' Queen Elizabeth, right? Why so dressy?"

"I wanted to look nice. Today's an important day. Grand reopening, first author reading, big party...I wanted to dress for the occasion."

Preston flashes his old Mr. Bean grin, with a thumbs-up. "Mission accomplished. You just . . . you oughta be goin' on a hot date."

"Well maybe I am." I smirk playfully, tilt my head, and raise my eyebrows.

He makes a fishy face, pooching out his lips. "Oh! I'll shut up then. Milliana Smith is one lucky lady."

I shove Preston's shoulder as he marches past. He chortles as if he's the cleverest man alive. After stowing his briefcase and lunch cooler in his office, he helps me sort out the day's schedule.

\* \* \*

Crowds begin to gather by five, come to see all the improvements on the bookstore, and to wish us luck. Our previous, loyal customers arrive first, eager to return to their favorite Hideaway, as well as masses of new faces here to check out what makes us so unique. All of them seem excited when they find out about the other events planned for the upcoming months.

The turnout is exhilarating. Our customers take flyers that list our new monthly Book-to-Film Adaptation Night, where we plan to show films based on novels. We've created a theater nook in the back, with a few oversized couches, a popcorn machine, candy counter, and a supersized flatscreen.

A half hour before the event is scheduled to begin, Milliana Smith still hasn't arrived. Needless to say, I'm freaking out just a tad. Sure, there's the whole concept of arriving fashionably late, but this is cutting it a bit close. I'm a bundle of wired nerves.

So many people arrive that finally Preston and I are forced to dig out extra folding chairs from the storage room. Even so, some people will have to stand during the reading. I am profusely apologetic, but they assure me they don't mind one bit.

Cristin rushes over as I welcome a few more customers. "Sorry, but you have a phone call. In the office."

I thank her and scurry off. But when I get there no one's on the other end. Then it rings again, a book jobber calling. That does it. After I finish with him, the ringer will be silenced for the rest of the night.

Preston taps on my door and sticks his head in. I'm still on the phone because of an issue with one of the orders I just placed. I point to the phone, making a they-won't-stop-talking face. He mouths, *Milliana is finally here.*

My stomach performs flip-flops. I persistently 'yes, yes' the guy on the other end until he's satisfied with the new billing arrangement we've put in place, and I can hang up.

"God, finally!" I glance at Preston, who for some reason is beaming almost literally from ear to ear. "Is it time? Let's get the show on the road." I clumsily bump one hip into the desk making a mad dash for the door.

"Now, hold on a sec. Okay, so here's the thing," he begins, blocking the doorway so I can't leave the office. "I know you're probably gonna say no, but hear me out."

He's making that face, the one that means he has something up his sleeve. I don't like it. Not tonight. "What are you planning now?"

"There's a ton of people here, you look exquisite, and . . well, you've been doin' so amazing these past few months."

"The answer is no."

"No, what?" he asks.

"I know what you're about to suggest. You want to play matchmaker and set me up to start dating again. Look, I'll date when I meet the right guy."

"But what if the right guy is here, now?" His eyes are filled with eagerness. He's bouncing on his toes like a three year old.

"Who are you trying to hook me up with this time?"

"Who, indeed. I mean, I don't know him. It's a customer that just walked in."

I fling my head back and guffaw. "I'm *not* going to date the customers, Preston."

"Just take a look at him. Please! Oh, the things I would do to this man." He rolls his eyes and bites one knuckle.

"Oh, very nice. That's so classy and professional," I reply in a snarky tone, not impressed by his crude comment. "What would Jack say if he heard that?"

With perfect timing, Jack suddenly pops into my office wearing his own bizarrely asinine grin. "Pres! Did you catch the hottie that just strolled in? Man, I'd love to leave teeth marks on that!"

Preston flourishes a hand at Jack. "See, it's unanimous. I get the sense the guy is straight, though." He turns to Jack. "You get that vibe?"

Jack nods soberly in disappointed agreement.

Preston turns back and lunges at my chest. He grabs the underwire on my bra and gives my boobs a good shaking.

"*Excuse me!*" I shout, swatting his hands away.

"Perk those girls up." He reaches out again. "He's not wearin' a ring."

I smack him away more forcefully. "I don't care. Male or female, bite-able or not, ring or no ring. I can find a date in my own time. Today is *not* that day." I push past Preston and Jack, appalled by the pair of them, and storm out of the office. They follow close behind.

It doesn't take long to scan the crowd and locate the toothsome stranger Preston and Jack are salivating over. Several women are practically drooling on themselves, gazes glued to a tall guy with wavy chestnut hair and slight facial scruff, wearing dark gray slacks, a long-sleeved white button down, with the sleeves rolled to the elbows. The top two buttons are undone, revealing a patch of muscular chest.

My heart heavily thumps once, sharply. I stop so short, Preston and Jack crash into my back. Preston grabs my arm and studies my face, as I stand silently gaping at the man. "You okay?" He follows my gaze. "Yes, yah see now? I told you. Gorgeous."

"But . . . what is he *doing* here?" I manage to utter. My legs, supported only by the thin stilettos of the strappy gold heels, feel ready to collapse.

Looking mystified, Preston says, "What are you talkin' about?"

I turn to look at him, with equal parts hope and dread. "What am I talking about? The man over there. That's Jared."

# Chapter 33

# Face to Face

I back away and frantically shepherd Preston and Jack into my office again, then quickly slam the door. I pace the room, feeling as if I am hyperventilating.

They hover, doing their best to console me, but I try to block out their garbled yapping so I can process my own thoughts. *Jared is here – in my bookstore. Never expected to see his face again. Yet, here he is! But . . . how can he be? Why?*

"Okay, what happens now?" Jack says, for about the fifth time. "You still have an event to host. We have to get back out there."

"You gonna be able to handle this?" Preston poses, laying a consoling hand on my arm.

"Yes! Of course I can handle it."

"Okay, well, good. But you might want to dab your mouth right there." He taps his index finger at one corner of his mouth. "Got a bit of spittle happenin' there."

Oh my God. Jack examines my face as I frantically wipe at both corners of my mouth. "Please try not to drool on yourself anymore," he urges. "It's very unbecoming."

"No promises," I joke darkly, then something occurs to me. I grab Preston's arm. "Hang on. Did you say, a few minutes ago, that there was no ring on his left hand?"

He frowns thoughtfully. "Nope, not that I saw."

"Hmm. . . ." I sigh. What are the odds? "Never mind, that doesn't matter right now. Right now I just have to keep it professional and not throw up." I open the door and march out again to greet my guests.

I spot Desi standing off to one side, and make sure to give her a hug, welcoming her properly. She graciously congratulates me on the amazing renovation, and wishes me all the luck in the world. Next, I catch sight of Liv's bridesmaid, Amelia. She is standing a few paces from Jared. She smiles and excitedly waves when she spots me, then tugs on his sleeve.

Jared turns and watches as I snake through the sea of people toward them. Preston and Jack trail behind, pausing now and then to thank our regulars in the crowd.

"Laina, my God," Amelia cries, throwing her arms around me, "you look absolutely gorgeous! Your hair! I *love* it!"

"It's great to see you again," I exclaim, pulling her into a tight hug. "And I'm . . . so surprised you're here."

"I felt so bad we didn't keep in touch after the wedding. When I found out you were having this event, well, I just *had* to come."

I beam, a hand over my heart, touched by her support. "That's so incredibly nice of you."

"And of course I wanted to share the news." She grins and flashes the back of her left hand, revealing a platinum princess-cut engagement ring, its diamond at least a carat and a half.

"Wow!" I grab her hand for a closer look. "Congratulations, it's breathtaking! When did this happen?"

"About two months ago. Adam said he couldn't wait any longer to propose. He's incredible, Laina, and I have you to thank. He loves me for me, quirks and all."

"I'm so thrilled for you both."

Jared steps up to her side then. She glances at him and quickly excuses herself. "Gonna grab a drink now!" She scurries off.

"Hey, Norton," Jared greets in that familiar, smoky voice.

*You will not throw up*, I remind myself. Holding out a hand in a formal manner, I say, "Hello, JP. Welcome to Viola's Hideaway."

He chuckles and his grin widens.

*Oh, I wish he wouldn't do that.*

My knees tremble. "What's so funny? As I recall, you once said you wouldn't laugh when I called you JP."

"No, I said I would *try* not to laugh," he corrects. Our eyes are fixed on each other. He hesitates before releasing my hand. "I almost didn't recognize you with the short hair."

"Yeah, felt like I needed a change."

His face softens. "I think I like this look better, actually." Not being subtle at all, he takes in my entire outfit, head to foot, then clears his throat.

*Keep it together, Laina.*

"This is Preston," I tell Jared, nudging my old friend closer. "And this is his partner, Jack." I turn to them. "Preston and Jack, I'd like you to meet Jared Hartley."

Jared extends his hand. "Great to finally meet you, Preston. I've heard a lot of good things about you."

Preston giggles. His cheeks flush. "Probably not as much as I've heard about you, I'm sure." Preston takes me aside and says he and Jack will begin rounding up the crew. Then Jared and I are left to ourselves. The smile briefly slips from his face as he asks, "Can we talk?"

"Well, it's only a couple of minutes until we kick this thing off. How about after?"

"Yeah." He nods. "Of course. Go get 'em."

I have to practically peel myself away bodily. Once I reach the podium at the front of the store, I tap the microphone, which squeaks, then echoes through the new high-tech sound system.

Preston comes up to stand by my side, easing my nerves a bit.

"Hello, everyone. Can you all hear me?"

People nod, others shout, "Yes!"

I take another breath. "Okay, great. First off, my name is Laina Jorden. I co-own Viola's Hideaway with my best friend, Preston De Luca." I put an arm around Preston for a moment. "We'd like to thank each and every one of you for joining us here tonight."

I pause a moment to collect my thoughts, wondering why I didn't write an actual speech, on paper, so I could look down at it now.

"Sometimes life presents us with obstacles – Hurricane Tyler, for example." Many in the crowd somberly nod. "But Preston and I, and everyone on our staff, are now thrilled to have a second chance to bring Viola's Hideaway back to you. New and improved, that is. Tonight is the first of many events to come, and we have an extremely talented author here with us tonight."

I meet Jared's gaze and he grins, sending a pleasant shiver down my spine. To avoid losing my train of thought, I have to look away, at the rest of the crowd.

"Her romantic comedy novel, *Twisted Fate*, is currently number eleven on the New York *Times* Best Seller list. So please, give a warm welcome to Milliana Smith!"

The crowd claps and cheers as Milliana—a single, thirty-something soccer mom from Westchester, with two teenage daughters—steps up to the podium in a blush-pink sundress, her novel cradled in one hand. She pushes back long, auburn hair, smiles at the crowd, and thanks everyone for attending tonight. Then she clears her throat, opens to a bookmarked page, and begins.

Preston and I stand off to the side. He leans in and says teasingly under his breath, "You can stop tremblin' now. You did great."

"I can barely believe this is all happening right now," I mutter.

Preston glances out at Jared, who is staring up at me. Shrugging, he says, "I can believe it."

I turn my head to peer at him, confounded.

"What," he begins, "you think this was all a coincidence?"

"I don't know what to think. Feels like I'm in a fog."

Preston snorts. "Sure. Maybe a magical one that drifted in all the way from Camelot. You are the Queen of Fate, honey, after all."

# Chapter 34

# Twisted Fate

At the signing after Milliana's reading, there's a line all the way to the door. She holds a meet and greet with readers, and then the store begins to clear out once guests notice our staff gathering chairs and closing down the coffee machines in the café. Jared approaches as we are clearing away the remains of complimentary cheese and crackers, and drinks set out earlier. Preston and I carry a few trays behind the café counter. Though we didn't ask, Jared lends a hand. After a while, though, he walks around to the other side of the café counter and leans on his elbows, watching me intently.

I soon find I'm so self-conscious; I nearly drop a whole bowl of avocado dip on my shoes.

My curiosity gets the better of me, finally, and I flash a glance at Jared's left hand, trying not to make it too obvious I'm checking for a wedding band.

Just as Preston said, there's no wedding ring on his left hand, which is not definitive proof of anything, of course. I desperately want to question him, but ultimately decide it isn't any of my business. There could be a million reasons the ring isn't there. It could be getting re-sized and polished. It could be in his pocket. Maybe he forgot to put it on after a shower tonight. Who knows? It's not *my* place to inquire.

So I fixate on the other looming question in the forefront of my mind – where is Liv?

I realize I'm standing around as if lost in my own bookstore, with nothing to do. So I grab a nearby cloth and wipe down the counter, even though Preston just finished taking care of that five minutes ago.

"Laina," Jared says, "is now a good time to steal you away?"

I whirl back toward him. Preston perks up like a prairie dog noticing an interesting sound. *Steal me away?* I fumble the cloth, drop it at my feet, then lunge to snatch it from the floor. But Preston reaches it first, and escorts me out from behind the café counter.

"Now's a *perfect* time to . . . steal her away." He grins at Jared, looking amused.

I turn back to Preston. "Sure it's all right, me leaving you with the clean up?"

"Of course! We're nearly done. Besides, I've got backup." He motions to our staff, Tammy and Cristin. "Why don't you and Jared go and talk in your office? It's much cozier...I mean, more private...in there." I shoot him a hard look, insinuating I want him to zip his lips. Right now.

He leans in close, and whispers, "Don't fuck this up or I *will* disown you."

Jared motions for me to lead the way. We enter my office, and I close the door behind us, then linger there a moment.

Jared takes a look around. "No pictures?"

"I had pictures on my old desk but they were ruined during the hurricane."

"Right. Sorry." He steps over to the desk and sits on the edge. He hangs his head then looks back up, at me. "You never said goodbye."

"*What?*" I squeak. "What're you talking about?"

"The Bahamas," he flatly replies. "You left without saying goodbye."

"Oh. Is that why you're here?" I frown. "Just for a proper goodbye?"

"No. There's a lot I need to talk to you about."

I pace around the office trying to decide where to situate myself. I decide I'll be most comfortable leaning against the wall, near the door. I'm too amped up with nervous energy to sit. Or maybe subconsciously I want a handy escape route.

"So guess what?" He says. "I finally did it. Finished the first draft of my novel."

"Get out! That's amazing!" I shout, sounding a bit too high-pitched and squeaky. "What made that happen?"

"Found the drive to keep going, I guess. The words poured out when I got back home. I couldn't stop writing. Now I'm thinking it would be a good idea to have someone read the manuscript and give me feedback before I revise and send it out."

"Yeah!" I clap excitedly. "You should definitely do that."

He folds his arms. "So, um, I want you to be the first to read it."

"What? Why me?"

"Because you'll tell me what you really think. I need someone I can trust to tear it apart."

Wow, he wants me to be the first person to read his book? My stomach jitters. I'm hardly able to hold still. "Of course, I'm flattered you asked. I'd love to read it."

Before I have time to think of what to say next, he blurts out, "Laina. What happened with you and Mason?"

*Oh my God. Please don't tell me you're here to convince me to get back with him.*

"Um . . .why do you want to know?"

"Guess I just feel like I *need* to know. I hope it wasn't my fault, somehow."

"No, absolutely not." I raise my eyebrows in surprise. "Not like it matters anymore, but I wasn't feeling what I ought to for him, especially at that point in a relationship. After I ended things, it seemed awkward to stick around, so I packed up and left."

He looks as though he's about to comment but I cut him off. "Okay, my turn to ask a question now."

"But wait, what if my follow-up question is related to what you just said?" He smirks.

"Nope. Those are the rules."

He nods and motions for me to proceed.

"Where's Liv?"

He takes a deep breath. "California." Without pausing he jumps right into *his* next question. "When did you find out I was Mason's stepbrother?"

"Wait," I say in a tremulous voice, "that's not a complete enough answer."

"Don't go breaking the rules," he teases. "Did you know I was his stepbrother before you arrived?"

"No! Originally, I was going to leave the Bahamas the day after the wedding. Shortly after we arrived, I realized I didn't feel the way I should, so I decided to end things the day after the wedding." Heat courses through my body from fingertips to my chest, then rushes to my cheeks, like a full-body blush. I must be breaking out in hives or something. Oh, awesome.

Jared rubs his forehead. "So why did you end up staying?"

Pursing my lips, I say, "Uh-uh. That's a new question."

He sighs. "Come on, why did you stay?"

"Why are you here without Liv?"

"I'll get to that in a second." He stubbornly holds my gaze, arms crossed. Clearly he won't say another word until I answer the last question.

So he's going to make me say it. All of it. As if I hadn't already made my feelings perfectly clear during the sun shower. "Okay, fine." I fold my arms, too, like a mirror image of him. "This will make me seem like a horrible person. Even though you were married, I stayed and didn't break things off with Mason right away, because I wanted to be around you. Even though you had found Liv and moved on with your life, I couldn't bring myself to leave."

"Okay. Then answer me this." He frowns as if confused. "When you *did* finally leave, why not say goodbye?"

"Because I couldn't!" I cry. "I was terrified if I allowed myself to say goodbye, it might have been the last thing you and I ever said to each other. So, I left and didn't let myself look back."

Desperate to throw the focus back onto him, I say, "Okay, now me again." My gaze shifts to his left hand. "Why aren't you wearing a wedding ring?"

He glances down at it, too. "You might want to sit for this one."

"Don't dance around the question," I protest, but I do take a second to lean against the back wall.

"I promise, I won't." He shakes his head. "The ring . . . it's just . . . Liv is one of the sweetest people I've ever known. Smart, caring, genuine. I felt sure she was the one. Then all of a sudden there you were again – this amazingly clever, quirky, sarcastic, klutzy, horrible dancer from my past."

"Hey!" I snap.

He smiles, but also looks a little sad. "Before you left, you said you were happy I finally found my soulmate. The truth is, I met her when I was four. And even though I tried each day to be the husband Liv deserved, I eventually realized I could either spend my life with someone who I love, simply because she's sweet, smart, and sincere, or I could spend my life with someone who makes me feel as alive as that four year old kid, every time I look into her eyes. Someone who really gets me. Who knocks the breath right out of me, just by standing there, wearing a simple black dress, because she's the most incredible thing I've ever seen."

*Oh. My. God.*

"So I *couldn't* stop thinking about you, but I also didn't *want* to stop. I hated myself. But I knew what I needed to do. The last thing I wanted to do was hurt Liv, but I also couldn't lie to her anymore." He reaches for a paperweight on my desk and nervously tosses it from one hand to the other. "I got home from work one day about a month ago, and decided to be honest with her, about everything."

"By *everything*," I say nervously, "you mean she knows now that we grew up together?"

"She deserved to know the whole truth."

"Oh, no." I stumble over to sit on the couch in the far corner of the office. "That couldn't have gone well."

"I don't think she believed me at first. Then, when it was clear I wasn't kidding, once she understood, she began to cry."

A black pit opens deep in my stomach. I feel so sorry for Liv, a nice person and who doesn't deserve to be hurt. Overcome with guilt, I wonder, *Should I call to apologize? Try to explain?* Probably not. I can't imagine that conversation going well, either.

Somewhat croaky, I utter, "God, she must hate me so much."

"She doesn't, Laina. I promise. She was mainly confused. Couldn't understand why we played it off the whole time as if we'd never met."

"Well, we didn't want to cause any weirdness."

"Yet in the end it still did. Can't change that now." He clears his throat. "But then something else happened," he continues. "She said she wasn't crying because she was sad, but because she was relieved. That was a weird moment, seeing the look on her face, like I'd just made something difficult easier for her. Then the entire conversation shifted." He scratches his head. "She confessed that she had feelings for someone else."

"No!" My jaw flies open and hangs there like a sprung Venus fly trap. "But . . . who?"

"Brace yourself. It's Mason."

"What?" I shout. "How? How did this happen?"

"I know, imagine that." He raises his eyebrows and nods. "They started talking, when she got after him about the way he was treating you. Guess it kinda snowballed from there. She confessed they wanted to be together and, well . . . I wasn't about to stop them. I've seen them twice since we split up. I can't lie, it's weird. But once I actually watched how they were together, I understood. Something between them just . . . fits, so much more than Liv and I ever did. Mason was such a very one-sided person. Kind of selfish. Always had to win, to get his way. Not anymore. Not with her." He laughs. "Blew my mind."

I recall them sitting together at the bar then, back in the Bahamas, eating conch and drinking like old friends. Even then, they had kind of seemed to fit. To look, well . . . *natural* together. "So, he knows about our past now, too, huh?"

"Yep." Jared rises to pace the room while I sit in shock, trying to catch up. "He had a *lot* of questions."

Stunned, I stare at the floor. "Here I thought my whole scenario was messed up. Yet this shit has just gotten weirder."

"What do you mean?"

I think back to when I locked myself in the bathroom before the ceremony, plotting to stop him from getting married. "Uh...nothing."

"I'm not buying it. Spill." He crosses his arms sternly. I really don't want to reveal how pathetically desperate I was back in the Bahamas.

"Come on, Laina, I'm baring my soul over here. Your turn."

"Okay, fine." I rise from the couch and walk back and forth. My turn to pace. "But please don't judge me for what I'm about to say."

"Deal." He chuckles. "How bad can it be?"

"Pretty appalling, actually." I stop walking because my knees are shaking. "In fact, I can't believe I'm about to tell you this," I mumble.

*Just spit it out! Tell him!*

"Okay, before the ceremony I bumped into your mom. That was when I realized I was at *your* wedding. I rushed back to the villa and accidentally locked myself in the bathroom. But I only realized it after I'd decided to find you and stop the wedding, which of course didn't happen, but only because of the stupid, defective door handle. Was it fate that I met Mason at one wedding and then ended up at yours? Was it fate that made that bathroom door handle hold me prisoner? I don't have any answers. Maybe it was just me, being selfish. I mean, who the hell stops a wedding, except in a movie?"

Jared shrugs. "I prefer to believe everything happens for a reason. I don't care how or why things turned out the way they did. I believe I was supposed to meet Liv and you were supposed to meet Mason. Maybe that too was part of our fate, so they could reunite us and then meet each other." He wanders over, stopping only a few inches away, looking intently at me. "I don't have the answers either, Laina. But I don't need to know. All that matters now is where we choose to go from here."

I exhale and put my hands on my head, feeling as if I've lost my bearings. Jared reaches out and gently pulls one of my hands to him. He doesn't let go, nor do I. He gazes at our entwined hands a moment. Then he reaches into his shirt pocket, and pulls outs a tiny bunch of Forget-Me-Nots, only slightly wilted, tied up with twine. "It's corny, but I don't care," he says, and hands me the flowers.

He takes another step closer, and rests his forehead against mine. Brushing a thumb against my cheek, he says softly, "Laina, I love you. I've loved you my whole life."

The words are like a melody. Their musical hum courses through me, bringing with them a level of joy I never imagined possible. And why not? I've waited an eternity to hear them.

"I love you too," I say, and a single tear trickles down one cheek.

He lifts the same thumb to wipe it away. A magnetic force is pulling us toward each other once again. I clutch the fabric of his shirt, and he leans in and kisses my lips, then draws me closer until our bodies are pressed one against the other. Our lips fit together seamlessly. Eventually, when we are forced to part, to draw breath again, we gaze at each other and smile.

Jared and I first met when we were four years old. Yet it has taken this long to reach the starting point, the moment when we can finally begin to spend our lives together. After far too many years of keeping us apart, fate has shown it always had other plans in store for us.

"What now?" I whisper.

Running a hand over my short brown hair, he sighs. "Well, Norton, I thought we'd start off the traditional way. With a first date."

*A date?* I want to squeal with delight, but do my best to play it cool. "Oh, I see. Okay. When?"

"How's tomorrow, after work?"

As I open my mouth to say yes, I remember tomorrow is Sunday, a day for which I have already made plans.

"Oh, shoot!" I grimace. "Tomorrow's no good." I smack a palm on my forehead. "Preston and I are supposed to see *Twelfth Night*. You know, Shakespeare in the Park."

Suddenly, from the other side of my office door, Preston bellows, "He can have my ticket!"

Jared and I smirk at each other. Preston has been creeping on us the entire time, an ear glued to the other side of the door.

"Thanks, bud!" Jared shouts back, then turns to me again. "What do you say? Is it a date?"

Draping my arms around his neck, I lean in, lightly kiss his lips once more, and whisper, "All I can say is, it's sure as hell about time."

## THE END

DANA MILLER enjoys sappy romantic comedies, obsessing over *Pride and Prejudice,* creating recipes for her food blog, and eating way too much sushi. *Twisted Fate* was conceived on Paradise Island, Bahamas. She holds an MFA in creative writing from Wilkes University, and lives in Pennsylvania with her fiancée and their two Sphynx cats.

## Acknowledgements

I would like to thank my parents for supporting my decision to go back to school to pursue writing, for always pushing me to do what I love, and for telling stories during dinner when I was young, just to get me to eat. To my sister Dorrie: Laina wouldn't be Laina without you. Thank you for helping me name her. To my sister Darlene, thanks for all the times I asked you to read the first few chapters over and over, even with minor edits. You always encouraged me to keep writing. And my fiancé, Dustin, I don't know how I ever became so lucky. Thank you for not allowing me to worry about the laundry, dishes, or house cleaning anytime I wanted to write. You've always supported me, and your faith has kept me going, even when I felt too tired to open my laptop. To Lenore Hart and David Poyer, I can't thank you enough for believing in this story and for working tirelessly to help my dream come true. To Renee Butts, the first person to read and assess my manuscript at NHP, I cannot thank you enough for your amazing feedback, editing suggestions, and for recommending *Twisted Fate* for publication. To my wonderful mentors at Wilkes University, Nina Solomon and Susan Cartsonis, for all your guidance and advice along the way. To Trilby, my Victorian apartment roomie and Wilkes bestie, thank you for keeping me going during our late-night writing sessions. And, finally, to my Mobies, my Wilkes writing family – you all inspire me. Grad school wouldn't have been the same without each and every one of you.

# Northampton House Press

Northampton House publishes selected fiction – historical, romance, thrillers, fantasy – and lifestyle and literary nonfiction, memoir, and poetry. Our logo represents the Greek muse Polyhymnia. See our list at www.northampton-house.com, and Like us on Facebook – "Northampton House Press" – for more great reading.

CPSIA information can be obtained
at www.ICGtesting.com
Printed in the USA
LVHW091451240119
605099LV00003B/418/P

9 781937 997892